Apothecary Jars

THE FABER MONOGRAPHS ON POTTERY AND PORCELAIN

Former Editors: W. B. HONEY, ARTHUR LANE and SIR HARRY GARNER
Present Editor: R. J. CHARLESTON

APOTHECARY JARS

Pharmaceutical Pottery
and Porcelain
in Europe and the East
1150–1850

with a Glossary of Terms
used in Apothecary Jar Inscriptions

BY

RUDOLF E. A. DREY

FABER AND FABER
London & Boston

First published in 1978
by Faber and Faber Limited
3 Queen Square London WC1
Printed in Great Britain by
BAS Printers Limited, Over Wallop, Hampshire
All rights reserved

British Library Cataloguing in Publication Data

Drey, Rudolf E A
    Apothecary jars. —(The Faber monographs on
    pottery and porcelain).
    1. Apothecary jars —Collectors and collecting
    I. Title
    738   NK4695.A6

    ISBN 0-571-09965-3

FOREWORD

In the history of ceramic art often all too little attention is paid to the commercial basis on which the ceramic industry rested in a given country or period. Much study is lavished on the outward forms of pots, their styles of decoration and the artists to whom they may be attributed, but nothing is said of the innumerable plain pieces which were made for everyday use and which, being much used and commonplace, were soon broken and discarded. On these, however, very often depended the economic health of the enterprise, and on this in turn depended its capacity to meet the special commissions and exceptional orders which normally provide the material of art-historical investigation.

In Renaissance Europe, and particularly in the sixteenth and seventeenth centuries, a special economic base was furnished for the makers of tin-glazed earthenware (maiolica, faience, or 'delftware') by the demands of the apothecary, whether in the pharmacy of a great monastery or of a palace, or in a more humble commercial establishment. On the practical plane, jars by the hundred were needed for the conservation of drugs, both solid and liquid, but the visual aspects of the pharmacy were not neglected, and a splendid decorative array of drug-jars was the ambition of any pharmacist who disposed of the necessary means. This side of the market, therefore, made both practical and artistic demands on the potter, and in this sense the pharmacist was perhaps the ideal customer. Some potters indeed seem to have lived almost exclusively by supplying the pharmacies. Masséot Abaquesne, of Rouen, is recorded as making little else, apart from tiles, and this is perhaps not surprising when it is realised that a single order consisted of some four thousand jars.

In the present book the author has traced the history of all centres of significance which produced pharmaceutical ceramic wares, and in so doing has also provided a conspectus of the pottery industry, mainly of Europe and mainly of the sixteenth to eighteenth centuries; but he has also outlined the Near Eastern origins of the drug jar, and not omitted the exceedingly rare examples in Chinese porcelain. Over and above this he has recorded and interpreted many hundreds of drug-names written on the jars, and has produced an authoritative list which supersedes all others. The book will therefore not only be of particular interest to the student and collector of ceramics, but an important source for the history of *materia medica*.

R. J. CHARLESTON

CONTENTS

ILLUSTRATIONS

Unless an indication is given to the contrary the objects illustrated are made of tin-glazed earthenware.

Colour Plates

Monochrome Plates

Map

Photographic Credits

Where no acknowledgement is made in this section, the illustration was supplied by the museum or private collector owning the object (see the captions to the plates)

Arts Graphiques de la Cité (AGRACI), Paris. Plates 45A, 47C, 49D, 51B, 66B, 76D, 79A,B

Claude Basnier, Paris. Plates 12A, 19D, 25A, 34C, 37C, 38, 39D, 41B,C, 43, 44B, 46B, 50B,D 53A, 55B, 60B, 61C, 64B, 78C, 84F, 95

René Basset, Lyons. Plates 9A, 11C, 12C, 14A,C, 15B, 16B, 17D, 18C, 19A, 22A,B,

31A, 37A,D, 45C,D, 46C,D, 91, 92, 93

Heinz Blum, Heidelberg. Colour Plate E, Plates 35A, 56A, 62E, 77D, 80C, 84A,B

Piet Boonstra, Groningen. Plate 61A

Studio Borchi, Faenza. Plates 19B, 28B, 32A, 34B

Henri Bouscarle, Narbonne. Plate 72B

Paul Bublex, Lyons. Plate 37B

M. Chopard, Nyon. Plates 7C, 25B, 28A, 32B, 36B, 84E

Studio Conteri, Genoa. Plates 8A, 21A, 30A,C, 31D

A. C. Cooper, London. Colour Plates A, C, Plate 14B

Henry Cooper, Northampton. Plates 7A,B

Studio Ellebé, Rouen. Plates 39C, 47D, 48A,B

Pierre Feuillade, Limoges. Plates 6B, 22C,D

Jupp Franz, Strasbourg. Plates 31C, 54C, 55C

Studio Frequin, Voorburg, The Hague. Plates 28D, 72D

Studio Gabriel, Paris. Colour Plate F, Plates 50A, 51A,C, 52A,B,C, 56B

Studio Gérondal, Lomme, Lille. Plates 44C,D, 47A

Peter Heman, Basle. Colour Plates B, D, Plates 20D, 23D, 28C, 33C, 35C, 45B, 53B, 55D, 56E, 77B, 78B, 82C, 85B,C, 86C

Studio Meusy, Besançon. Plate 94

O. E. Nelson, New York. Plates 6A, 89A

Claude O'Sughrue, Montpellier. Plates 41A, 44A

M. Platteeuw, Bruges. Plates 60A, 64A

Dominguez Ramos, Madrid. Plate 3A

G. Rampazzi, Turin. Plates 31B, 36C

J. D. Schiff, New York. Plates 2A,B

Soprintendenza Gallerie Napoli, Naples. Plates 9B, 10A, 17A

Sperryn's, London. Plate 2C

A. Struiksma, Leeuwarden. Plates 58B, 61B

R. Todd-White and Son, London. Colour Plate G, Plates 6C, 8C, 10B,C, 12B, 20A,B, 26B,C, 29B, 34D, 35D, 36A, 39A,B, 56C, 68C, 69A,B, 70A,C, 77A, 79D, 84C

Dick Wolters, Rotterdam. Plates 4C, 16A, 29A, 60C

Author. Plate 96

ACKNOWLEDGEMENTS

In the preparation of this book I have received generous assistance from many museum officials, private collectors and others. I am particularly grateful to the following for helpful discussions: Mrs. Agnes Lothian Short, formerly Librarian of the Pharmaceutical Society of Great Britain; Monsieur Louis Cotinat, co-editor of the *Revue d'Histoire de la Pharmacie*; Dr. D. A. Wittop Koning, Curator of the Medisch-Pharmaceutisch Museum, Amsterdam; Mrs. Lydia Mez-Mangold, Curator of the Schweizerisches Pharmazie-historisches Museum, Basle; Pharmazierat Dr. Werner Luckenbach, Curator of the Deutsches Apothekenmuseum, Heidelberg; Dr. Günther Schiedlausky, Landeskonservator, Germanisches Nationalmuseum, Nuremberg; Professor Giuseppe Liverani, Director of the Museo Internazionale delle Ceramiche, Faenza; Professor Guillermo Folch Jou, Curator of the Museo de la Farmacia Hispana, Madrid; Mr. Henry Brocksom, M.P.S., London. I am much indebted to the museums, private collectors and pharmaceutical companies who have provided photographs of objects in their possession, or who have granted permission for such items to be photographed. Others whose help I gratefully acknowledge are Mr. Robert Charleston, who undertook the onerous task of editing the manuscript, and Mr. Giles de la Mare of Messrs. Faber and Faber, who gave me advice and encouragement at every stage of the project. Lastly more than conventional thanks must be expressed to my wife, both for assistance in elucidating the botanical problems posed by the plant names occurring in drug jar inscriptions, and for her patience and forbearance during the many years the work has been in progress.

Blackheath, London   RUDOLF E. A. DREY
1977

ABBREVIATIONS

Books

Crellin, *English and Dutch Medical Ceramics:* J. K. Crellin, *Medical Ceramics: A Catalogue of the English and Dutch Collections in the Museum of the Wellcome Institute of the History of Medicine*, London, 1969

Giacomotti, *Catalogue MN:* Jeanne Giacomotti, *Catalogue des Majoliques des Musées Nationaux (Musées du Louvre et de Cluny; Musée National de Céramique à Sèvres; Musée Adrien-Dubouché à Limoges)*, Paris, 1974

Honey, *European Ceramic Art: Dictionary:* W. B. Honey, *European Ceramic Art from the End of the Middle Ages to About 1815: A Dictionary of Factories, Artists, Technical Terms, et cetera*, London, 1952

Honey, *European Ceramic Art: Illustrated Survey:* W. B. Honey, *European Ceramic Art from the End of the Middle Ages to About 1815: Illustrated Historical Survey*, London, 1949

Kohlhaussen *et al.*, *Alte Apothekengefässe:* H. Kohlhaussen, G. Schiedlausky and H. Stafski, *Alte Apothekengefässe*, Biberach an der Riss, 1960

Kremers and Urdang, *History of Pharmacy:* E. Kremers and G. Urdang, *History of Pharmacy*, 3rd ed., revised by G. Sonnedecker, Philadelphia and Toronto, 1963

Rackham, *Catalogue VAM:* Bernard Rackham, *Catalogue of Italian Maiolica*, London (Victoria and Albert Museum), 1940. Volume I: text; Volume II: plates

World Ceramics: R. J. Charleston (ed.), *World Ceramics: An Illustrated History*, London, New York, Sydney and Toronto, 1968

Periodicals

Cahiers: Cahiers de la Céramique, du Verre et des Arts du Feu, Sèvres

Faenza: Bollettino del Museo Internazionale delle Ceramiche in Faenza

Rev. Hist. Pharm.: Revue d'Histoire de la Pharmacie, Paris

Vrienden: Mededelingenblad van de Vrienden van de Nederlandse Ceramiek, Amsterdam

THE WARES

Principal centres of production of drug jars in Europe.

Chapter 1

INTRODUCTION

The Evolution of the Tin-Glazed Earthenware Apothecary Jar with Pharmaceutical Inscription

Among the earliest skills developed by man was the art of fashioning earthenware articles such as pots and jugs. *Homo sapiens* has always been an acquisitive animal, and the pottery jar offered him a convenient means of storing his commodities for everyday usage. Only simple techniques were needed to make earthenware receptacles, and the raw materials required—clay, water and wood (the latter to provide a source of heat for hardening the pot) were readily available. Coating of the surface with an appropriate slip would confer resistance to penetration by liquids, and render the vessel suitable for storage of fluids. Finally, using a suspension of a ferruginous earth such as ochre, ornamental patterns could be traced on the surface of the container, thus satisfying man's innate urge to embellish his objects of domestic usage.

The earthenware jar was well suited to the storage of the roots, seeds, berries and herbal extracts of the early healer of the sick.[1] Its shape and size could be varied in accordance with the user's requirements, and the vessel could be closed with a parchment membrane, or with a seal of wax or chalk, thus guarding against loss of volatile constituents.

In primitive society the healer's range of materia medica was restricted to a relatively small number of herbal remedies and some mineral compounds, and a local craftsman employing simple methods could supply the drug vessels needed. However, with the introduction in the Middle Ages of pharmacopoeias and *antidotaria*, each listing some hundreds of herbs, roots, syrups, juleps, aromatic waters, pills, ointments, electuaries, lohochs, spices and sweetmeats to be prepared and held in store by the apothecary, there arose an ever-increasing demand for vessels for use in pharmacies and dispensaries attached to hospitals and monasteries. This demand for drug containers in turn acted as a stimulus to the foundation of potteries, and there is little doubt that

---

[1] In ancient times not only earthenware vessels, but also containers hollowed out of wood, marble, basalt and some other materials served for storage of drugs (cf. e.g. St. Mark, xiv, 3; St. Luke, vii, 37).

many workshops in ceramic centres such as Florence, Cafaggiolo, Siena, Faenza, Savona, Castelli, Antwerp, Lambeth, Talavera, Lyons and Montpellier owed much of their prosperity, if not their actual existence, to commissions for drug vessels placed by pharmacies and monastic foundations. Indeed at Montpellier, the seat of an important school of medicine, the *faïencerie* during the first hundred years of its existence appears to have been engaged exclusively on production of tin-enamelled apothecary jars.

Finds made on archeological sites have revealed that both the use of drugs for treatment of disease, and the manufacture of earthenware storage vessels had their origin in the East, in districts of Turkey, Persia and Mesopotamia. Excavations on the sites of ancient cities such as Nippur, south of Baghdad, yielded on the one hand pottery jars which might have been used for storage of drugs, and, on the other, archival clay cylinders inscribed in cuneiform, some of which carried inventories of vegetable drugs—hellebore, opium, mandrake root, sweet flag root and others.[2] Records attesting the use of drugs have also been found in other pottery-producing regions. At Knossos, on the island of Crete, excavations initiated by Sir Arthur Evans afforded clay tablets bearing inscriptions in Linear B which are thought to designate drugs and spices.[3] In ancient Egypt a papyrus dating from c.1550 B.C., discovered by Professor Georg Ebers, provides evidence of the use of medicaments of vegetable and mineral origin for healing purposes,[4] including acetate of copper, which was the principal ingredient of an ointment known in later times under the name *Unguentum Aegyptiacum* (Plates 22A, 26B, 46A). At a later date pottery and medicine flourished on the Greek mainland and in Rome. Physicians such as Hippocrates, Dioscorides and Galen introduced new drugs into medical practice and enunciated the principles of a system of therapy which was to

---

[2] Kremers and Urdang, *History of Pharmacy*, p. 6; R. Campbell Thompson, 'Assyrian medical texts', *Proceedings of the Royal Society of Medicine, Section of The History of Medicine*, vol. 17, 1923, pp. 1–34; vol. 19, 1925, pp. 29–78.

[3] M. Ventris and J. Chadwick, *Documents in Mycenaean Greek. Three Hundred Selected Tablets from Knossos, Pylos and Mycenae with Commentary and Vocabulary*, Cambridge, 1959, pp. 221–3.

[4] C. P. Bryan, *The Papyrus Ebers*, London, 1930; B. Ebbell, *The Papyrus Ebers: The Greatest Egyptian Medical Document*, Copenhagen and London, 1937.

Plate 1A   Albarello, with carved decoration and coloured glazes
            PERSIA (RAYY or KASHAN), middle of the 12th century. H. 14 cm (5.5 in)
            London, Victoria and Albert Museum. See page 26
Plate 1B   Albarello, painted in lustre and touches of underglaze blue
            PERSIA (RAYY), late 12th century. H. 23.5 cm (9.2 in)
            London, British Museum. See page 26
Plate 1C   Albarello, painted in black and covered in a tuquoise-blue glaze
            SYRIA, 13th or 14th century. H. 33 cm (13 in)
            London, Victoria and Albert Museum. See page 26
Plate 1D   Albarello, painted in blue and black
            SYRIA, late 13th or early 14th century. H. 25.5 cm (10 in)
            Lucerne, Collection Mr. E. Kofler-Truniger. See page 26

dominate pharmaceutical practice until well into the seventeenth century. The period of Classical Greek medicine is also notable for an early documentary reference to the use of earthenware vessels for storage of roots, leaves and flowers.[5]

After the decline of the Roman Empire the ascendancy in the domains of pottery and medicine passed again to the Near East. New drugs and spices such as cassia bark, tamarind, nux vomica, senna, galanga root, sandalwood, musk, cloves, nutmeg[6] and dragon's blood (a resinous exudation on the fruits of certain palms) were placed at the disposal of the physician. Schools of medicine and hospitals were founded at Jundishapur (Western Persia), Damascus, Baghdad, Cairo and other cities of Islam, and these establishments undoubtedly offered important outlets to the wares of the Near Eastern potters.

Western Asia, as well as being a source of important developments in medicine and pharmacy, was also noteworthy for a number of innovations in techniques of pottery decoration.[7] Foremost among these was the use of glazes for enhancing the imperviousness of vessels intended to hold fluids, and for imparting a lustrous surface to an otherwise matt body. The early glazing compositions—powdered sand mixed with soda (alkaline glaze) or mixed with oxide or sulphide of lead (lead glaze), sometimes pigmented with a compound of copper—suffered from the disadvantage of failing to adhere to the body of the vessel after firing in the kiln, or of running during the process of firing and smudging any decorative designs previously applied. These difficulties were overcome by coating the vessel with a suspension in water of a finely-ground three-component mixture—oxide (ashes) of tin, oxide of lead, and a melt of powdered sand and potash; any ornamental design applied to a surface coated

[5] P. Dorveaux, 'Les pots de pharmacie dans les vieux auteurs', *Bulletin des Sciences Pharmacologiques*, vol. 29, 1922, pp. 530–8.
[6] Spices such as cloves, nutmeg and cinnamon served not only for flavouring of foodstuffs but entered also into the composition of drug mixtures.
[7] For accounts of the technique of manufacture of Islamic pottery see Arthur U. Pope and Phyllis Ackerman, *A Survey of Persian Art from Prehistoric Times to the Present*, London and New York, vol. 2, 1939, pp. 1697–1702; Jean Lacam, 'La céramique Musulmane des époques Omeyyade et Abbasside, VIIe au Xe siècle', *Cahiers*, No. 20, 1960, pp. 244–93; Alan Caiger-Smith, *Tin-Glaze Pottery in Europe and the Islamic World*, London, 1973, pp. 199–217.

Plate 2A   Albarello, painted in dark blue and golden lustre
            VALENCIA (MANISES), first half of 15th century. H. 28.5 cm (11.2 in)
            New York, Collection Dr. R. C. Bak. See page 28
Plate 2B   Albarello, painted in dark blue and golden lustre, with coat of arms of City
            of Valencia
            VALENCIA (MANISES), second half of 15th century. H. 31 cm (12.2 in)
            New York, Collection Dr. R. C. Bak. See page 28
Plate 2C   Albarello, painted in blue and golden lustre
            VALENCIA (MANISES), second half of 15th century. H. 33 cm (13 in)
            New York, Collection Dr. R. C. Bak. See page 28
Plate 2D   Albarello, painted in blue and golden lustre
            VALENCIA (MANISES), third quarter of 15th century. H. 39.5 cm (15.5 in)
            London, Victoria and Albert Museum. See page 28

with this composition was immune from distortion in the subsequent high-temperature firing. This technique, which is believed to have had its origin in Mesopotamia in about 600–400 B.C., was to gain wide acceptance at a later date in Europe for decoration of ornamental and useful earthenware, the wares coated with this composition (tin glaze) being known as *maiolica, faïence,* delftware, etc., according to the country of manufacture.

Only a limited range of colours was available to the potter-artist; all were pigments of mineral origin, in order to withstand the heat of the kiln. The colours were blue derived from cobalt oxide, purple obtained from pyrolusite or other manganese ore, yellow obtained from antimony, and brown and green derived from compounds of iron and copper, respectively. Using these basic colours the Islamic artisans were able to achieve rich polychrome effects.

A refinement in technique of decoration was the use of compositions made from oxide of silver or copper mixed with sulphur and a ferruginous clay such as ochre. The mixture was applied to the previously-glazed and fired vessel; a second firing in the presence of carbonaceous (black) smoke at a relatively low temperature resulted in reduction of the metallic oxide, and formation of a thin film of metal, imparting an iridescent sheen to the surface of the vessel.[8] This technique of ornamentation (lustering) was used extensively in the twelfth and thirteenth centuries at Raqqa in Northern Mesopotamia, and at Kashan and Rayy in Persia (Plate 1B), and at a later date, with certain modifications, in Spain and in Italy, at Deruta and Gubbio. Another important innovation attributable to Islamic potters is the storage jar known as the albarello; this was a cylindrical vessel having a flange at its open end (Plates 1A,B,C,D) over which a parchment cover could be tied (Plates 79A,B). Albarelli were used in the home and in apothecaries' shops for storage of solid and viscous materials such as herbs, spices, candied fruits, honey, ointments and electuaries. They were exported in considerable quantities from Persia and Syria, particularly in the thirteenth and fourteenth centuries, for use in the pharmacies of Europe.[9] The

[8] A. Lane, *Early Islamic Pottery*, London, 1958, p. 14.
[9] W. Bode, *Die Anfänge der Majolikakunst in Toskana*, Berlin, 1911, p. 11; A. Lane, *Later*

Plate 3A   Oil jar, painted in blue and golden lustre
             VALENCIA (MANISES), middle of 15th century. H. 29 cm (11.4 in). Inscription 'Oly d̄ mirta' (*Oleum de myrtus*)
             Madrid, Instituto de Valencia de Don Juan. See page 28

Plate 3B   Albarello, painted in green and manganese-purple
             TERUEL, second half of 15th century. H. 37 cm (14.6 in). Inscription 'AVE MARIA GRACIA PLENA DOMINUS TECUM' (Hail Mary, full of Grace, the Lord be with You)
             Madrid, Museo de la Farmacia Hispana. See page 142

Plate 3C   Albarello, painted in blue monochrome
             VALENCIA, first half of 15th century. H. 40.5 cm (16 in)
             London, Victoria and Albert Museum. See page 142

Plate 3D   Albarello, painted in dark blue
             CATALONIA, late 15th or early 16th century. H. 28 cm (11 in)
             London, Victoria and Albert Museum. See page 142

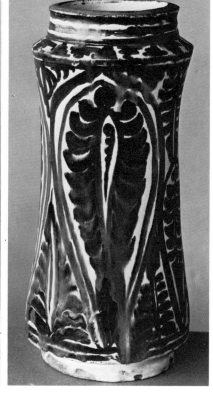

albarello shape was to be widely adopted at a later date by the pharmaceutical potters of Europe, and was also used, although sparingly, in China from the fifteenth century onwards (Plate 88).

Islamic potters did not only make their wares in the East. Following the conquest of Southern Spain by the forces of the caliphate of Damascus in the eighth century they set up kilns, initially at Seville and Cordova (the seat of a school of medicine) and later at Málaga and Granada. The principal products of these early Iberian (Hispano-Moresque) potteries were dishes and storage jars decorated in traditional Eastern style, and tiles for the revetment of walls of mosques and palaces. The fourteenth century saw the establishment of factories at Teruel in the province of Aragon, and at Paterna and Manises in Valencia. The potteries of Manises were notable for the production of tin-glazed lustreware of rare nobility of shape and splendour of design; the wares included richly lustred albarelli decorated with arabesques (Plate 2A), coats of arms (Plate 2B) and cyphers which are believed to be apothecaries' marks (Plates 2C,D). Hispano-Moresque lustreware was shipped in considerable quantities from Spain to Italy and to other countries such as France, England and the Netherlands, and eventually offered serious competition to pottery exported from the Levant to Western Europe.

The manufacture of decorated tin-glazed earthenware was initiated in Italy at a somewhat later date than in Spain, probably at the beginning of the thirteenth century. The earliest productions, made in the Umbria-Latium region, particularly at Orvieto and Viterbo, in Tuscany, and in certain other regions, were small dishes and jugs, painted in green and brown colours or incised with simple geometric designs or representations of animals.[10] At the beginning of the fifteenth century more ambitious articles were attempted — large ornamental dishes with green and manganese-purple decoration, pitchers, bottles and albarelli, sometimes with portraits in relief. This class of pottery, which owed little to foreign influence, was followed by wares painted predominantly in cobalt-blue, the decoration not infrequently being copied from Hispano-Moresque importations.

The beginning of the production of drug jars inscribed with the name of the contents dates from about the middle of the fifteenth century, such wares being produced on a small scale in Spain (Plate 3A) and in Italy (Rackham, *Catalogue VAM*, No. 24, Plate 2). Non-inscribed vessels continued however to be widely used in pharmacies, since containers on which the drug name was painted restricted the freedom of the apothecary to change the contents of the vessel as circumstances dictated. On non-inscribed jars the nature of the contents was indicated by means of a label affixed to the side of the vessel or, at a later date, by reference to a painted number (Plate 54B). Some centres of production of

---

Islamic Pottery: Persia, Syria, Egypt, Turkey, London, 2nd ed., 1971, p. 17; G. Fehérvári in *World Ceramics*, p. 88.

[10] David Whitehouse, 'The medieval glazed pottery of Lazio', *Papers of the British School at Rome*, 1967, pp. 40–86; Giuseppe Liverani in *World Ceramics*, pp. 146 and 147.

pharmaceutical pottery, such as Kreussen, Narbonne and the factory of Masséot Abaquesne at Rouen produced only uninscribed jars; similarly, the pharmaceutical wares of Sicily seldom carry the name of a drug. Evidence that non-inscribed jars were used for storage of medicaments is provided by contemporary paintings or prints, depicting pharmacies with uninscribed drug vessels on their shelves;[11] additional evidence is afforded by surviving old pharmacies and *apothicaireries* which have retained their original sets of uninscribed containers (Plates 93, 96). In the seventeenth and eighteenth centuries jars with blank cartouches were occasionally produced; on such vessels the apothecary would arrange for the drug name to be painted in unfired cold colours on the empty panel after purchase (Plates 53A, 55C, 74B, 83C, 87C).

---

[11] Cf. an eighteenth-century engraving by H. Bölmann of the interior of the Stern-Apotheke in Nuremberg (reproduced by H. Stafski in *Aus Alten Apotheken*, Munich, 4th ed., 1967, plate 14) which was furnished with uninscribed albarelli of the type shown in Plate 83A. See also Henry Wallis, *Oak-Leaf Jars*, London, 1903, fig. 83.

Chapter 2

ITALY: PART I
Pharmaceutical Pottery of the 'Classical' Factories

It has been seen in the preceding chapter that the mainstream of Italian tin-glazed earthenware (maiolica) was derived from two sources: the early native products manufactured in various regions of the peninsula, and the more highly developed Hispano-Moresque wares imported from Eastern Spain. Each of these tributaries made distinctive contributions to the evolution of Italian ceramic art, contributions which may be perceived in two classes of pottery dating from *c*.1400–70: the green-and-purple dishes, jugs and drug jars made at Orvieto, in the province of Umbria, and some other cities (Plate 4A), which were successors to the primitive native wares, and the albarelli of Tuscan manufacture decorated with blue-and-purple vine leaves (Plate 4B) or with blue geometrical patterns,[1] which had their origin in importations from Valencia.

In the second half of the fifteenth century the Italian ceramic industry

[1] Cf. Rackham, *Catalogue VAM*, Nos. 50–2; Giacomotti, *Catalogue MN*, No. 54.

Plate 4A Albarello, painted in green and manganese-purple
UMBRIA (ORVIETO) or TUSCANY, first half of 15th century. H. 19.5 cm (7.7 in)
London, Victoria and Albert Museum. See pages 30 and 32

Plate 4B Albarello, painted in blue and manganese-purple
TUSCANY, *c*.1460–70. H. 24.5 cm (9.6 in)
London, Victoria and Albert Museum. See page 30

Plate 4C Albarello, painted in blue, green, brown and manganese-purple
TUSCANY or FAENZA, end of 15th century. H. 22 cm (8.7 in). Inscription 'DIA·CAPTOL' (*Diacatholicon*)
Rotterdam, Museum Boymans-van Beuningen. See pages 32 and 48

Plate 4D Bottle, painted in dark blue and orange
TUSCANY or FAENZA, *c*.1500. H. 30.5 cm (12 in). Inscription 'A·DI MATRICHA' (*Acqua di matricale*)
London, Victoria and Albert Museum. See page 32

entered a period of rapid development. New factories were established in Tuscany, Umbria and at Faenza. Fuller use was made of the range of colours available to the maiolica painter, and novel shapes of vessel made their appearance. Concurrently the artists enlisted a multitude of ornamental motifs to embellish their wares—palmettes, masks, cupids, portrait heads (Plates 14C, 16B, 17B,D), strapwork designs (Colour Plate B), leaves of pyramidal form (Plate 4D), Gothic foliage (stylised leaves coiled into a volute) (Plate 4C), grotesques (mythical figures combining animal and human forms, or having foliated limbs) (Plates 10A, 15C), and many others. Wares with a pharmaceutical or medical theme are surprisingly rare. A Deruta albarello in the Victoria and Albert Museum depicts a youth pounding a drug in a mortar (Rackham, *Catalogue VAM*, No. 405); other drug jars portray Asclepius, God of Medicine (Giacomotti, *Catalogue MN*, No. 1443), the Persian physician Avicenna (Plate 20A) and the figure in medieval medical literature known as Mesuë.[2] St. Roch, a saint invoked against pestilence, is also occasionally represented on apothecary jars (Plate 11C). After about 1525 representations of subjects drawn from religion, mythology or the history of Greece and Rome (Plates 7A, 18A) assumed importance, particularly at Faenza and Urbino. Towards the end of the sixteenth century decorative treatment became more austere; colour was used more sparingly, and there were fewer innovations of design. Production of maiolica continued well into the eighteenth century and beyond, but with relatively few exceptions the *seicentesche* and *settecentesche* wares did not attain the standard of excellence set by the earlier productions.

The maiolica potter's preoccupation with ornamentation and attention to detail is perhaps nowhere more in evidence than on pharmacy jars, particularly those of the Renaissance. Distinctive treatment was customarily accorded to the individual members of a series of vessels,[3] and on occasion even the drug name label was made to conform to the overall ornamental design (Plates 16B, 28C, 36C). On some jars the reverse of the vessel was decorated as elaborately as the front,[4] a practice which paralleled the custom at Deruta and in certain other regions of Italy of painting the backs of dishes with geometrical or flowery designs.

The earliest tin-glazed earthenware drug jars to be produced in Italy were in all probability albarelli and syrup jars with green and manganese-purple decoration. These productions, which date from the first half of the fifteenth century, were manufactured at ORVIETO and perhaps other places in Umbria, and at one or more centres in Tuscany (Plate 4A). Of slightly later date than the productions of Orvieto are the dignified oak-leaf wares—albarelli and globular jars with short strap-handles—made in the neighbourhood of FLORENCE in the period *c.*1430–55. The vessels are painted in a thickly-applied dark blue or near-black pigment (*zaffera in rilievo*), generally outlined in manganese-purple,

[2] See page 214.
[3] See Colour Plate A, Plates 14B, 9B,C, 12B,C, 18A.
[4] See Plates 10B,C, 20A,B, 22C,D, 26B,C, 27B,C, 29C,E.

A. Albarello
DERUTA, first quarter of 16th century. H. 24 cm (9.4 in). Inscription
'EMP·DE·BACHE L^AVR' (*Empiastro di bacche di lauro*, poultice of bay berries)
London, Courtauld Institute Galleries (Gambier-Parry Collection). See page 48

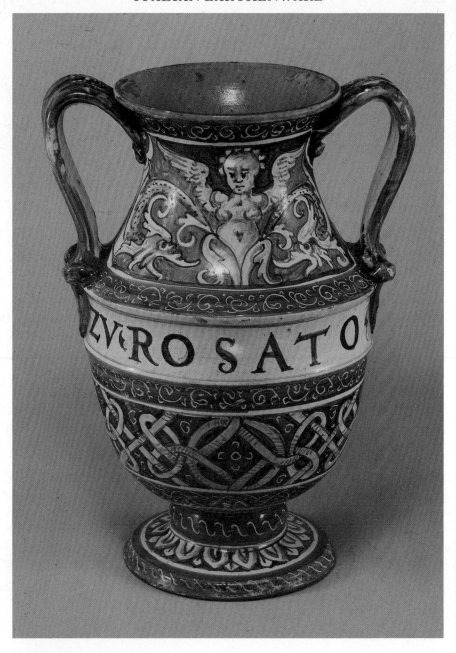

B. Double-handled drug jar
Probably FAENZA, first quarter of 16th century. H. 34 cm (13.4 in). Inscription
'ZV·ROSATO' (*Zuccaro rosato*)
Basle, Collection F. Hoffmann-La Roche & Co. See page 32

Double-handled globular jar, painted in dark blue and manganese-purple, with details in green FLORENTINE, second quarter of 15th century. H. 21 cm (8.3 in) *London, Victoria and Albert Museum.* *See page 40.*

Twin-handled albarello, painted in dark blue and manganese-purple FLORENTINE, second quarter of 15th century. H. 32 cm (12.6 in) *London, Victoria and Albert Museum.* *See page 40*

6A   Albarello, painted in blue and
      yellow, with touches of brown and
      green
      TUSCANY, perhaps CAFAGGIOLO,
      early 16th century. H. 29.5 cm
      (11.6 in). Inscription C°L°QVINTIDA'
      Author's collection. See page 40

6B   Double-handled drug jar, painted
      in blue, yellow, brown and green
      TUSCANY, last quarter of 15th
      century. H. 21 cm (8.3 in).
      Inscription 'DIaCALAMENTA'
      *Limoges, Musée National Adrien-
      Dubouché. See page 40*

6C   Double-handled drug pot,
      displaying arms of Aldobrandini di
      Lippo, painted in blue and ochre
      TUSCANY, perhaps CAFAGGIOLO,
      *c.*1510–20. H. 13 cm (5.1 in).
      Inscription 'pll·BIChIChE' (*Pillole
      bechiche*)
      Author's collection. See page 40

7A Double-handled drug jar, painted in blue, green, yellow and brown
TUSCANY (CAFAGGIOLO or MONTELUPO), middle of 16th century. Inscription
'SYᴼ DI BETTONICA'
Castle Ashby, Collection the Marquess of Northampton. See page 40

7B Reverse of 7A

7C Albarello, painted in blue, green, ochre and yellow
TUSCANY, perhaps CAFAGGIOLO, *c*.1520. H. 17 cm (6.7 in). Inscription
'COF·AMECH' (*Confezione Hamech*)
Nyon (Switzerland), Musée au Château. See page 40

7D Double-handled syrup jar, painted in blue, green, ochre and yellow
TUSCANY (CAFAGGIOLO or MONTELUPO), middle of 16th century. H. 47 cm
(18.5 in). Inscription 'SYᴼ·ROSᴼ·SOLVTᵛᴼ' (*Siroppo rosato solutivo*)
Milan, Museo d' Arte Antica. See page 40

8A   Twin-handled drug pot, painted in blue, green and yellow
MONTELUPO, last quarter of 16th century. H. 32 cm (12.6 in). Inscription 'SYᴼ·DI·ANTUF'*
Genoa, Museo degli Ospedali Civili. See page 40

8B   Double-handled syrup jar, painted in polychrome
MONTELUPO, second half of 16th century. H. 36 cm (14.2 in). Inscription 'SYᴼDI·BISANTISᶜᴱ'
London, British Museum. See page 40

8C   Spouted jar, displaying arms of Franciscan Order, painted in blue, yellow, ochre and green
Probably MONTELUPO, c.1570. H. 25 cm (9.8 in). Inscription 'Â·DI·AGRIMᴬ' (*Acqua di agrimonia*)
London, Collection Mr. H. E. Brocksom. See page 40

* See page 181.

9A Albarello, painted in yellow, blue, ochre and green
SIENA, *c*.1500–10. H. 24 cm (9.4 in).
Inscription 'dia·boraginato'
Lyons, Musée Lyonnais des Arts Décoratifs (Collection Paul Gillet).
See page 46

9B Albarello, painted in blue and brown, with touches of green
SIENA, *c*.1500. Inscription 'ra·dacoro' (*Radice di acoro*)
Naples, Museo Nazionale di Capodimonte (de Ciccio Collection).
See page 46

9C Albarello, painted in blue, bluish black, brown, yellow and green
SIENA, dated 1501. H. 27.5 cm (10·8 in). Inscription 'benalbo'
(*Behen album*)
London, Victoria and Albert Museum. See page 46

10A   Albarello, painted in yellow,
        brown, blue and green
        SIENA, *c*.1510. Inscription
        'CASTOREO'
        Naples, Museo Nazionale di
        Capodimonte (de Ciccio
        Collection). See page 46
10B   Albarello, painted in blue, ochre
        and yellow
        Probably SIENA, *c*.1510–20. H.
        20 cm (7.9 in)
        Author's collection. See page 46
10C   Reverse of 10B

11A   Albarello, painted in blue, green,
ochre and yellow
SIENA or DERUTA, *c.*1500–5.
Inscription 'ELLO DE PISILIO'
(*Elettuario di psillio*)
Paris, Musée des Arts Décoratifs.
See page 46

11B   Albarello, painted in blue, ochre
and yellow, with touches of green
SIENA or DERUTA, dated 1507.
H. 21 cm (8.3 in). Inscription
'ATA^{N}AS·MAGᾹ·' (*Athanasia magna*)
The Hague, Gemeentemuseum.
See page 46

11C   Albarello, painted in blue, green,
ochre and yellow
Probably DERUTA, beginning of
16th century, H. 23 cm (9 in).
Inscription 'ELLE·CONTR^A·PESTA'
(*Electuarium contra pestem*, anti-
pestilential electuary)
*Lyons, Musée Lyonnais des Arts
Décoratifs (Collection Paul
Gillet). See page 46*

with patterns of stylised leaves, which have been variously interpreted as oak leaves or fern fronds; supplementary ornamentation is provided by motifs such as fleurs-de-lis, heraldic beasts, harpies, fishes, hares or birds.[5] Some of the jars carry a monastic emblem, either on the body of the vessel or on the handles, of which the ladder surmounted by a cross (the badge of the hospital of Santa Maria della Scala in Siena) (Plate 5B) and the crutch (insignia of the hospital of Santa Maria Nuova in Florence) (Plate 5A) are well known.[6]

Production of oak-leaf jars in Tuscany came to an end after the middle of the fifteenth century, but the pot of globular form remained a favourite shape of drug vessel (Plates 6B,C), although after about 1530 the handle in the form of a short looped strap was supplanted by the handle fashioned in the form of plaited rope (Plates 7A,B) or in the shape of a dragon's head (Plate 7D). On occasion a coat of arms was featured, showing that the jar was intended for a ducal or princely pharmacy (Plate 6C). Decorative themes favoured by Tuscan potters in the first half of the sixteenth century included formal foliage, daisy-like flowers springing from an urn (Plate 6A) and stylised pine cones (Plates 6C, 7B,C), the latter an ornament particularly associated with the Tuscan potteries of CAFAGGIOLO and MONTELUPO.[7]

The pharmaceutical maiolica of Montelupo includes drug jars of barrel form (Plate 8A), as well as the conventional albarello and spouted jar (Plates 8B,C). These wares, which date from c.1540–80, generally carry a decoration of leaves divided into dark and light halves, with the inscription in a dark brown hue. Another class of pharmaceutical pottery assignable to Montelupo comprises drug jars of late sixteenth-century date, decorated with grotesque winged demi-figures (Plate 8B). The drug vessels of this class appear to be related to a group of armorial pilgrim bottles in the Victoria and Albert Museum and elsewhere;[8] they were probably inspired by decorative wares of Urbino origin, but they lack the delicate colouring of the Urbinesque productions.

SIENA and DERUTA, ceramic centres situated south of Florence and south of Perugia, respectively, produced some of the most splendid ornamental and pharmaceutical maiolica of the Renaissance. The wares are characterised by effective use of traditional maiolica motifs allied to careful execution of the decoration. Additionally Deruta is celebrated for production in the sixteenth century of pottery painted in blue and in yellow lustre, a technique of ornamentation applied mainly to non-pharmaceutical wares, only one lustred drug jar of Deruta manufacture appearing to have been recorded (Plate 13B).

---

[5] Henry Wallis, *Oak-Leaf Jars*, London, 1903; Rackham, *Catalogue VAM*, Nos. 34–45 (plates 7–9); Giacomotti, *Catalogue MN*, Nos. 29–37; Galeazzo Cora, *Storia della Maiolica di Firenze e del Contado. Secoli XIV e XV*, Florence, 1973, plates 55–95, 112–14.
[6] For other emblems on early Tuscan pharmacy jars see Cora, loc. cit. (note 5, above), plate 335.
[7] See also M. Bellini and G. Conti, *Maioliche Italiane del Rinascimento*, Milan, 1964, pp. 74 and 79; Rackham, *Catalogue VAM*, Nos. 332 and 333.
[8] Rackham, *Catalogue VAM*, Nos. 951 and 952 (plate 153); Bellini and Conti, loc. cit. (note 7, above), p. 81, figs. B and C; G. Cora, 'Sulla fabbrica di maioliche sorta in Pisa alla fine del '500', *Faenza*, vol. 50, 1964, plates V and VI.

12A   Albarello, painted in blue, yellow, orange and green SIENA or DERUTA, *c*.1500–10. H. 22 cm (8.7 in). Inscription 'LOCH·DE PAPAVS' (Probably *Lohoch de papavere simplex*) *Sèvres, Musée National de Céramique. See page 46*

12B   Albarello, painted in blue, green, yellow and orange Probably DERUTA, dated 1524. H. 23 cm (9 in). Inscription 'ZVCC°·VIOLATO' *Author's collection. See page 46*

12C   Syrup jar, painted in blue, green, yellow and orange Probably DERUTA, *c*.1525. H. 23 cm (9 in). Inscription 'SY°·DE·ABSENZ°' (*Syrupus de absinthio*) *Lyons, Musée Lyonnais des Arts Décoratifs. See page 46*

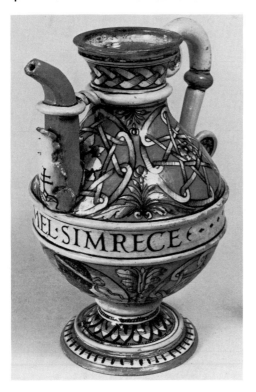

13A   Spouted jar, painted in polychrome
DERUTA, dated 1501. H. 26 cm (10.2 in). Inscription 'OXIMEL·SIMRECE' (*Oxymel simplex*)
London, British Museum. See page 46

13B   Spouted jar, painted in yellow lustre, brown and black, outlines in blue and details in green
DERUTA, dated 1502. H. 26 cm (10.2 in). Inscription 'OXIZACARA' (*Oxysacchara*)
London, British Museum. See page 40

14A Spouted jar, painted in blue, ochre, green and yellow DERUTA, *c.*1520–30. H. 27 cm (10.6 in). Inscription 'A·PLÂTAGINIS' (*Aqua plantaginis*) *Lyons, Musée Lyonnais des Arts Décoratifs (Collection Paul Gillet). See page 48*

14B Albarello, painted in blue, yellow, green and ochre DERUTA, *c.*1510–20. H. 24 cm (9.4 in). Inscription 'ZVCA^{RO}·BVGLOSSATO' *London, Courtauld Institute Galleries (Gambier–Parry Collection). See page 48*

14C Albarello, painted in yellow, blue, ochre and green DERUTA, *c.*1510–20. H. 22 cm (8·7 in). Inscription 'ELL·INDI·MA' (*Electuarium Indum majus*) *Lyons, Musée Lyonnais des Arts Décoratifs (Collection Paul Gillet). See page 48*

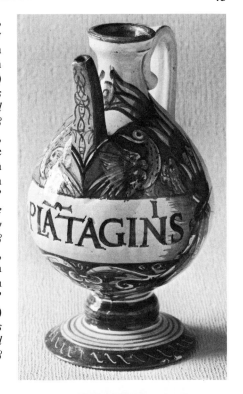

15A   Albarello, painted in blue,
           yellow, brown and green
           FAENZA, *c*.1510. H. 18 cm
           (7.1 in). Inscription
           'ell·dia·sebesten·s'
           London, Victoria and Albert
           Museum. See page 48

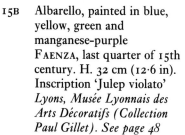

15B   Albarello, painted in blue,
           yellow, green and
           manganese-purple
           FAENZA, last quarter of 15th   15C   Double-handled albarello, painted in
           century. H. 32 cm (12·6 in).   blue, green and yellow
           Inscription 'Julep violato'   FAENZA, *c*.1525. H. 35 cm (13.8 in).
           Lyons, Musée Lyonnais des   Inscription 'COMINO·PESTO' (Crushed
           Arts Décoratifs (Collection   caraway)
           Paul Gillet). See page 48   *London, British Museum. See page 32*

16A   Shallow drug pot with cover, painted in blue, ochre, green and yellow
FAENZA, *c.* 1510. H. 11 cm (4.3 in) Inscription 'colloq̃tida' (*Coloquintida*)
Rotterdam, Museum Boymans-van Beuningen. See pages 48 and 52

16B   Syrup jar, painted in blue, green
and yellow
FAENZA, end of 15th century. H.
25 cm (9.8 in). Inscription
'Sy·de·asiendo' (*Syrupus de
assentio*)
*Lyons, Musée Lyonnais des Arts
Décoratifs. See page 48*

16C   Syrup jar, painted in colours
FAENZA, end of 15th century. H.
23 cm (9 in). Inscription 'S
de·bixãtis' (*Syrupus de Byzantiis*)
*Present ownership unknown.
See page 48*

Although Siena and Deruta were geographically in different provinces, the
first in Tuscany, the second in Umbria, the wares of the two localities have
certain characteristics in common, which may be explained by migrations of
potters between the two centres, as well as by ceramic links of each city with
Faenza. In particular the members of a large class of albarelli, bottles and
spouted jars, dating from the first quarter of the sixteenth century, with
inscriptions and main decorative motifs framed by oval wreaths, generally
incorporating fruits or ribbons (Plates 11A,B,C, 12A,B,C) are difficult to attribute
with certainty to one centre or another, and they have been variously assigned
to Siena,[9] to Deruta,[10] and to a more general Siena-Deruta category.[11]

In addition to this group of wares of indeterminate origin there are several
series of drug jars which can be given with some degree of confidence to either
Siena or Deruta. The Sienese wares comprise albarelli with a predominantly
yellow, ochre, or near-black ground, decorated with grotesques, masks,
dolphins, cornucopias, vases, chequer patterns and other motifs (Plates 9A,B,C,
10A,B,C). Evidence of origin for these wares is afforded by stylistic affinities
with pavement tiles of Sienese manufacture made for the palace of Pandolfo
Petrucci (1452–1512) in Siena.[12]

An early non-lustred pharmacy vessel unambiguously assignable to Deruta
is a spouted jar dated 1501 with strap-work decoration (Plate 13A), probably
made from the same mould as the previously mentioned blue-and-yellow

[9] Cf. Bernard Rackham, *Islamic Pottery and Italian Maiolica*, London, 1959, No. 321, plate
135B.
[10] Rackham, *Catalogue VAM*, Nos. 390, 404, 405, 406, 420.
[11] Jeanne Giacomotti, *La Majolique de la Renaissance*, Paris, 1961, pp. 51–2; id., 'Les
majoliques de la Collection Paul Gillet au Musée Lyonnais des Arts Décoratifs', *Cahiers*, No. 25,
1962, pp. 21–45; figs. 14, 15, 16, 18, 19.
[12] Otto von Falke, *Majolika*, Berlin, 2nd ed., 1907, fig. 55, p. 124; Rackham, *Catalogue VAM*,
No. 386, plate 62.

Plate 17A   Albarello, painted in yellow, brown, blue and green
              FAENZA, end of 15th century. Inscription 'dia· iris'
              *Naples, Museo Nazionale di Capodimonte (de Ciccio Collection). See page
              48*
Plate 17B   Albarello, painted in blue, yellow, brown, green and manganese-purple
              FAENZA, end of 15th century. H. 26 cm (10.2 in). Inscription 'Cata·ticum
              iperialis'
              London, Victoria and Albert Museum. See page 48
Plate 17C   Albarello, painted in blue, green, ochre and yellow
              FAENZA, *c.*1525. H. 22 cm (8.7 in). Inscription 'U. MARTIAδô' (*Unguentum
              Martiatum*)
              The Hague, Gemeentemuseum. See page 52
Plate 17D   Albarello, painted in blue, green, yellow, ochre and manganese-purple
              FAENZA, *c.* 1475–85. H. 30 cm (11.8 in). Inscription 'S·de·limonibus'
              *Lyons, Musée Lyonnais des Arts Décoratifs (Collection Paul Gillet). See
              page 48*

lustred ewer. Other pharmaceutical wares for which there is strong presumptive evidence in favour of a Deruta origin are albarelli, spouted jars and bottles whose general decorative treatment is related to the Siena-Deruta class, but which are painted in a fuller palette and a freer style, 'd'un faire plus libre'[13] (Colour Plate A, Plates 14A,B,C).

Manufacture of tin-glazed earthenware at FAENZA began towards the end of the fourteenth century. By the end of the fifteenth century Faenza rivalled Umbria and Tuscany as a source of maiolica of distinction, and eventually was to become the most prolific of all centres of production of tin-glazed pottery in Italy.

As a consequence of intermigration of potters between Faenza, Florence, Siena, Deruta and certain other localities, particularly in the period c.1480–1515, the wares of Faenza are not always distinguishable from those of other ceramic centres of the period. Thus the decorative feature known as a contour panel—a compartment following at a distance the outline of a portrait or animal—occurs both on wares of Faventine origin (Plates 17A,B) and on pottery of Tuscan manufacture.[14] Similarly the stylised rosette (Plate 15A),[15] the stylised peacock feather (Plate 15B), the coiled leaf ornament known as Gothic foliage (Plates 4C, 16C) and the sinuous lines known as Rays of San Bernardino (Plates 16C, 58A), although much in favour with Faenza potters, are also to be found on maiolica made elsewhere in Italy. On the other hand, ornamental patterns of stylised flowers on thin coiling stems surrounded by clusters of small dots (Plates 16A,B, 17B,D) do not appear to have been used away from Faenza, and wares decorated with this motif may reasonably confidently be assigned to this city.

Decorative treatments used on ornamental and pharmaceutical wares made

---

[13] Giacomotti, *Catalogue MN*, p. 113.
[14] Rackham, *Catalogue VAM*, Nos. 56–8.
[15] Melisanda Lama, 'Temi ornamentali del Quattrocento', *Faenza*, vol. 29, 1941, plates VIII and IX; J. Giacomotti, *La Majolique de la Renaissance*, Paris, 1961, plate VI–3.

Plate 18A   Pair of drug bottles, depicting Europa riding the Bull, and David holding the head of Goliath, painted in blue, green, yellow and ochre
FAENZA, c. 1530. H. of each 42 cm (16.5 in). Inscriptions 'Aq·lupulor' and 'Aq·pimpinelle'
Amsterdam, Rijksmuseum. See page 52

Plate 18B   Twin-handled drug bottle, painted in blue, green, ochre and yellow
FAENZA, c. 1515–20. H. 46 cm (18 in). Inscription 'Aq·boragini'
London, British Museum. See page 52

Plate 18C   Double-handled drug jar on low foot, painted in blue, green, ochre and yellow
FAENZA, c.1525. H. 23 cm (9 in). Inscription 'confetio am' (*Confectio hamech*)
Lyons, Musée Lyonnais des Arts Décoratifs (Collection Paul Gillet). See page 52

at Faenza after about 1515–20 are more distinctive, and include *berettino* (or *bianco sopra azzurro*) ornamentation, in which an opaque white pigment, sometimes supplemented by other colours, was applied on to a uniform blue ground (Plate 20C), and *a quartieri* decoration, in which the walls of the vessel, or the surface of the dish or plate, were apportioned into equally spaced panels, adjacent compartments being painted in different colours (Plates 19A,B). The apothecary jars of the middle of the sixteenth century were frequently embellished with formal foliage—acanthus, palmettes, etc., whilst figures in medallions provided additional decoration (Plates 19C,D).

After the middle of the sixteenth century there was a gradual return to restraint in decorative treatment. Ornamentation was used more sparingly, much of the white tin-glaze being left exposed (*bianchi di Faenza*) (Plate 21A). At the same time there was greater discrimination in the use of colour, the painter's palette being pared to ochre, yellow and blue, and on occasion, reduced to a single colour. This more austere form of ornamental treatment may be illustrated by reference to a set of drug jars with blue monochrome decoration (Plate 20D), probably by the same hand as a ewer and basin in the Victoria and Albert Museum.[16] After the sixteenth century Faenza appears to have lost much of its importance as a source of pharmaceutical maiolica, the supremacy in this field passing to other factories, notably those of Liguria, Sicily and the Abruzzi. Pharmaceutical pottery of merit was however still occasionally produced, particularly in the eighteenth century at the

---

[16] Rackham, *Catalogue VAM*, No. 1028; Rackham, *Italian Maiolica*, London, 1963, plate 82A.

Plate 19A   Albarello, painted in blue, green, ochre and yellow
                FAENZA, middle of 16th century. H. 26 cm (10.2 in). Inscription 'ung^tu·populionis' (*Unguentum populeum*)
                Lyons, Musée Historique des Hospices Civils. See page 50

Plate 19B   Albarello, painted in brown, blue, yellow, green and manganese-purple
                FAENZA, middle of 16th century. H. 31 cm (12·2 in). Inscription 'Sy° Cidonior' (*Syrupus cydoniorum*)
                Faenza, Museo Internazionale delle Ceramiche. See pages 50 and 52

Plate 19C   Jar of globular form, painted in blue, green, ochre and yellow
                FAENZA, middle of 16th century. H. 33 cm (13 in). Inscription 'teifera magna' (*Trifera magna*)
                Birmingham, City Museum and Art Gallery. See page 50

Plate 19D   Globular jar, painted in polychrome, with the portrait of the Prophet Jonah
                FAENZA, third quarter of 16th century. H. 33 cm (13 in). Inscriptions 'PROFETA ION', 'veru(m) tame(n) rursus videbo templum' ('Yet I will look again toward Thy Holy Temple', Jonah, ii, 4) and 'Sy°·violati·d·v^e' (*Syroppo violato delle viole*)
                Sèvres, Musée National de Céramique. See page 50

factory of Count Annibale Ferniani,[17] which remained active until 1900.

Faventine potters were responsible for a number of notable drug jar services. A set dating from about 1510 is of interest in that the members of the series — covered cylindrical pots of shallow form, decorated with formal flowers and tendrils on coiling stems (Plate 16A) — have a shape which is only rarely encountered among the wares of the pharmaceutical potter.[18] Of somewhat later date is a heterogeneous group of albarelli, bottles, dragon-spouted syrup jars and other shapes painted in ochre, yellow, blue and green hues with portraits (Colour Plate C, Plate 18c) and subjects drawn from the Bible, Classical history or mythology (Plate 18A). Not infrequently the portraiture is marked by an 'element of caricature and a distinctive handling which has not been recognised in any other maiolica-painting'[19] (Plate 17C). These vessels were evidently produced in considerable numbers at Faenza and may have been copied at other factories. They are sometimes referred to as Orsini-Colonna drug jars by reason of a certain stylistic affinity with a two-handled bottle inscribed with the legend 'ET SARRIMO BONI AMICI' and painted with a bear (orso) clasping a pillar (colonna) (Plate 18B), a subject which is believed to commemorate the reconciliation of the Orsini and Colonna families in 1517.[20]

Assignable to the middle of the sixteenth century is a group of albarelli and globular jars with ornamentation of strawberry leaves or other foliage, and medallion portraits of persons famous in history or legend, or characters drawn from literature (Plate 19B).[21] Also from the middle of the cinquecento is a set of

[17] Saul Levy, *Maioliche Settecentesche Piemontesi, Liguri, Romagnole, Marchigiane, Toscane e Abruzzesi*, Milan, 1964, plate 207.
[18] Other vessels from this set are reproduced in Rackham, *Catalogue VAM*, No. 215; G. Liverani, *Five Centuries of Italian Majolica*, New York, Toronto and London, 1960, colour plate 11.
[19] B. Rackham, loc. cit. (note 9), p. 71.
[20] For other examples see e.g. Rackham, *Catalogue VAM*, Nos. 250–7; Giacomotti, *Catalogue MN*, Nos. 247–51, 253–60.
[21] See also L. Zauli Naldi, *Faenza*, vol. 42, 1956, plate LXIV, fig. c and p. 124; B. Rackham, loc. cit. (note 9), Nos. 303, 305, 306 and plate 132; Giacomotti, *Catalogue MN*, Nos. 960–3.

Plate 20A   Albarello, painted in blue, green, yellow and ochre
              Probably FAENZA, second half of 16th century. H. 23.5 cm (9.2 in).
              Inscriptions 'VICENA' (Avicenna) and 'loch·de·pino'
              Author's collection. See page 32
Plate 20B   Reverse of 20A
Plate 20C   Spouted jar, displaying arms of Salviati of Florence, painted in dark
              blue and opaque white, with touches of green and brown
              FAENZA, dated 1531. H. 25 cm (9.8 in). Inscription 'OLLIO' (*Olio*)
              London, Victoria and Albert museum. See page 50
Plate 20D   Albarello, painted in blue monochrome
              FAENZA, c.1570. H. 22 cm (8.7 in). Inscription 'Aspalto'
              Basle, Collection F. Hoffmann-La Roche & Co. See page 50

albarelli with decoration of garlands, medallion heads and monogram 'RB' (probably the initials of the apothecary who commissioned the set) (Plate 22A); the vessels have stylistic similarities with wares of Castel Durante manufacture and may have been made at the latter locality.[22]

Some of the finest ceramic productions of the Italian Renaissance originated in the potteries of the duchy of Urbino; these were situated at Castel Durante, at Gubbio, at Pesaro, in the vicinity of the city of Urbino and, for a brief period only, in the township of Fabriano. The first of these factories to have been engaged in manufacture of tin-glazed earthenware is believed to have been CASTEL DURANTE: decorative maiolica was produced there from about 1490 onwards, whilst production of drug vessels dates from about 1525. Ornamental features associated with Castel Durante pharmaceutical pottery include medallion portraits and scroll-work, often supplemented by garlands of laurel or other foliage at the shoulder and base of the vessel (Plates 22B,C). More specific are the so-called trophies—medleys of weapons, shields, helmets (Plate 22D), drums (Plate 22B), music books, etc.—among which a rectangular tablet inscribed with the date of manufacture is sometimes to be found. Evidence of origin of these wares is afforded on occasion by an inscription such as 'fato in tera duranti apreso a n cita durbino.'[23] Production of drug jars with decoration of trophies continued well into the seventeenth century (Plate 23B).

The earlier wares of Castel Durante comprise a series of urn-shaped jars, painted predominantly in blue and orange colours (Plate 21C), and albarelli of

---

[22] For another vessel from this set see (Sir) Victor Negus, *Artistic Possessions at the Royal College of Surgeons of England*, Edinburgh and London, 1967, frontispiece.
[23] Rackham, *Catalogue VAM*, No. 615; J. Chompret, *Répertoire de la Majolique Italienne*, Paris, 1949, vol. 1, p. 35; vol. 2, figs. 159, 162 bis, 163; Giacomotti, *Catalogue MN*, Nos. 794–6.

exceptional size intended for display in pharmacies (Plate 23A). Of slightly later date is a group of small pill jars marked with a patriarchal cross or papal cross interlaced with the letter 'S' (Plate 21D), probably the emblem of the Order of the Celestines, or of the Monastery of Santo Spirito de Sulmona, which belonged to the Celestine Order.[24] Some of the vessels carry the date 1541 and the inscription 'mariotto da gubio', believed to be the name of a potter whose home town was Gubbio, but who was temporarily working at Castel Durante (cf. Rackham, *Catalogue VAM*, No. 815).

Dating from the third quarter of the sixteenth century is a group of albarelli and spouted jars which are decorated with trophies and a cherub's head. Some members of the group are inscribed with the date of manufacture (Plates 23C,D). Another group of drug containers assignable to Castel Durante comprises syrup jars, vessels of globular form with serpentine handles, albarelli and other shapes; the members of the service are decorated in predominantly blue and ochre colours with a standing female figure, variously designated as Venus Marina, Fortune or Amphitrite, standing on a dolphin and holding aloft a sail (Plates 24C,D). This subject was much in vogue during the Renaissance, and is also encountered on decorative maiolica from Siena (Giacomotti, *Catalogue MN*, No. 413) and Castel Durante (Rackham, *Catalogue VAM*, No. 599), in sculpture[25] and, at a somewhat later date, on Dutch ceramic tiles.[26]

Contemporaneous with the Venus Marina jars, and perhaps from the same workshop, is a covered pill pot (presumably one of a series), depicting an enthroned queen with crown and sceptre (Plate 24B), a subject occurring also on a group of pharmacy jars made in the third quarter of the sixteenth century

---

[24] Monsieur Bertrand Jestaz of the Musée du Louvre has pointed out that a similar emblem was displayed on the exterior of the old Convent of the Celestines in Paris. See also Giacomotti, *Catalogue MN*, No. 790.
[25] L. Planiscig, *Venezianische Bildhauer der Renaissance*, Vienna, 1921, figs. 432–40.
[26] Anne Berendsen *et al.*, *Tiles: A General History*, London, 1967, p. 120.

Plate 22A   Albarello, painted in ochre, yellow, green and blue
              FAENZA or CASTEL DURANTE, *c.* 1560. H. 32 cm (12.6 in). Inscription
              'VNG™ EGIPTIAC$\tilde{\text{V}}$' (*Unguentum Aegyptiacum*)
              *Lyons, Musée Lyonnais des Arts Décoratifs (Collection Paul Gillet). See
              page 54*
Plate 22B   Albarello, painted in ochre, yellow, green and blue
              CASTEL DURANTE, *c.*1550–60. H. 30 cm (11.8 in). Inscription 'Sy⁰. de
              endivia'
              *Lyons, Musée Lyonnais des Arts Décoratifs (Collection Paul Gillet).
              See page 54*
Plate 22C   Ovoid jar, painted in colours, with the portrait of the Prophet Jonah
              CASTEL DURANTE, *c.*1570. H. 32.5 cm (12.8 in). Inscription 'Trifera:
              Mag:'
              Limoges, Musée National Adrien-Dubouché. See page 54
Plate 22D   Reverse of 22C

at URBINO (Plate 24A). The same theme occurs on an amphora inscribed 'FATTO IN VRBINO' (Rackham, *Catalogue VAM*, No. 836). The drug vessels, which comprise albarelli and syrup jars with short stub-like spouts, are reputed to have been made in the workshop of Orazio Fontana for the Court Pharmacy of Guidobaldo II della Rovere, Duke of Urbino (1538–74). These and a group of related vessels (Colour Plate D) are painted in a vigorous polychrome palette.

Patterns of grotesques rendered in yellow, brown, green and sometimes manganese-purple tones, which were much in favour at Urbino for decoration of ornamental ware and tableware, are also found on drug jars made at this centre (Plates 25B,C); however the quality of the decoration on these pharmaceutical wares seldom attains the level of excellence of the ornamental productions. The same type of decor is to be found on an albarello (Plate 25A) inscribed on the reverse with the words 'ROMA FECIT' (Giacomotti, *Catalogue MN*, No. 1299), but whereas the Urbinesque productions are painted in a three- or four-colour palette, the range of colours on the Roman albarello is restricted to pale blue and yellow.

GUBBIO, an ancient city south of Urbino, gained renown early in the sixteenth century for production of maiolica with ruby-red lustre decoration. Only one set of drug jars with this type of decoration appears to have been recorded (Plate 21B); the members of the series have affinities with Faenza wares, and the vessels may have been painted at Faenza and sent to Gubbio for lustering.

The pharmaceutical ceramic wares of VENICE may be broadly grouped into three categories, each distinct in style and date. The earliest productions, dating from *c*.1530–55, are albarelli and globular jars decorated with large fruits and stylised foliage rendered in a strong polychrome palette (Plates 26A,B,C), a type of ornamentation also found on other forms of Venetian

---

Plate 23A   Cylindrical drug pot, painted in blue and olive-green
CASTEL DURANTE, *c*.1550. H. 41.5 cm (16.3 in).
Inscription 'Mostarda·f·' (*Mostarda fina*)
London, Victoria and Albert Museum. See page 56

Plate 23B   Drug bottle, painted in blue, yellow, brown and manganese-purple, with details in green
CASTEL DURANTE, dated 1638. H. 21.5 cm (8.5 in). Inscription 'A·DE·CAMOMLLA' (*Acqua di camomilla*)
London, Victoria and Albert Museum. See page 54

Plate 23C   Albarello, painted in colours
CASTEL DURANTE, dated 1569. H. 21 cm (8.3 in). Inscription 'PHILONIO RO' (*Philonium Romanum*)
Paris, Musée du Louvre. See page 56

Plate 23D   Oil jar, painted in blue, green, yellow, orange and grey
CASTEL DURANTE, dated 1569. H. 25 cm (9.8 in). Inscription 'OL·SAMBUCIN' (*Oleum sambucinum*, oil of elder flowers)
Basle, Collection F. Hoffmann–La Roche & Co. See page 56

maiolica (cf. Rackham, *Catalogue VAM*, No. 970). Drug jars of this type are believed to have been made at Faenza and Antwerp as well as in Venice, and the productions of these centres are not readily separated from each other.[27] A class of vessels of somewhat later date comprises jars with polychrome decoration of flowers and acanthus scrolls, usually with the addition of portrait heads or saints in medallion (Plates 27B,C). These jars were made in large numbers and the quality of their decoration ranges from casual to meticulous workmanship, suggesting that the wares emanated from more than one factory. Some of the vessels, such as large albarelli inscribed 'Mostarda' or 'Mostarda f' (Plate 27A), intended for display in pharmacies, are of exceptional quality, and are attributable to the hand of Maestro Domenigo, a leading potter in Venice in the period *c*.1560–80 (cf. Rackham, *Catalogue VAM*, No. 978). At a somewhat later date copies were made in Sicily[28] and at Gerace in Calabria.[29]

A third group comprising syrup jars, straight-sided albarelli and dumb-bell shaped albarelli is characterised by decor of foliage shaded half light, half dark (Plates 28A,B,C), an ornamental motif which occurs also on pottery of Montelupo manufacture. The members of this class of maiolica have generally a lavender ground on which the ornamentation is executed in dark blue tones (*berettino* decoration), sometimes with the addition of other pigments, a form of ornamentation evolved at Faenza at an earlier date. These wares are datable by reference to an armorial albarello from this group in the Victoria and Albert

---

[27] B. Rackham, *Guide to Italian Maiolica*, London, 1933, p. 72; Honey, *European Ceramic Art: Dictionary*, pp. 445 and 642; ibid., *Illustrated Survey*, plate 49C; T. Hausmann, *Majolika. Spanische und Italienische Keramik vom 14. bis zum 18. Jahrhundert*, Berlin, 1972, No. 245.
[28] Bellini and Conti, loc. cit. (note 7), p. 174, fig. D; Giacomotti, *Catalogue MN*, Nos. 1326–8.
[29] Mario Jung, 'Ulteriori notizie sulla maiolica Calabrese', *Faenza*, vol. 57, 1971, pp. 94–6, plate LXXVIII.

Plate 24A   Albarello, painted in blue, green, yellow, ochre and touches of manganese-violet
URBINO, workshop of Orazio Fontana, *c*.1565. H. 23 cm (9 in).
Inscription 'CŌ·VIOLATO' (*Conserva violato*)
Paris, Musée du Louvre. See page 58

Plate 24B   Covered drug pot, painted in blue, yellow, brown and black
Probably CASTEL DURANTE, *c*.1575. H. 13 cm (5.1 in). Inscription
'T·DE·EVPATOR' (*Trochisci de eupatorio*)
London, Victoria and Albert Museum. See page 56

Plate 24C   Globular drug jar, painted in green, blue, ochre and yellow
CASTEL DURANTE, dated 1579. H. 21 cm (8.3 in). Inscription
'S·DE·ANETI' (Probably *Seme di aneti*, dill seed)
Munich, Bayerisches Nationalmuseum. See page 56

Plate 24D   Syrup jar, painted in green, blue, ochre and yellow
CASTEL DURANTE, dated 1579. H. 22 cm (8.7 in). Inscription
'SYᴼ·BISANTINO'
Munich, Bayerisches Nationalmuseum. See page 56

25A Albarello, painted in pale
blue and yellow
ROME, beginning of 17th
century. H. 21 cm (8.3 in).
Inscriptions 'ROMA FECIT'
(at back) and
'HIERA LOGOD'
*Sèvres, Musée National de
Céramique. See page 58*

25B Syrup jar, painted in blue,
green, ochre and yellow
URBINO, last quarter of
16th century. H. 20.5 cm
(8 in).
Inscription 'SY^{O}·D·TRIBES'
(Probably intended to read
'SY^{O}·D·TRIBUS' or 'SY^{O}·D·RIBES')
*Nyon (Switzerland), Musée
au Château. See page 58*

25C Spouted drug jar, painted
in yellow, brown and blue
URBINO, *c*.1570–80. H.
38 cm (15 in). Inscription
'AQ D·LATTVCA' (*Acqua di
lattuca*) *Geneva, Musée
Ariana. See page 58*

24A Globular jar, painted in blue, green, ochre and yellow
VENICE, *c*.1540–50. H. 30.5 cm (12 in). Inscription 'peri· quonditi' (*Pere condite*, candied pears)
Milan, Museo d'Arte Antica. See page 58

26B Albarello, painted in blue, green, yellow and ochre
Probably VENICE, *c*.1530. H. 18 cm (7·1 in). Inscription 'u·egiptiago' (*Unguento Egittiaco*)
Author's collection. See page 58

26C Reverse of 26B

27A Albarello, painted in blue,
yellow, brown and green
VENICE (Maestro Domenigo),
c.1565–75. H. 41 cm (16.1 in).
Inscription 'Mostada f'
(*Mostarda fina*)
*Hamburg, Museum für Kunst
und Gewerbe. See page 60*
27B Albarello, painted in blue,
yellow, brown and green
VENICE (Workshop of
Maestro Domenigo),
c.1565–75. H. 25 cm (9.8 in).
Inscription
'Scorsa·de·cedro·C.'
*Geneva, Musée Ariana. See
page 60*
27C Reverse of 27B

C. Syrup jar
   FAENZA, c.1520. H. 22.5 cm (8.9 in). Inscription 'Syo.de pomis' (*Syrupus de pomis*)
   London, Courtauld Institute Galleries (Gambier-Parry Collection). See page 52

D. Spouted jar
URBINO, third quarter of 16th century. H. 29.5 cm (11.6 in). Inscription
'A·D·FARFARA' (Acqua di farara)
Basle, Collection F. Hoffmann-La Roche & Co. See page 58

Museum, inscribed 'iacomo vasellaro a ripa granni fecit 1593' (Rackham, *Catalogue VAM*, No. 983).

Production of pharmaceutical earthenware at Venice continued into the eighteenth century, the more notable wares of later date including drug jars with *petit feu* decoration from the factory of Geminiano Cozzi.[30]

---

[30] *World Ceramics*, p. 180, plate 38; Laura Campanile, *I Vasi di Farmacia*, Milan, 1973, p. 30.

Chapter 3

ITALY: PART II
Pharmaceutical Pottery of the
Later Factories

SICILY has been the scene of developments in medicine since the Middle Ages, a period during which the island came succesively under the domination of the Arabs, Normans, Germans and the House of Aragon. The Hohenstaufen Emperor Frederick II in particular made significant contributions to the evolution of medicine in Sicily: during his reign a Law for the Separation of Medicine and Pharmacy was promulgated,[1] and hospitals and leproseries were founded in various parts of the island. Supplies of pharmacy vessels for these establishments were secured initially from Spain and later from the Italian mainland, but in the last quarter of the sixteenth century Sicilian hospitals and pharmacies began to entrust their requirements for pharmacy jars to local factories which had sprung up at Palermo, Caltagirone, Trapani, Sciacca and

[1] Kremers and Urdang, *History of Pharmacy*, pp. 420–1.

Plate 28A   Albarello, painted in blue monochrome
VENICE, last quarter of 16th century. H. 19.5 cm (7.7 in). Inscription 'HIERA LOGOD'
Nyon (Switzerland), Musée au Château. See page 60

Plate 28B   Albarello, painted in blue and opaque white on a pale blue ground
VENICE, last quarter of 16th century. H. 19 cm (7.5 in). Inscription 'VNG·DE·PLVMBO' (*Unguentum de plumbo*)
Faenza, Museo Internazionale delle Ceramiche. See page 60

Plate 28C   Oil jar, painted in blue and opaque white, with touches of yellow and brown
VENICE, last quarter of 16th century. H. 22 cm (8.7 in). Inscription 'ol· ?tra· Verm' (*Oleum contra vermes*)
Basle, Schweizerisches Pharmazie-Historisches Museum. See page 60

Plate 28D   Albarello, painted in pale blue
Probably GENOA, c.1570. H. 22 cm (8.7 in)
The Hague, Gemeentemuseum. See page 72

29A   Albarello, painted in blue, yellow, brown and green
SICILY, probably TRAPANI, first half of 17th century. H. 29 cm (11.4 in)
Rotterdam, Museum Boymans-van Beuningen. See page 70

29B   Albarello, painted in green, yellow and manganese-purple on a blue ground
SICILY, probably CALTAGIRONE, middle of 17th century. H. 15 cm (5.9 in)
Author's collection. See page 70

29C   Albarello, painted in blue, green, yellow and ochre
SICILY (PALERMO), *c.*1600. H. 30 cm (11.8 in).
London, British Museum. See page 70

29D   Albarello, painted in blue, yellow, ochre and light green
SICILY (PALERMO), beginning of 17th century. H. 20 cm (7.9 in). Inscription
'SYᴼ·DI·CICORIA·COMPTO' (*Syroppo di cicoria composto*)
London, Royal College of Surgeons of England. See page 70

29E   Reverse of 29C

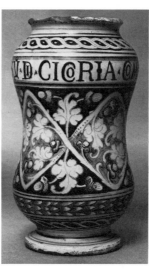

30A Twin-handled jar (*idria*),
painted in blue on a pale
blue ground
SAVONA or ALBISSOLA,
c.1600–15. H. 52 cm
(20·5 in). Inscription
'A.bethonice' (*Aqua
betonicae*)
*Genoa, Museo degli
Ospedali Civili. See page
74*

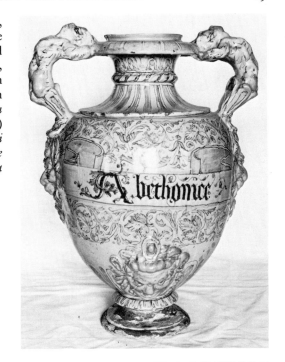

30B Double-handled jar (*idria*), painted
in blue
SAVONA or ALBISSOLA, *c*.1615–35.
H. 40.5 cm (16 in). Inscription
'Aq.Boraginis.'
*Milan, Museo d' Arte Antica.
See page 74*

30C *Idria* painted in blue
SAVONA or ALBISSOLA,
c.1615–35. H. 40.5 cm (16 in).
Inscription 'Aq.Endivie.'
(*Aqua endiviae*)
*Genoa, Museo degli Ospedali
Civili. See page 74*

Collesano. The wares, which date principally from the period c.1585–1670, were albarelli, globular vases and spouted jars, almost invariably decorated in polychrome pigments.

Sicilian maiolica exhibits rather less originality than the pottery of other regions of Italy, the ornamental themes being generally copied from wares of an earlier date made at Faenza, Castel Durante, Venice or in Tuscany.[2] In particular the albarelli with chain patterns of guilloche and figures of saints and others in medallions (Plates 29C,D,E), which were made in profusion at PALERMO in the first half of the seventeenth century, had antecedents in albarelli with this type of decoration made in the middle of the sixteenth century at Faenza.[3] Sicilian drug vessels are therefore not always readily separable from wares made on the mainland, although characteristics such as pronounced waisting of albarelli and a certain superficiality in the execution of the ornamentation often enables a differentiation to be made between the respective productions. In addition certain motifs are peculiar to Sicilian potteries; these include large petals customarily ascribed to CALTAGIRONE (Plate 29B) and an ornament of crumpled ribbon assignable to TRAPANI (Plate 29A). On occasion the jars carry initials such as 'SPQP'[4] (*Senatus populusque Panormitanus*), 'SPQD'[5] (*Senatus populusque Drepanensis*) and 'SPQS'[6]

[2] M. Bellini and G. Conti, *Maioliche Italiane del Rinascimento*, Milan, 1964, p. 173, figs. B and C; p. 174, figs. C and D; pp. 175 and 176; Giacomotti, *Catalogue MN*, Nos. 1326–8.
[3] J. V. G. Mallet, 'Alcune maioliche Faentine in raccolte Inglesi', *Faenza*, vol. 60, 1974, pp. 3–23; plates XVIII-a,b, XIX-b.
[4] Rackham, *Catalogue VAM*, No. 1019; Bellini and Conti, loc. cit. (note 2, above), p. 174, fig. B; p. 175.
[5] E. Mauceri, 'Le officine Siciliane di ceramica', *Faenza*, vol. 18, 1930, plate VI-d.
[6] N. Ragona, *La Ceramica Siciliana dalle Origini ai Giorni Nostri*, Palermo, 1955, p. 57.

Plate 31A   Covered twin-handled jar (*idria*), displaying arms of the Franciscan Order, decoration in blue monochrome
Probably SAVONA, first half of 18th century. H. 48 cm (18.9 in). Inscription 'Aqu· Borag:'
Lyons, Musée Historique des Hospices Civils. See page 74

Plate 31B   Triple-handled drug jar with cover, decoration in polychrome
SAVONA (perhaps painted by G. Berti), first half of 18th century. H. 50 cm (19.7 in). Inscription 'Aq. Flor. Camamille' (*Aqua florum chamomillae*)
Turin, Museo Civico d'Arte Antica. See page 74

Plate 31C   Reverse of two-handled drug jar, painted in blue, yellow, brown, green and manganese-purple
SAVONA, c.1685–1715. H. 45 cm (17.7 in). Inscription 'Aq. Cicorie' (at front)
Strasbourg, Musée des Arts Décoratifs. See page 74

Plate 31D   Reverse of double-handled drug jar, painted in blue monochrome
SAVONA, workshop of G. Valente, first quarter of 18th century. H. 49 cm (19.3 in). Inscription 'Aqu.Scorson.' (at front)
Genoa, Museo degli Ospedali Civili. See page 74

(*Senatus populusque Saccensis*), which are indicative of a Palermo, Trapani or Sciacca origin, respectively, whilst jars made at Palermo and Collesano are sometimes inscribed with the names of these localities.[7]

Another major source of pharmaceutical pottery as well as decorative maiolica was the province of LIGURIA, in North-Western Italy. The factories were situated in or around the coastal towns of GENOA, ALBISSOLA and SAVONA, the last being the principal centre of production of Ligurian earthenware.

Many of the Ligurian drug jars bear factory marks, of which the ducal *berretto* with triple palm, branches and initials 'GM' (attributed to G. Marchiano of Savona), the sun-face mark (ascribed to Girolamo Salomine, also of Savona), the beacon light (mark of the Levantino family, potters at Albissola) and the orb surmounting the letters 'LL' (also mark of the Levantinos) are the most important.[8]

The earliest pharmaceutical productions which can be assigned with some degree of confidence to Liguria are jars with blue spiral ornaments dating from about 1565–80, probably made at Genoa (Plate 28D); the ornamentation on the vessels was derived from Turkish (Isnik) wares,[9] which were imported at this

---

[7] Mauceri, loc. cit. (note 5, above), plate V-a,b; Mario Jung, 'Maioliche Siciliane nella Collezione Reber al Museo di Nyon', *Faenza*, vol. 58, 1972, pp. 41–3; plate XV, Giacomotti, *Catalogue MN*, No. 1319.

[8] A comprehensive list of potters' marks on Ligurian pharmacy jars is given in G. Pesce, *Maioliche Liguri da Farmacia*, Milan, 1960, pp. 48–65.

[9] A. Lane, *Later Islamic Pottery: Persia, Syria, Egypt, Turkey*, London, 2nd ed., 1971, plate 29A.

Plate 32A   Waisted cylindrical drug pot on short foot, painted in blue, outlines and inscription in manganese-purple
SAVONA, second quarter of 17th century. H. 21 cm (8.3 in). Inscription 'Ell·d·hiera·picra·d·gal·' (*Electuarium de hiera picra de Galeno*)
Faenza, Museo Internazionale delle Ceramiche. See page 74

Plate 32B   Albarello, painted in blue monochrome
SAVONA, probably first quarter of 18th century. H. 21 cm (8.3 in). Inscription 'Ung· Populeon·'
Nyon (Switzerland), Musée au Château. See page 74

Plate 32C   Waisted drug pot on short foot, painted in blue, inscription in black
SAVONA, 18th century. H. 19 cm (7.5 in). Inscription 'El·di·Suc·di·Ros·' (*Elettuario di succo di rose*)
Copenhagen, Universitets Medicinsk Historiske Museum. See page 74

Plate 32D   Waisted ointment jar on short foot, painted in blue, inscription in manganese-purple
SAVONA or ALBISSOLA, middle of 18th century. Inscription 'U. Malvinu' (*Unguentum malvinum*, ointment of mallow)
London, Royal College of Surgeons of England. See page 74

period in substantial quantities from Asia Minor. Sometimes a portrait head was incorporated into the design.[10]

The beginning of the seventeenth century saw the production of large *idrie* with handles in the form of arched figures (Plate 30A) or coiled serpents (Plates 30B,C), a shape derived from ornamental vases made in Tuscany and at Urbino at an earlier date. This class of earthenware was decorated in blue monochrome with foliage or figures and animals set amongst plants and flowers. A *mascherone* in relief, whose mouth was generally pierced to receive a spigot for delivery of the contents of the vessel, provided additional embellishment. Albarelli with this genre of painted decoration are also known (Plate 32A).

In the second half of the seventeenth century new shapes of vessel, particularly globular jars provided with handles moulded in the shape of heads of horses, lions, griffins, etc., were introduced (Plates 31A,B,C,D). These later wares, ascribed to the Savona potters Giuseppe Valente, Giacomo Berti and others, were decorated with religious or mythological subjects, the ornamentation being sometimes allowed to spread on to the foot of the vessel and the cover. On occasion the arms of the Franciscans (Plate 31A) or other religious order were displayed, indicating that the vessel had been commissioned by a monastic pharmacy. Both monochrome and polychrome examples of this type of ware are known, the latter including large amphorae for medicated waters, with triple handles in the form of heads of animals arranged around the neck of the container (Plate 31B).

In addition to these productions, which were made for the hospitals dei Cronici and Pammatone in Genoa, the hospital Santa Maria di Misericordia at Albenga, and other infirmaries,[11] there was a considerable output of vessels intended for *spezierie* in Liguria and perhaps other regions of Italy such as Piedmont. These wares include drug jars painted with stylised foliage (Plate 32D) or with mock gadroons, sometimes with the addition of the initials of the proprietor of the pharmacy (Plate 32C). The decoration on these wares was generally executed in blue monochrome, whilst the inscription was rendered in manganese-violet. Other Ligurian drug vessels, commissioned by individual pharmacies, may be exemplified by reference to a service made for a Farmacia alla Trinità (Plate 32B) and a set of jars with graceful manganese-violet chinoiserie decor from the workshop of Luigi Levantino (Plate 33C).

The requirements for pharmaceutical pottery of the Kingdom of Naples were met principally by the kilns of the ABRUZZI region, which were situated in

---

[10] G. Morazzoni, *La Maiolica Antica Ligure*, Milan, 1951, plate 13; G. Liverani, *Five Centuries of Italian Majolica*, New York, Toronto and London, 1960, fig. xlvi.
[11] Drug jars made for the Ospedale di San Paolo at Savona depict the standing figure of St. Paul (M. Labò, 'La ceramica di Savona', *Dedalo*, vol. 4, 1923–4, p. 437; Morazzoni, loc. cit. (note 10, above), plate 27; Agnes Lothian, 'Saints on drug jars', *Chemist and Druggist*, vol. 159, 1953, p. 600, fig. 10).

33A   Covered syrup jar, painted in pink,
      blue, green, orange and purplish
      black
      PESARO, workshop of A. Casali and
      F. A. Caligari, c.1765–75. H. 29.5 cm
      (11.6 in). Inscription 'Sir: di Cedro'
      (*Siroppo di cedro*)
      London, Victoria and Albert Museum.
      See page 81

33B   Oil jar, painted in blue, outlines
      and inscription in manganese-
      purple
      Probably NOVE, second half of
      18th century. H. 21 cm
      (8.3 in). Inscription
      'Ol.d.Camamilla.'
      Nuremberg, Germanisches
      Nationalmuseum. See page 81

33C   Syrup jar, painted in manganese-
      purple. Mark: Orb and letters LL
      SAVONA or ALBISSOLA, workshop of
      Luigi Levantino, first half of 18th
      century. H. 18 cm (7.1 in).
      Inscription 'Sӱr·Capil·Vener·'
      (*Syrupus capillorum Veneris*)
      Basle, Schweizerisches Pharmazie-
      Historisches Museum. See page 74

or near the small town of CASTELLI, in the foothills of the Gran Sasso. The first ceramic wares of the Abruzzi, dating from the close of the sixteenth century, were tiles, dishes and wall plaques; manufacture of pharmacy jars does not appear to have commenced until the last quarter of the seventeenth century.

Among the earliest of the *abruzzese* officinal productions was a service of albarelli, bottles and other shapes painted in polychrome with the subject of St. Martin sharing his cloak with the beggar (Plate 34C). This set, which was made for the Carthusian monastery of San Martino at Naples, stemmed probably from the workshop of Carlo Antonio Grue (1655–1723), a leading artist at Castelli. The members of the series bear dates from 1697 onwards. A related set, probably of later date, comprising double-handled jars for medicinal waters, painted with portraits of the Apostles, is noteworthy for the beauty of its painting (Colour Plate E, Plate 35A).[12]

In the first half of the eighteenth century a number of Castelli potters, notably Dr. Francesco Antonio Saverio (Xaverio) Grue (1686–1746), son of Carlo Antonio Grue, established themselves in the city of NAPLES[13] and trained apprentices, of whom Donato Massa (active 1711–48),[14] P. Criscuolo[15]

---

[12] Other jars from this set are illustrated in G. C. Polidori, *La Maiolica Antica Abruzzese*, 2nd ed., Milan, 1952, plate 57; W. Luckenbach, 'Apotheken-Gefässe aus der Majolika-Manufaktur in Castelli', *Beiträge zur Geschichte der Pharmazie*, vol. 23, 1971, pp. 17–18.

[13] Guido Donatone, 'Maiolica Napoletana dei secoli XVII–XVIII', *Napoli Nobilissima*, 1967, pp. 58–70.

[14] Donatone, loc. cit. (note 13 above), fig. 47; id., *La Farmacia degli Incurabili e la Maiolica Napoletana del Settecento*, Naples, n.d. (1972?), fig. 15.

[15] O. Ferrari and G. Scavizzi, *Maioliche Italiane del Seicento e Settecento*, Milan, 1965, p. 135.

Plate 34A   Spouted jar, painted in blue, green, yellow and brownish orange
             CASTELLI (ABRUZZI), c.1690–1710. H. 26 cm (10.2 in). Inscription 'MEL·
             VIOLATVM'
             Cambridge, Fitzwilliam Museum (Glaisher Collection). See page 78

Plate 34B   Spouted jar, painted in blue, green, yellow and brown
             CASTELLI (ABRUZZI), c.1690–1710. H. 39.5 cm (15.5 in). Inscription 'AQ·
             D· ACETOSA'
             Faenza, Museo Internazionale delle Ceramiche. See page 78

Plate 34C   Drug bottle, painted in blue, yellow, brown, green and manganese-
             purple. At back insignia of Carthusian Order.
             CASTELLI or NAPLES, dated 1702. H. 27.5 cm (10.8 in). Inscription 'AQ
             ROS· PERSIC·' (*Aqua rosarum Persicarum*, water of Persian roses)
             Sèvres, Musée National de Céramique. See pages 76 and 78

Plate 34D   Drug bottle, painted in yellow, green and blue
             CASTELLI (ABRUZZI), c.1710–30. H. 28 cm (11 in). Inscription 'AQVA·
             CARD· SANCT·' (*Aqua cardui sancti*)
             London, Collection Mr. W. A. Beare. See page 78

and Carmine Porreca (Plate 35D)[16] made drug vessels for local pharmacies. The Neapolitan craftsmen worked generally in the style of Castelli, and their wares are not readily distinguished from the productions of the *castellani* kilns.

Shapes of drug container of *abruzzese* and Neapolitan manufacture are the spouted jar, bottle, strap-handled vase and albarello of tall form; in addition to these vessels of conventional shape there was also a substantial production of albarelli of wide diameter (Plates 35C,D). The drug label is usually to be found at the base of the container, and a distinctive mark such as a lozenge or scallop often occurs at the foot or on the spout (Plates 34A,B,C,D, 35B). Both polychrome and blue monochrome palettes were used for the execution of the decoration. The polychrome wares were mostly decorated with religious or biblical subjects, whilst the monochrome wares generally carry a view of buildings or a landscape; occasionally the badge of a monastery or religious order such as that of the Minims (Plate 35C) is displayed.

Finally mention must be made of a number of factories at which production of pharmaceutical maiolica appears to have been confined to the eighteenth century. These were Turin,[17] Lodi,[18] Pavia,[19] Nove, Pesaro, Bassano and possibly others. Some of the productions of these workshops, such as a large group of vessels with decoration of festoons, probably of Nove manufacture

---

[16] Naples, Palazzo Reale, and Teramo, Museo Civico, *Mostra dell' Antica Maiolica Abruzzese, Catalogo*, 1955, plate LXXV, No. 179; Ferrari and Scavizzi, loc. cit. (note 15, above), p. 133.
[17] Saul Levy, *Maioliche Settecentesche Piemontesi, Liguri, Romagnole, Marchigiane, Toscane e Abruzzesi*, Milan, 1964, plates 13 and 16.
[18] Saul Levy, *Maioliche Settecentesche Lombarde e Venete*, Milan, 1962, plates 202B and 214B.
[19] ibid., plate 228.

Plate 35A   Double-handled drug jar, painted in polychrome
             CASTELLI (ABRUZZI), probably first quarter of 18th century. H. 36 cm
             (14.2 in). Inscription 'AQ: RVTH: CAPR:' (*Aqua rutae caprariae*)
             Heidelberg, Deutsches Apothekenmuseum. See page 76

Plate 35B   Spouted jar with cover, decoration painted in blue, yellow, ochre, green,
             manganese-purple and black
             CASTELLI (ABRUZZI), first quarter of 18th century. H. 28 cm (11 in).
             Inscription 'OXIMEL SICILLIT' (*Oxymel scilliticum*)
             London, Royal College of Surgeons of England. See page 78

Plate 35C   Albarello, displaying emblem of Order of Minims, decoration in blue
             monochrome.
             ABRUZZI, dated 1734. H. 24 cm (9.4 in)
             Basle, Schweizerisches Pharmazie-Historisches Museum. See page 78

Plate 35D   Albarello, painted in polychrome
             NAPLES or CASTELLI, probably work of Carmine Porreca. Dated 1759.
             H. 28.5 cm (11.2 in). Inscription 'SYR. POMOR. DULC.' (*Syrupus pomorum dulcium*, syrup of sweet apples)
             London, Collection Mr. H. E. Brocksom. See page 78

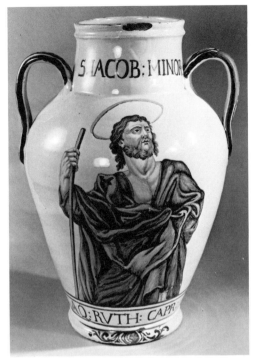

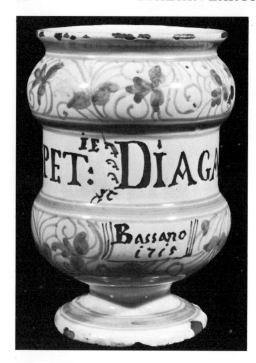

(Plate 33B), and a set of dated albarelli and bottles of BASSANO origin (Plate 36A), were painted in the traditional style of maiolica ornamentation, but the greater part of the Italian eighteenth-century pharmaceutical earthenware was decorated with naturalistically painted flowers in the colours of the *petit feu*, the palette often including an attractive olive-green and a delicate pink or bright crimson.

Wares of this type may be exemplified by reference to a large service of albarelli, spouted jars, bottles and covered vases, attributable to the Rossetti factory at TURIN, which was made for the Ospedale Maggiore della Carità at Novara (Plate 36C).[20] Other sets of *settecentesche* drug vessels with floral decoration include a group of jars from the workshop of Antonio Casali and Filippo Antonio Caligari at PESARO (Plate 33A), and a set of ewers and urns from the factory of Pasquale Antonibon at Nove. The latter service is noteworthy in that the jars have a fluted profile (Plate 36B); the same ribbed profile and ornamentation of star-shaped flowers occur also on a service of tableware from this workshop.[21]

---

[20] C. Pedrazzini, *La Farmacia Storica ed Artistica Italiana*, Milan, 1934, pp. 283–4 and 289; O. Ferrari and G. Scavizzi, *Maioliche Italiane del Seicento e Settecento*, Milan, 1965, p. 117.
[21] Levy, loc. cit. (note 18, above), plate 309B.

Plate 36A   Waisted drug pot on short foot, decoration painted in pale blue, inscription in manganese purple
BASSANO, 1715. H. 13 cm (5.1 in). Inscriptions 'Bassano 1715' and 'SPET^{IE}: DIAGALANGA·'
London, Pharmaceutical Society of Great Britain. See page 81

Plate 36B   Covered drug jar, painted in polychrome
NOVE, factory of Pasquale Antonibon, *c.* 1780–90. H. 21 cm (8.3 in). Inscription 'Ping: Equi:' (*Pinguedo equi*)
Nyon (Switzerland), Musée au Château. See page 81

Plate 36C   Covered twin-handled jar, painted in polychrome
Probably TURIN, Rossetti factory, middle of 18th century. H. 47 cm (18.5 in). Inscriptions 'HOSP· MAI· CHAR· CIV· NOV·' (Hospitalis Maioris Charitatis Civitatis Novariae) and 'Cort. Peruvian' (*Cortex Peruvianus*)
Turin, Museo Civico d'Arte Antica. See page 81

Chapter 4
FRANCE

Production of tin-glazed earthenware drug jars in France had its origin in the sixteenth century at Lyons, Rouen and the Languedoc district in the south. In the next two centuries factories in other regions took up manufacture of these vessels, and it is probable that most of the great ceramic factories in France were at one time or another engaged in the making of pharmaceutical faience or porcelain, notable exceptions being Aprey, Mennecy, Sèvres and Vincennes.

Although many of the vessels were intended for the shelves of urban and princely pharmacies, the majority of the wares were commissioned by hospitals and Hôtels-Dieu, some of which have survived to the present day with their original sets of albarelli, *pots sur piédouche* (jars on short spreading foot) and *chevrettes* (spouted vessels) (Plates 91 to 95). Sets of drug jars were generally

---

Plate 37A   Albarello, painted in blue, green and yellow
                 LYONS, last quarter of 16th century. H. 23 cm (9 in). Inscription 'Philoniü Ro' (*Philonium Romanum*)
                 Lyons, Musée Historique des Hospices Civils. See page 84

Plate 37B   Drug bottle, painted in blue, green and ochre
                 LYONS, *c.*1590–1610. H. 30 cm (11.8 in). Inscription 'A: scabiose' (*Aqua scabiosae*)
                 Lyons, Musée Historique des Hospices Civils. See page 84

Plate 37C   Syrup jar, painted in blue, ochre, yellow and green
                 LYONS, beginning of 17th century. H. 22 cm (8.7 in). Inscription 'S. de cichoreo. sim.' (*Syrupus de cichorio simplex*)
                 Sèvres, Musée National de Céramique. See page 84

Plate 37D   Albarello, painted in blue, ochre, yellow and green
                 LYONS, beginning of 17th century. H. 23 cm (9 in). Inscription 'E. de baccis l.' (*Electuarium de baccis lauri*)
                 Lyons, Musée Historique des Hospices Civils. See page 84

extensive, some of the series numbering more than 150 individual vessels.[1] Drug jars destined to hold one or other of the Sovereign Remedies — *Theriaca*, *Mithridatium*, *Confectio Alkermes*, *Confectio de Hyacintho* and *Orvietanum* — were sometimes of greater height or more elaborate in their decoration than the other jars in the series, in recognition of the superior medicinal properties attached to these *grandes compositions galéniques* (Plates 43, 48B,C, 94).

Probably the first potter to make tin-enamelled drug jars in France was Benedetto Angelo, an artisan of Italian origin, who established himself at LYONS in about 1512. Angelo was awarded a contract to supply local hospitals with pharmacy vessels, and in return he undertook to instruct a number of orphans (*Enfants de l'Aulmone*) in the craft of pottery manufacture. Few of the drug jars of the early Lyonnais period have survived, but they are believed to have been albarelli and spouted jars decorated in Italian style with motifs such as Gothic foliage.[2] The drug jars of the second half of the sixteenth century were more individual in conception, the ornamentation including fanciful foliage (Plate 37B) and broadly painted strap-work designs (Plate 37A). The dominant colour of the decoration was generally dark blue, while details were traced in pale green, yellow and ochre. One of the most attractive productions of Lyons is a group of albarelli and spouted jars depicting a pelican feeding its young, symbol of charity, which was made for the Hôpital de la Charité in Lyons (Plates 37C,D).

Pharmaceutical pottery was also produced at an early date at ROUEN, in a factory founded by Masséot Abaquesne in the second quarter of the sixteenth century. The vessels — uninscribed albarelli and spouted jars decorated with portrait heads set among foliage on coiled stems — are noteworthy for the use of subdued colours allied to vigorous brushwork which resulted in a design of unusual strength (Plate 38). From the relatively large number of surviving drug jars and from documentary evidence, particularly a contract providing for the supply of 346 dozen jars to a wholesaler in apothecary's requisites named Pierre Dubosc, it is clear that the Abaquesne workshop was a major source of pharmacy jars in North-Western France in the two decades 1545–65.

Other wares from this workshop were wall tiles, pavement tiles, dishes and pilgrim bottles. Abaquesne died in 1564, and his factory ceased production a few years later.

Hospitals in the south of France secured their drug jars from potteries at Narbonne, Nîmes and Montpellier, all in the Languedoc district. The wares of Nîmes and Montpellier betray the influence of Italy; on the other hand the productions of NARBONNE bear the imprint of Spanish models. Thus the vine-leaf decoration on a group of lustred earthenware jars of Narbonne

---

[1] An inventory of the inscriptions on the drug jars of the Hôtel-Dieu at Gray in the Department of the Haute-Saône (Eastern France) has been compiled by Claudius Brocard, *Rev. Hist. Pharm.*, vol. 20, 1970–1, pp. 386–404.

[2] L. Cotinat, 'Faïences pharmaceutiques du XVe au XIXe siècle', *Bulletin de la Société de Pharmacie de Strasbourg*, vol. 8, 1965, pp. 107–24, fig. 5.

38   Spouted jar, painted in blue, green, ochre, yellow and manganese-purple
      ROUEN, workshop of Masséot Abaquesne, *c*.1540–50. H. 21 cm (8.3 in)
      Sèvres, Musée National de Céramique. See page 84

manufacture (Plate 72B) is derived from Valencian vessels of earlier date, and motifs such as large fleurs-de-lis (Plate 72C) and half-palmettes[3] on a group of lustred albarelli (one of which bears the date 1584[4]) have counterparts in lustred dishes made in nearby Catalonia. These pharmacy vessels in all likelihood were the creation of Catalonian potters working at Narbonne.

The pharmaceutical ceramic wares of NîMES were the work of Antoine Syjalon (or Sigalon), a potter who was active from about 1560 until his death in 1590. His vessels are decorated with portraits or friezes of acanthus; the drug name is inscribed in Gothic characters (Plates 39A,B,C,D). Albarelli from the Nîmes factory are usually fluted at the shoulder, whilst syrup jars carry gadroon-like indentations on the body. Besides producing drug jars Syjalon was responsible for a number of heraldic dishes and pilgrim bottles of remarkable quality, one of which is inscribed 'Nismes 1581'.

The output of Syjalon was on a relatively small scale; on the other hand the production of the MONTPELLIER potters, which extended over two centuries, from about 1565 to the middle of the eighteenth century, was substantial. The wares have been extensively studied and described by Jean Thuile.[5] The earliest drug vessels were spouted jars and cylindrical pots on splayed foot, decorated with dolphins, fleurs-de-lis and portraits of saints, popes or kings of France (Plates 40, 41B,C). The syrup jars often carry a small vertically disposed ring between the spout and the body of the vessel (Plate 41C), in contrast to spouted jars of Italian manufacture, where the link is effected by a horizontal tie

---

[3] Alice W. Frothingham, *Lustreware of Spain*, New York, 1951, p. 250, fig. 201.

[4] J. Chompret, *Les Faïences Françaises Primitives d'après les Apothicaireries Hospitalières*, Paris, 1946, pl. 59, fig. 236; Frothingham, loc. cit. (note 3, above), fig. 200.

[5] (a) J. Thuile, *La Céramique à Montpellier du XVIe au XVIIIe Siècle; ses Rapports avec la Faïence Nîmoise*, Paris, 1943; (b) id., 'Faïences anciennes de Montpellier. XVIe–XVIIIe siècles', *Cahiers*, No. 32, 1963, pp. 232–51; (c) id., 'Les pots de pharmacie à l'Exposition de l'Ancienne Faïence de Montpellier du Musée Fabre', *Rev. Hist. Pharm.*, vol. 16, 1963, pp. 129–32 and 204–7.

Plate 39A   Albarello, painted in blue, green, ochre and yellow
              NîMES, workshop of Antoine Syjalon, c.1570–80. H. 24 cm (9.4 in).
              Inscription 'D. catholico.' (*Diacatholicon*)
              London, Collection Mr. W. A. Beare. See page 86

Plate 39B   Reverse of 39A

Plate 39C   Syrup jar, painted in blue, green, ochre and yellow
              NîMES, workshop of Antoine Syjalon, c.1570–80. H. 24 cm (9.4 in).
              Inscription 'S·di·glicirrhisa:' (*Syrupus de glycyrrhiza*)
              Rouen, Musée des Antiquités. See page 86

Plate 39D   Albarello, painted in blue, green, ochre and yellow
              NîMES, workshop of Antoine Syjalon, c.1570–80. H. 23.5 cm (9.2 in).
              Inscription 'C·hamech' (*Confectio Hamech*)
              Sèvres, Musée National de Céramique. See page 86

40   Ointment jar, painted in polychrome, with the portrait of Clodion, chieftain of
      the Franks
      MONTPELLIER, probably workshop of Pierre Estève, *c.*1590. Inscriptions
      'Clodio, Rex Franc. II' and 'V. Mun. de A.' (*Unguentum mundificativum de apio*)
      Private French collection. See page 86

41A   Albarello on low foot, painted in blue, yellow, brown and green
MONTPELLIER, workshop of Daniel Ollivier, first half of 17th century. H. 24 cm (9.4 in).
Inscription 'Cerat. Stomachic G.' (*Ceratum stomachicum Galeni*)
Montpellier, Musée Fabre. See page 92

41B,C   Spouted jar, painted in blue, green, yellow and ochre, with portrait of Merovée III
MONTPELLIER or NÎMES, *c.*1570–80. H. 27 cm (10.6 in). Inscription 'M. Violatun' (*Mel violatum*)
Sèvres, Musée National de Céramique. See page 86

42A   Covered drug pot on short foot, painted in yellow and ochre on a deep blue ground MONTPELLIER, probably workshop of Daniel Ollivier, first half of 17th century. H. 26.5 cm (10.4 in). Inscription 'Co.R.Simphitu' (*Conserva radicis symphyti*) *The Hague, Gemeentemuseum. See page 92*

42B   Covered syrup jar, painted in yellow, ochre and touches of green on a deep blue ground MONTPELLIER, probably workshop of Daniel Ollivier, first half of 17th century. H. 30 cm (11.8 in)' Inscription 'S. Acetos sim:' (*Syrupus acetosus simplex*) *Paris, Collection Monsieur L. Cotinat. See page 92*

42C   Syrup jar with cover, painted in yellow and ochre on a deep blue ground MONTPELLIER, probably workshop of Daniel Ollivier, first half of 17th century. H. 29.5 cm (11.6 in). Inscription 'S.d papave R:' (*Syrupus de papavere rhoeas*) *The Hague, Gemeentemuseum. See page 92*

43 Covered jar with serpentine handles, painted in polychrome
MONTPELLIER, second half of 17th century. H. 55 cm (21.6 in).
Inscription 'Theriaca. A.' (*Theriaca Andomachi*)
Sèvres, Musée National de Céramique. See page 92

(Plates 8C, 12C, 13A,B). The early Montpellier wares have certain affinities with the drug vessels of Syjalon, to whom they were at one time attributed, but Thuile has shown that they were the work of Pierre Estève (active 1570–96) and others.

The first half of the seventeenth century saw the manufacture at Montpellier of covered jars decorated with stylised foliage, fleurs-de-lis and animals rendered in yellow and ochre on a deep blue ground (Plates 42A,B,C); these productions have been assigned by Thuile to the workshop of Daniel Ollivier (1593–1682). Of about the same date as these wares is a group of albarelli and spouted jars painted in polychrome colours with large leaves, formal rosettes and ribbed fruit (Plate 41A).[6] These vessels are stylistically close to drug jars made at an earlier period at Antwerp; they were perhaps the work of Flemish potters who had migrated to Montpellier at the close of the sixteenth century to escape religious persecution in their homeland.[7]

After the middle of the seventeenth century the last traces of Italian influence vanished; at the same time there was a transition, echoing trends elsewhere in Europe, to a blue or blue-and-purple palette. Decorative motifs of this period included diademed heads and festoons (Plates 43, 44A,C). Some of the vessels were provided with covers shaped in the form of effigies of prelates or physicians (Plates 43, 44C), one of whom has been identified as Pierre Richer de Belleval, Professor of Anatomy and Botany at the University of Montpellier at the close of the sixteenth century.[8] Other jars carried the emblem of a

---

[6] See also Thuile, loc. cit. (note 5(a), above), plate 1, figs. 45, 46; plate 2, fig. 49; Chompret, loc. cit. (note 4, above) plate 17, fig. 49; plate 46; J. Giacomotti, *French Faience*, London, 1963, p. 15.
[7] E. Segers, 'Origine et évolution des faïences pharmaceutiques en Belgique', *Revue de Médecine et de Pharmacie*, 1957, No. 4.
[8] Thuile, loc. cit. (note 5(c), above), p. 132 and plate X (opp. p. 129); Montpellier, Musée Fabre, *La Faïence de Montpellier*, 1962, Cat. Nos. 52 and 53.

Plate 44A   Theriac jar, painted in blue and manganese-purple
             MONTPELLIER, end of 17th or beginning of 18th century. H. 41 cm
             (16.1 in). Inscription 'Theriacque. A.' (*Thériaque d'Andromaque*)
             Montpellier, Musée Fabre. See page 92
Plate 44B   Spouted jar, painted in blue and black
             MONTPELLIER or SAINT-JEAN-DU-DÉSERT, *c.*1690–1710. H. 26 cm
             (10.2 in). Inscription 'M. Violatū·' (*Mel violatum*)
             Sèvres, Musée National de Céramique. See page 94
Plate 44C   Drug jar with cover, painted in blue and manganese-purple
             MONTPELLIER, end of 17th or beginning of 18th century. H. 53 cm
             (20.9 in). Inscription 'E·Pectoral' (*Electuarium pectorale*)
             Lille, Musée des Beaux-Arts. See page 92
Plate 44D   Covered theriac jar, painted in blue, inscription in manganese-purple
             Probably SAINT-JEAN-DU-DÉSERT, late 17th century. H. 57 cm
             (22.4 in). Inscription 'Theriaca·A·' (*Theriaca Andromachi*)
             Lille, Musée des Beaux-Arts. See page 94

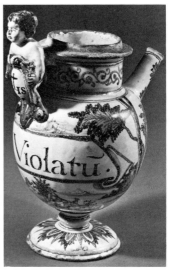

religious order such as that of the Jesuits (Plate 44B), indicating that the vessel had been commissioned for a monastic pharmacy.

The hill town of MOUSTIERS, to the east of Montpellier, which was noted for decorative pottery of refined workmanship, had also a small production of pharmaceutical faience. The drug jars are decorated in blue monochrome, sometimes supplemented by manganese-purple or black, and were probably made at the factory of the Clérissy family. Decorative motifs include formal scrolls (Plate 45A), cherubs (Plates 45C,D) or lace-like patterns of lambrequins (Plate 45B). Additional ornamentation on some containers is provided by plaited handles[9] or by masks in the form of lions' heads (Plate 45B). Another locality in the south of France associated with the manufacture of decorative and pharmaceutical earthenware is SAINT-JEAN-DU-DÉSERT, on the outskirts of Marseilles, whose pharmacy jars are stylistically related to those of Montpellier (Plate 44D).

NEVERS in Central France was a source of ornamental pottery of distinction from the last quarter of the sixteenth century onwards, but the production of drug jars appears to date only from about the middle of the seventeenth century. The earliest pharmacy jars from this locality were probably made at a workshop founded in about 1632 by a potter of Italian descent named Pierre Custode. The jars comprised bottles, spouted vessels and covered cylindrical pots painted in opaque white (*blanc fixe*) on a dark blue (*bleu persan*) ground, a type of decoration which had been used in slightly modified form at Faenza

---

[9] *Rev. Hist. Pharm.*, vol. 13, 1957–8, plate XI (opp. p. 102).

Plate 45A   Drug pot on low foot, decoration painted in blue with manganese-purple outlines, inscription in black
SOUTHERN FRANCE, perhaps MOUSTIERS, *c*.1700. H. 24 cm (9.4 in). Inscription 'Estr. Degeieure' (*Extrait de genièvre*)
Paris, Faculté de Pharmacie. See page 94

Plate 45B   Drug jar of baluster shape on short foot, painted in blue monochrome
MOUSTIERS, first quarter of 18th century. H. 46 cm (18 in). Inscription 'M.DAMOCRato' (*Mithridatium Damocratis*)
Basle, Collection F. Hoffmann-La Roche & Co. See page 94

Plate 45C   Drug jar on low foot, displaying Jesuit emblem, decoration painted in blue, inscription in black
Probably MOUSTIERS, second quarter of 18th century. H. 20 cm (7.9 in). Inscription 'C. Capil. Ven.' (*Conserva capillorum Veneris*)
Lyons, Musée Historique des Hospices Civils. See page 94

Plate 45D   Syrup jar, painted in blue monochrome, inscription in black
Probably MOUSTIERS, second quarter of 18th century. H. 21 cm (8.3 in). Inscription 'S. Pap. Alb.' (*Syrupus papaveris albi*)
Lyons, Musée Historique des Hospices Civils. See page 94

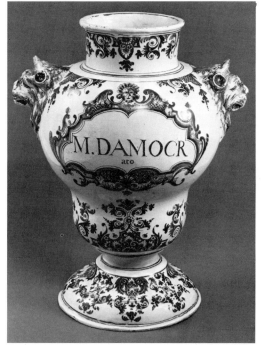

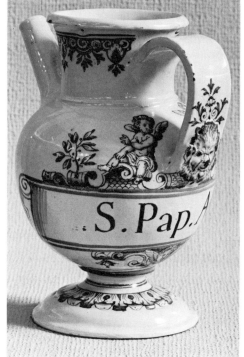

(Plate 20C) and at the Daniel Ollivier factory at Montpellier. Ornamental motifs were splashes of white, simulating molten candle wax (*décor à la tache de bougie*) (Plate 47A), and flowers, foliage and birds (Plates 46A,B,C,D). Of somewhat later date than the *bleu persan* wares are a number of services of drug jars painted in blue and manganese-purple with chinoiserie subjects (Plate 47C) or in green, yellow and purple with floral motifs (Plate 47B); this genre of ornamentation occurs also on tableware and ornamental ware made at Nevers.[10]

Production of tin-glazed earthenware at ROUEN, which had ceased shortly after the death of Masséot Abaquesne, was revived in about 1644 when Nicolas Poirel, sieur de Grandval, received the grant of a privilege to make tin-glazed pottery. Little is known of Poirel's activities in the domain of faience manufacture but in 1647 the concession was transferred to Edmé Poterat (d.1687), who erected kilns at Saint-Sever-les-Rouen on the road to Elbeuf. Poterat's earliest wares included a pyriform bottle with decoration of heads of cherubim and foliage, inscribed 'Nenuphar' and 'faict a Rouen 1647'.[11] A number of craftsmen were recruited from Nevers, this circumstance no doubt accounting for a certain *nivernais* influence on some of the seventeenth-century wares from Rouen (Plate 47D).

After the expiry of Poterat's privilege in 1696 new workshops sprang up at Rouen, and eventually eighteen factories were engaged in the making of tin-glazed pottery. In the eighteenth century Rouen became a prolific source of pharmaceutical faience, the wares ranging from simple pots with scrolled cartouche (Plate 49B), to large jars with floral decoration or patterns of

[10] Cf. Arthur Lane, *French Faïence*, London, 2nd ed., 1970, plates 9B, 11, 13A; Honey, *European Ceramic Art: Illustrated Survey*, plate 78B.

[11] J. Giacomotti, loc. cit. (note 6, above), p. 54; H.-P. Fourest and J. Giacomotti, *L'Oeuvre des Faïenciers Français du 16e à la Fin du 18e Siècle*, Paris and Lausanne, 1966, p. 88.

Plate 46A   Covered cylindrical ointment jar on short foot, painted in white on a deep blue ground
              NEVERS, probably middle of 17th century. H. 28 cm (11 in). Inscription 'V·AEgyptiac.' (*Unguentum Aegyptiacum*)
              London, Victoria and Albert Museum. See page 96

Plate 46B   Spouted jar, painted in white on a deep blue ground
              NEVERS, probably middle of 17th century. H. 24 cm (9.4 in). Inscription 'H.Laurin' (*Huile de laurier*; oil of bayberries)
              Sèvres, Musée National de Céramique. See page 96

Plate 46C   Drug bottle, painted in white on a deep blue ground
              NEVERS, probably middle of 17th century. H. 29 cm (11.4 in). Inscription 'E·De Cichoree' (*Eau de chicorée*)
              Lyons, Musée Historique des Hospices Civils. See page 96

Plate 46D   Reverse of 46C

E.   Double-handled drug jar
     CASTELLI (ABRUZZI), probably first quarter of 18th century. H. 36 cm (14.2 in).
     Inscription 'AQ: CHAMAEMEL.'
     Heidelberg, Deutsches Apothekenmuseum. See page 76

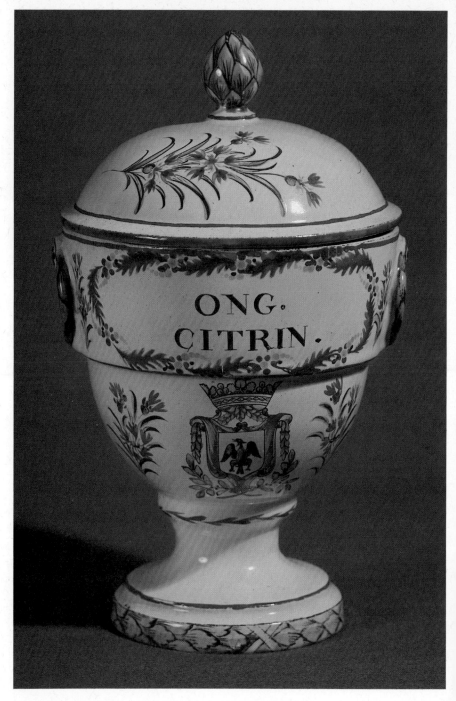

F.   Covered drug jar, displaying arms of Nicolas Beaujon
     Probably SCEAUX, second half of 18th century. Inscription 'ONG· CITRIN.'
     Paris, Musée de l' Assistance Publique. See page 100

lambrequins, sometimes supplemented by modelled embellishments (Plates 48A,B,C). Among the more notable eighteenth-century drug vessels of Rouen manufacture are covered urns of exceptional size decorated in predominantly red and blue *grand feu* colours, probably from the factory of Jean-Baptiste Guillibaud (Plate 48c), and pots and spouted jars decorated in polychrome with the royal arms of France (crown and triple fleurs-de-lis) (Plate 49A).[12] These last vessels are believed to have been made for the hospital at Évreux, in Normandy, which had been endowed by a member of the French royal family.

Decorative and pharmaceutical pottery was produced at a number of localities in south-western France. The most important of these was BORDEAUX, where Jacques Fautier established a small factory in 1709. This workshop was taken over three years later by Jacques Hustin and subsequently considerably enlarged. Jacques Hustin died in 1749; thereafter the enterprise was directed by Hustin's son Jacques-Denis-Ferdinand Hustin, and after the death of the latter in 1778, by Hustin's widow in partnership with a potter named Jean-Étienne Monsau. The factory closed in 1783. A substantial part of the production of the Hustin *atelier* appears to have been pharmaceutical pottery for hospitals in Bordeaux and neighbouring cities.[13] The early wares, probably made by migrant workers from Nevers, were painted in blue monochrome colours in the *nivernais* style; jars of later date were decorated in polychrome colours which included a dark red and a characteristic olive-green (Plate 49D). One of the most attractive pharmaceutical services from the Hustin *faïencerie* was a series of vessels made for a Carmelite monastery; the jars bear

[12] Other jars of Rouen manufacture emblazoned with the royal arms are known; e.g. see *Rev. Hist. Pharm.*, vol. 21, 1972–3, plate LXIX, No. 73, and pp. 371–2.
[13] Méaudre de Lapouyade, *Essai d'Histoire des Faïenceries de Bordeaux du XVIIIᵉ Siècle à Nos Jours*, Mâcon, 1926, pp. 37, 48–50 and plates VI and XIII; G. Devaux, 'Les faïences pharmaceutiques de l'Hôpital de Dax', *Rev. Hist. Pharm.*, vol. 22, 1974–5, pp. 435–6.

Plate 47A   Syrup jar, painted in white on a dark blue ground
             NEVERS, late 17th or early 18th century. H. 22 cm (8.7 in). Inscription
             'S·Myrtinus' (*Syrupus myrtinus*)
             Lille, Musée des Beaux-Arts. See page 96
Plate 47B   Syrup jar, painted in green, ochre, yellow and black
             NEVERS, second half of 17th century. H. 25 cm (9.8 in). Inscription
             'S·Ramno' (*Syrupus rhamni*)
             Paris, Musée des Arts Décoratifs. See page 96
Plate 47C   Spouted jar, painted in blue and manganese-purple
             NEVERS, second half of 17th century. H. 23.5 cm (9.2 in). Inscription
             'Mel. Rosatum'
             Paris, Faculté de Pharmacie. See page 96
Plate 47D   Syrup jar, decoration painted in blue, inscription in black
             ROUEN, factory of Edmé Poterat, 1650–80. H. 28 cm (11 in). Inscription
             'S·Cichorij sim.' (*Syrupus cichorii simplex*)
             Rouen, Musée des Beaux-Arts. See page 96

the monastic blazon (arms of the Shod Carmelite Order) and decoration of cherubs and festoons of flowers or fruit (Plate 49C). Other centres of production of pharmaceutical faience in South-Western France were Montauban and La Rochelle.[14]

The requirements for drug jars of the French capital and its surroundings were met principally by the potteries of the PARISIAN REGION which were situated in Paris, and on the outskirts, at Saint-Cloud and Sceaux. Production of faience in this region is believed to have been initiated by François Dezon in the Faubourg Saint-Antoine, in the eastern quarter of Paris, in about 1675; later on manufacture of tin-glazed earthenware was taken up by other potters, of whom Jacques Chapelle working at Sceaux achieved considerable renown. Production of faience in and around Paris continued until the end of the eighteenth century and even beyond, latterly in competition with the porcelain factories of Paris and elsewhere in France.

The pharmacy jars of the Parisian region are mostly decorated with formal or naturalistically painted flowers (Plates 50A,B, 52C, 53B), with garlanded ribbons (Plates 50C,D, 51B,C) or with festoons (Colour Plate F, Plate 51A). As on drug jars of Rouen manufacture the ornamentation sometimes includes a representation of the serpent, attribute of Asclepius, Greek god of Medicine (Plates 52A,B). The pharmacy jars in general cannot be assigned to a particular factory; examples of wares of unproven origin are drug containers with monochrome or polychrome decor, made for the Abbess of Chelles, Louise-Adélaïde d'Orléans, whose coat of arms is displayed on the vessels (Plate 53A). Among wares of known manufacture is a set of covered armorial urns on pedestals of square form, inscribed 'A. . . . THORY, RUE DE LA ROQUETTE, À PARIS, 1er Octobre 1778', which were presented by the financier Jacques Necker and his wife to the hospital which bears their name (Plate 52A). Attributable to SAINT-CLOUD are vessels with decor of blue peony-like flowers outlined in manganese-violet or black (Plate 53B); a number of these jars are known to have been made for the Hôpital Civil at Versailles.[15] Jars are also known from this factory bearing the royal emblem.[16]

Services of drug containers assignable to SCEAUX include a set of 150 armorial vessels made for the pharmacy of the hospital founded by Nicolas Beaujon in 1784 (Colour Plate F, Plate 51A), and two series of jars and tureens

[14] E. Forestié, Les Anciennes Faïenceries de Montauban, Ardus, Nègrepelisse, Auvillar, Bressols, Beaumont, etc., Montauban, 1929, pl. XII; Giacomotti, loc. cit. (note 6, above), pp. 184 and 187; Giacomotti, 'La faïence de la Rochelle au XVIIIe siècle', Cahiers, Nos. 42–3, 1968, pp. 92–113, figs. 1 and 5; P. Julien, 'Faïences et hôpitaux rochelais du XVIIIe siècle', Rev. Hist. Pharm., vol. 20, 1970, pp. 65–6 and plates VII and VIII.
[15] Édouard Garnier, 'Les anciens vases de pharmacie des hôpitaux et hospices de Paris', Gazette des Beaux-Arts, vol. 38, 1888, p. 129; Émile Tilmans, Faïences de France, Paris, 1954, fig. 176; Giacomotti, loc. cit. (note 6, above), p. 98.
[16] Garnier, loc. cit. (note 15, above), p. 127; L. Cotinat, 'Quelques vases de pharmacie d'apothicaireries royales', Beiträge zur Geschichte der Pharmazie, vol. 23, 1971, pp. 25–7, figs. 1 and 2.

48A   Ointment jar on low foot, decoration
painted in blue, inscription in black
ROUEN, *c*.1700. H. 33 cm (13 in). Inscription
'V·Album Rh·' (*Unguentum album Rhasis*)
Rouen, Musée des Beaux-Arts. See page 98

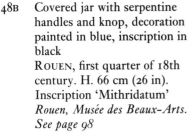

48B   Covered jar with serpentine
handles and knop, decoration
painted in blue, inscription in
black
ROUEN, first quarter of 18th
century. H. 66 cm (26 in).
Inscription 'Mithridatum'
Rouen, Musée des Beaux-Arts.
See page 98

48C   Covered jar with serpentine
handles, painted in red and blue,
with touches of green
ROUEN, probably Guillibaud
factory, *c*.1720–40. H. 49 cm
(19.3 in). Inscription 'Conf·
Alquermes·'
Paris, Musée des Arts Décoratifs.
See page 98

with the blazon of Condé, commissioned for the hospital at Chantilly (Plate 95).

In EASTERN FRANCE pharmaceutical faience was made at a number of localities, notably at Niderviller, Lunéville, Strasbourg, Saint-Clément and Poligny.[17] Whilst some of the drug jars were of conventional shape and were decorated as in the Parisian region with floral motifs or sprigs of foliage (Plates 55D,E), the greater part of the pharmaceutical productions conformed to the rococo style prevailing in Eastern France at the time. This style, which is characterised by the use of asymmetric shapes and irregular ornamental patterns, found particular expression on the faience of NIDERVILLER, in the province of Lorraine. The wares from this city include a number of armorial drug jars of refined workmanship, such as a service of covered urns with *rocaille* decoration displaying the arms of the Compagnie des Apothicaires et Épiciers de Paris, attributable to the factory of Baron Jean-Louis de Beyerlé (Plate 54C). Other drug jars from Niderviller which may be cited are two covered vases of exceptional size splendidly emblazoned in purplish-pink and other *petit-feu* colours with the arms of Stanislas Leczinski, Duke of Lorraine (Plate 54A), and a series of spouted jars commissioned by Stanislas Leczinski for the hospital of the Frères Hospitaliers de Saint-Jean de Dieu (Brothers Hospitallers of Saint John) at Nancy; the members of the series bear the shield of the order of the Frères de Saint-Jean (Plate 54B).[18]

---

[17] Suzanne de Buyer, 'Faïence de Franche-Comté. XVIIIième siècle. Poligny au Bailliage d'Aval', *Cahiers*, No. 34, 1964, pp. 104–19, figs. 3–8; ibid., 'Les apothicaireries hospitalières de Franche-Comté et leurs faïences', *Rev. Hist. Pharm.*, vol. 19, 1968–9, plates XXXIII, L, LI and LII.

[18] See also Lucien Wiener, 'Les vases de la pharmacie de Saint-Charles au Musée Lorrain', *Journal de la Société d'Archéologie Lorraine et du Musée Historique Lorrain*, vol. 30, 1881, pp. 138–46.

Plate 49A   Cylindrical ointment pot, painted in blue, green, yellow and black
               ROUEN, first quarter of 18th century. H. 21 cm (8.3 in). Inscription 'V:Neapolitan:simp·' (*Unguentum Neapolitanum simplex*)
               Paris, Collection Monsieur L. Cotinat. See page 98

Plate 49B   Drug pot, painted in green, blue, yellow and red
               ROUEN, middle of 18th century. H. 11 cm (4.3 in). Inscription 'Ext.Card.B.' (*Extractum cardui Benedicti*)
               Basle, Collection Ciba-Geigy. See page 98

Plate 49C   Covered theriac jar, displaying coat of arms of Carmelite Order, decoration painted in blue, green, brown, yellow and manganese-purple
               BORDEAUX, Hustin factory, middle of 18th century. H. 36 cm (14.2 in). Inscription 'THYRIACA'
               London, Wellcome Institute of the History of Medicine. See page 100

Plate 49D   Covered cylindrical jar, painted in blue, green, brown, yellow and manganese-purple
               BORDEAUX, c.1770–80. H. 21.5 cm (8.5 in). Inscription 'Bals. Cameroni.'
               Paris, Faculté de Pharmacie. See pages 98 and 181

LUNÉVILLE and STRASBOURG each had only a small output of pharmaceuti-cal pottery; to the first of these centres is assignable a series of jars and ewers decorated with floral sprays, scrolling foliage and other motifs painted in a *petit feu* palette which included a dark red and green (Plate 55A);[19] the set was commissioned by the hospital in Lunéville. Strasbourg was responsible for two series[20] of uninscribed jars with *rocaille* cartouche (Plate 55C), reputedly made by the potter Paul Hannong for a pharmacy whose franchise he acquired in 1747.

In Northern France LILLE is believed to have been a source of pharmaceutical pottery, but our knowledge of the wares from this centre is very incomplete. It is thought that two types of drug jars were made at Lille: a category comprising vessels with blue monochrome decoration of lambrequins made in imitation of Rouen ware (Plate 55B),[21] and a class of jars decorated with motifs such as peacocks or a satyr's head, which were derived from officinal earthenware made in Holland or Belgium.[22]

French pharmaceutical potters were slow to abandon the traditional faience in favour of porcelain as a material for drug containers, and it was not until the second quarter of the nineteenth century that porcelain apothecary jars found their way in any quantity on to the shelves of pharmacies. A soft paste porcelain service exceptional for its early date and refined workmanship was made at CHANTILLY in about 1735; the vessels are decorated in enamel colours with branches of berried foliage on the front (Plate 57A) and flowers in Kakiemon

[19] See also R. Schnyder, *Keramik-Freunde der Schweiz*, No. 86, 1974, pp. 38–9.
[20] Hans Haug, *Les Faïences et Porcelaines de Strasbourg*, Strasbourg, 1922, plate IX and p. 30; id., 'Strasbourg, entre Chantilly et Meissen (1744 à 1749)', *Cahiers*, No. 1, 1955, pp. 20–35, fig. 28.
[21] For other examples see Garnier, loc. cit. (note 15, above), p. 131; 'Pharmacie et médecine d'antan', *Rev. Hist. Pharm.*, vol. 21. 1972–3, plate LXVIII, Nos. 77 and 78.
[22] Cf. D. A. Wittop Koning, *Delftse Apothekerspotten*, Deventer, 1954, p. 161, fig. 91.

Plate 50A   Cylindrical drug pot on short foot, painted in blue monochrome
PARIS, 18th century. H. 28 cm (11 in). Inscription 'Lenit. Fin' (*Lénitif fin*)
Paris, Musée de l'Assistance Publique. See page 100

Plate 50B   Ointment pot of albarello shape, painted in blue monochrome
PARIS, c.1690–1740. H. 20 cm (7.9 in). Inscription 'Vnguent· Album Rhazis'
Sèvres, Musée National de Céramique. See page 100

Plate 50C   Covered cylindrical jar, decoration painted in green and violet, inscription in black
PARIS, c.1800. H. 24 cm (9.4 in). Inscription 'Crocus Martis Ap:'
Basle, Collection Ciba-Geigy. See page 100

Plate 50D   Covered cylindrical jar, painted in polychrome
SCEAUX, second half of 18th century. H. 22 cm (8.7 in). Inscription 'Cons: Apii' (*Conserva apii*, conserve of smallage)
Sèvres, Musée National de Céramique. See page 100

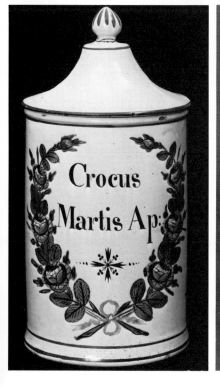

style on the reverse. The jars carry the Chantilly mark of a hunting-horn in red; some seventeen members of the series have been recorded.[23]

Hard-paste porcelain pharmacy jars were made from about 1800 onwards, at the *atelier* of the porcelain decorator Deroche in PARIS (Plate 56D) (workshop active *c*.1812–45; known in later years as Pochet-Deroche-Gosse), and at some other workshops. Ornamental subjects include floral patterns (Plate 56E)[24] and themes associated with the practice of pharmacy or medicine, such as the bowl of Hygeia, the winged caduceus, or portrait heads of famous physicians (Plates 56A,B,C,D). A set of jars from the Deroche *atelier*, decorated in blue and gold with the arms of France, believed to have been made for the old *apothicairerie* of the Tuileries and now in the pharmacy of the Hôtel des Invalides in Paris, has been described by Cotinat.[25]

After about 1850 production of porcelain drug jars increased steadily to meet the growing requirements of retail pharmacies in France and elsewhere for these prestige wares; however, quantity production of the containers was accompanied by a decline in standard of workmanship and artistic merit.

[23] R. E. A. Drey, 'Une série de vases de pharmacie en porcelaine tendre de Chantilly', *Rev. Hist. Pharm.*, vol. 20, 1970–1, pp. 475–8 and plate LXXXI.
[24] See also 'Porcelaines de Paris de 1800 à 1850', *Cahiers*, Nos. 46–7, 1970, Cat. No. 258; Régine de Plinval de Guillebon, *Paris Porcelain 1770–1850*, London, 1972, fig. 154.
[25] L. Cotinat, loc. cit. (note 16, above), fig. 6; L. Cotinat, 'Antiquités pharmaceutiques conservées dans les musées de Paris', *Rev. Hist. Pharm.*, vol. 21, 1972–3, p. 559.

Plate 51A   Drug container of tureen shape, displaying arms of Nicolas Beaujon, decoration painted in polychrome
Probably SCEAUX, second half of 18th century. H. 42 cm (16.5 in). Inscription 'ORVIÉTAN'
Paris, Musée de l'Assistance Publique. See page 100

Plate 51B   Covered cylindrical jar, painted in yellow, brown, green, blue and manganese-violet
Probably SCEAUX, second half of 18th century. H. 24.5 cm (9.6 in). Inscription 'EX: LUPULI·' (*Extractum lupuli*)
Paris, Faculté de Pharmacie. See page 100

Plate 51C   Covered cylindrical jar, painted in polychrome
SCEAUX or PARIS, 18th century. H. 14 cm (5.5 in). Inscription 'EXT. BORAGIN.' (*Extractum boraginis*)
Paris, Musée de l'Assistance Publique. See page 100

52A   Covered theriac jar on pedestal, displaying arms of Jacques Necker and his wife, decoration painted in blue monochrome
PARIS, Thory factory, dated 1778. H. 70 cm (27.6 in). Inscription 'Teriaque'
Paris, Musée de l'Assistance Publique.
See page 100

52B   Covered theriac jar, painted in blue monochrome
Probably PARIS, 18th century. H. 48 cm (18.9 in). Inscription 'THERIAQUE DE VENISE' (Venice theriac)
Paris, Musée de l'Assistance Publique.
See page 100

52C   Covered ointment jar, painted in polychrome
Probably SCEAUX, second half of 18th century. H. 39 cm (15.3 in). Inscription 'MVNDIFICAT· DE APIO·'
Paris, Musée de l'Assistance Publique.
See page 100

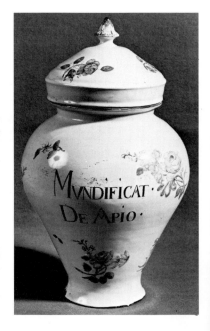

53A   Pharmacy bottle, displaying arms of Louise-Adélaïde d'Orleans, decoration in blue monochrome
PARIS or SAINT-CLOUD, c.1720–5. H. 28 cm (11 in) *Sèvres, Musée National de Céramique. See page 100*

53B   Drug bottle, painted in dark blue with manganese-purple outlines, insciption in black
SAINT-CLOUD, first quarter of 18th century. H. 27 cm (10.6 in). Inscription 'A. Buglossi.' (*Aqua buglossi*) *Basle, Schweizerisches Pharmazie-Historisches Museum. See page 100*

54A Covered display jar, painted in polychrome
NIDERVILLER, c.1760. H. 110 cm (43·2 in)
Nancy, Musée Historique Lorrain. See page 102

54B Spouted pharmacy jar, painted in blue monochrome
NIDERVILLER, third quarter of 18th century. H. 32 cm (12.6 in)
Nancy, Musée Historique Lorrain. See pages 28 and 102

54C Covered jar, emblazoned with arms of Compagnie des Apothicaires et Épiciers de Paris, decoration in blue and gold
NIDERVILLER, c.1755. H. 30 cm (11·8 in)
Strasbourg, Musée des Arts Décoratifs. See page 102

55A Double-handled drug jar with cover, painted in green, red, yellow, violet and blue LUNÉVILLE, second half of 18th century. H. 37 cm (14.6 in). Inscription 'Dyaprun Solutif.' (*Diaprunum solutivum*) *Basle, Collection Ciba-Geigy. See page 104*

55B Spouted jar, painted in dark blue Probably LILLE, first half of 18th century. H. 21 cm (8.3 in). Inscription 'S.Absinthii' (*Syrupus absinthii*) *Sèvres, Musée National de Céramique. See page 104*

55C Drug pot, painted in blue monochrome. Mark PH STRASBOURG, factory of Paul Hannong, middle of 18th century. H. 18 cm (7.1 in) *Strasbourg, Musée des Arts Décoratifs. See page 104*

55D Covered drug jar of baluster shape, painted in green, red and brown, inscription in black Probably SAINT-CLEMENT, second half of 18th century. H. 19.5 cm (7.7 in). Inscription 'Extract. Hiosciam.' *Basle, Schweizerisches Pharmazie-Historisches Museum. See page 102*

55E Cylindrical drug jar, painted in polychrome Probably EASTERN FRANCE (ALSACE), second half of 18th century. H. 20 cm (7.9 in). Inscription 'CONS: HAEDERAE· Ɐ:' *Zurich, Schweizerisches Landesmuseum. See page 102*

56A   Covered porcelain drug jar, with gilt decoration
       Probably PARIS, second quarter of 19th century.
       Inscription 'Ext: Rhei'
       *Heidelberg, Deutsches Apothekenmuseum. See page
       106*

56B   Covered porcelain jar, painted in red and gold
       Probably PARIS, middle of 19th century. H. 25 cm
       (9.8 in). Inscription 'POMM: CITRIN:'
       Paris, Musée de l'Assistance Publique. See page 106

56C   Covered porcelain jar, painted in pale lilac, red,
       black and gold
       FRANCE, 19th century. H. 25 cm (9.8 in)
       Inscriptions 'GALIEN' (Galen) and 'GEM POPUL:'
       (*Gemmae populi*)
       *London, Pharmaceutical Society of Great Britain.
       See page 106*

56D   Covered porcelain jar, painted in red, green, black
       and gold
       PARIS, Deroche workshop, 1816. H. 40 cm (15.7 in).
       Inscription 'PIL: BALS: M:' (*Pilulae balsamicae
       Mortonii*)
       Paris, Musée des Arts Décoratifs. See page 106

56E   Covered porcelain jar, painted in polychrome
       FRANCE, 19th century. H. 26.5 cm (10.4 in).
       Inscription 'ANIS ESTRELL.'
       *Basle, Collection F. Hoffmann–La Roche & Co.
       See page 106*

57A   Covered soft-paste
porcelain jar, with
polychrome decoration in
enamel colours
CHANTILLY, *c.*1735.
H. 15.5 cm (6.1 in). Inscription
'Cerat de Galien'
London, British Museum.
See page 106

57B   Set of covered porcelain jars, painted in polychrome and gilt
VIENNA, du Paquier factory, *c.* 1725–30. H. of each 11.5 cm (4.5 in).
Inscriptions 'CONFECTIO ALKERMES COMPLETA', 'OPOBALSAMI VERI OPTIMI',
'THERIACA ANDROMACHI'
Vienna, Österreichisches Museum für Angewandte Kunst. See page 164

Chapter 5

THE LOW COUNTRIES

Italian artistans in the first quarter of the sixteenth century set up kilns not only in France at places such as Lyons, but also established themselves further afield, at Seville in Spain, and at ANTWERP in the Southern Netherlands. The first potter to manufacture tin-glazed earthenware on a commercial scale at Antwerp was a craftsman from Castel Durante named Guido Andries (or Guido di Savino), whose wares were mainly tiles and ornamental dishes. The factory prospered and soon other potters from Italy settled in Antwerp. One of these, Pieter Frans van Venedigen, described in a contemporary document as 'faiseur de pots d'apothécaire demeurant en la rue de Cambreporte devant le Lyon d'Or à Anvers',[1] specialised in production of drug jars, and to him is ascribed much of the Netherlandish pharmaceutical pottery of the first half of the sixteenth century.

Guido Andries, Pieter Frans and their assistants worked mainly in Italian style and their wares, particularly the drug jars and ornamental dishes, are often difficult to separate from similar products made in Italy. Additional complications in the identification of early Netherlandish pharmacy vessels arise from the circumstance that albarelli and spouted jars decorated in Italo-Netherlandish style were made in the first half of the seventeenth century at Montpellier and perhaps other centres in Southern France.[2] Detailed studies by Rackham,[3] Nicaise,[4] Wittop Koning,[5] Dingeman Korf[6] and others have removed many of the uncertainties surrounding Netherlandish maiolica, but none the less the attribution of some of the wares remains conjectural.

Decorative motifs common to drug jars from Italy and the Antwerp region

[1] Dingeman Korf, *Nederlandse Majolica*, Bussum, n.d. (1969?), p. 22.
[2] Cf. Chapter 4, and 'Symposium Antwerps Plateel', *Vrienden*, Nos. 66–7, 1972, pp. 39, 42, 93–4.
[3] B. Rackham, *Early Netherlands Maiolica*, London, 1926.
[4] H. Nicaise, 'Les modèles italiens des faïences néerlandaises au XVIe et au début du XVIIe siècle', *Bulletin de l'Institut Historique Belge de Rome*, 1936, pp. 107–41.
[5] D. A. Wittop Koning, 'Van Antwerpse majolica tot Delfts aardewerk', (a) *Antiek*, vol. 1, No. 8, 1967, pp. 26–35; (b) *Antiek*, vol. 1, No. 9, 1967, pp. 22–31.
[6] Dingeman Korf, *Nederlandse Majolica*, Bussum, n.d. (1969?).

58A   Albarello, painted in blue,
ochre, green and touches of
manganese-purple
FAENZA, end of fifteenth
century. H. 20 cm (7.9 in)
*London, Victoria and Albert
Museum. See page 48*

58B   Albarello, painted in blue,
green and brown
NETHERLANDS, probably third
quarter of 16th century. H.
14 cm (5.5 in).
*Leeuwarden (Holland), Fries
Museum. See page 114*

58C   Small pot of albarello shape,
painted in blue and
manganese-purple
Probably LONDON, first half
of 17th century. H. 8 cm
(3.2 in)
*Manchester, City Art Gallery.
See page 129*

include patterns of elongated leaves arranged in zigzag fashion (Plate 58B), an ornamental form which may have been derived from Faenza productions of earlier date (Plate 58A), and the stylised rosette (Plate 59A) which is also known on pavement tiles and other products of Faenza manufacture (Plate 15A). Patterns of stylised leaves on slender stems which were widely used in Italy in the sixteenth century (cf. Plate 26B and Rackham, *Catalogue VAM*, No. 204) are also to be found on Netherlandish drug jars.[7]

In addition to these imitations of Italian wares Flemish potters made a number of sets of drug jars whose decoration was more individual in character, and whose workmanship invites comparison with that of the finer pharmaceutical productions of Italy (Plates 59B,C, 60B). Distinctive features of these wares include guilloche-like borders formed of short interlacing curves, encircling the neck and foot of the vessel (Plates 60A,B), or a diagonally descending band on which the name of the drug is displayed. Both monochrome and polychrome wares with this type of decoration are known; on occasion the jars are inscribed with the date of manufacture.[8]

The oppression of the Flemings by the forces of Philip II of Spain, particularly after the occupation of Antwerp by the Duke of Parma in 1585, caused many potters to leave their homeland. A few of the potters migrated to Montpellier and England, but the greater part sought refuge in the Northern Netherlands (Holland), where they established workshops at Rotterdam, Haarlem, Amsterdam and other cities. Concurrently, manufacture of pottery at Antwerp declined and virtually ceased towards the close of the sixteenth century. Production of tin-glazed earthenware on any scale in the Southern Netherlands was not resumed until the third quarter of the seventeenth century, and it is to be presumed that Netherlandish pottery made during the intervening period had its origin in Holland.

Amongst the earliest wares which may be attributed with some degree of

---

[7] Cf. 'Antwerps Plateel', *Vrienden*, Nos. 62–3, 1971, Cat. No. 2; Wittop Koning, loc. cit. (note 5(b), above), pp. 23–5.
[8] e.g. Plate 60B; Wittop Koning, loc. cit. (note 5(b), above), fig. 16.

Plate 59A   Pair of albarelli, painted in blue, green, yellow and brown
Probably NETHERLANDS (ANTWERP), *c.*1540. H. of each 25 cm (9.8 in).
Inscriptions 'u·populion' and 'adipis·capreti'
London, Victoria and Albert Museum. See page 116

Plate 59B   Albarello, painted in blue, green, yellow and brown
NETHERLANDS (ANTWERP), *c.*1550–60, H. 30.5 cm (12 in). Inscription
'JERA PIGRA·'
London, Victoria and Albert Museum. See page 116

Plate 59C   Albarello, painted in blue, green, yellow and brown
NETHERLANDS (ANTWERP), *c.*1550–60. H. 26 cm (10.2 in). Inscription
'TIRICA·M·G' (*Theriaca magna*)
Amsterdam, Rijksmuseum. See page 116

confidence to HOLLAND is a large group of albarelli, spouted jars and bottles with blue monochrome decor of false gadroons, bursting pods and dark-and-light shaded oak or vine leaves (Plates 61B,C). This distinctive decor, which is known as the *a foglie* motif, occurs also on Netherlandish tiles and dishes, and may have been derived from sixteenth-century Venetian or Tuscan maiolica. Their attribution to the Northern Netherlands rests in the main on stylistic similarities with a fragment from a gadrooned albarello in the Westfries Museum at Hoorn, north of Amsterdam, painted in Dutch style with a harbour scene.[9] The mock gadroon design occurs also on a group of vessels with motif of song-birds and basket of fruit above the cartouche (Plate 61A), which were predecessors of the well-known jars with peacock decor made at a later date at Delft.

Another design, probably evolved at the beginning of the seventeenth century in Holland, is the horned head or mask, sometimes referred to as the 'satyr motif'[10] (Plates 60C,D). Additional ornamentation on these jars comprises the head of a cherub or angel, whilst some of the vessels (Plate 60C) carry the guilloche-like borders which were a characteristic feature of some sixteenth-century drug jars of Antwerp manufacture (Plates 60A,B). On later jars of this type, attributable to BELGIUM and perhaps FRENCH FLANDERS (Lille and Tournay),[11] of which polychrome and blue monochrome examples are known,

---

[9] D. A. Wittop Koning, *Delftse Apothekerspotten*, Deventer, 1954, fig. 7; C. H. de Jonge, *Delft Ceramics*, London, 1970, fig. 8.

[10] Wittop Koning, loc. cit. (note 9, above), pp. 64–5, 216–17.

[11] Wittop Koning, loc. cit. (note 9, above), pp. 159–64, 213–17; H. E. Thomann, 'Die "Delftse Pottenkamer" der J. R. Geigy A. G., Basel', *Keramik-Freunde der Schweiz*, No. 65, 1964.

Plate 60A   Albarello, painted in blue monochrome
             NETHERLANDS (ANTWERP), middle of 16th century. H. 17.5 cm (6.9 in).
             Inscription 'CO·R⁰S⁴RV̂·PR⁰VENTIA' (Perhaps *Conserva rosarum Proventiae*,
             conserve of Provins roses*)
             Bruges, Museum Gruuthuse. See page 116

Plate 60B   Syrup jar, painted in blue, yellow, ochre, green and manganese-purple
             NETHERLANDS (ANTWERP), dated 1546. H. 25 cm (9.8 in). Inscription
             'S.CAPILL.VE.' (*Syrupus capillorum Veneris*)
             Sèvres, Musée National de Céramique. See page 116

Plate 60C   Syrup jar, painted in blue monochrome
             Probably NORTHERN NETHERLANDS (HOLLAND), first quarter of 17th
             century. H. 23 cm (9 in). Inscription 'S·FVMARIAE' (*Syrupus fumariae*)
             Rotterdam, Museum Boymans-van Beuningen. See page 118

Plate 60D   Drug pot, painted in blue monochrome
             Probably NORTHERN NETHERLANDS (HOLLAND), middle of 17th
             century. H. 11.5 cm (4.5 in). Inscription 'PVL·AVREVS' (*Pulvis aureus*)
             Basle, Collection Ciba-Geigy. See page 118

*See page 227 (*Rosa Provincialis*)

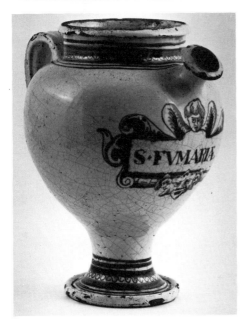

61A   Syrup jar, painted in pale and dark blue HOLLAND, probably *c*.1640. H. 23 cm (9 in). Inscription 's PAPAVERIS RHEA' (*Syrupus papaveris rhoeadis*) *Groningen, Groninger Museum. See page 118*

61B   Albarello, painted in blue monochrome. Probably HOLLAND, beginning of 17th century. H. 20 cm (7.9 in). Inscription 'HIERA·PICRA·C̄O·' *Leeuwarden (Holland), Fries Museum. See page 118*

61C   Syrup jar, painted in blue monochrome Probably HOLLAND, beginning of 17th century. H. 22 cm (8.7 in). Inscription 's·GRANATORVM' (*Syrupus granatorum*) *Sèvres, Musée National de Céramique. See page 118*

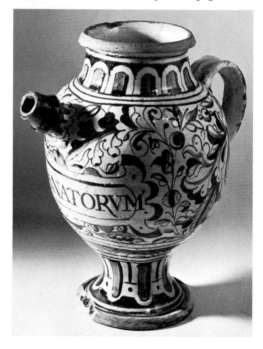

62A Syrup jar, painted in blue monochrome
BELGIUM or NORTHERN FRANCE (Brussels,
Tournay or Lille), *c*.1710–30. H. 21 cm (8.3 in).
Inscription 's·PAPAVERIS' (*Syrupus papaveris*)
Basle, Collection Ciba-Geigy. See page 122

62B Drug pot, painted in blue monochrome
BELGIUM or NORTHERN FRANCE (Brussels,
Tournay or Lille), first half of 18th century.
H. 27.5 cm (10.8 in). Inscription 'C ROSAR·RURÃR'
(*Conserva rosarum rubrarum*)
Basle, Collection Ciba-Geigy. See page 122

62C Drug pot, painted in blue monochrome
Probably BELGIUM (Brussels), 18th century.
H. 27 cm (10.6 in). Inscription 'C CALEND :'
(*Conserva calendulae*)
*Brussels, Musée de l'Assistance Publique. See
page 122*

62D Bottle with flanged neck, painted in blue and
manganese-purple
BELGIUM or NORTHERN FRANCE (Brussels,
Tournay or Lille), first half of 18th century.
H. 30 cm (11.8 in). Inscription 'A· ROSARVM·'
(*Aqua rosarum*)
Basle, Collection Ciba-Geigy. See page 122

62E Drug pot, decoration painted in blue with
manganese-purple outlines
BELGIUM or NORTHERN FRANCE (Brussels,
Tournay or Lille), *c*.1710–30. H. 27 cm (10 6 in).
Inscription 'S. Polych. Seig.' (*Sal polychrestum
Seignetti*)
*Heidelberg, Deutsches Apothekenmuseum.
See page 122*

the decor is enriched by the addition of carnation-like flowers, song-birds, peacocks and other motifs (Plates 62A,B,C,D,E). On occasion the satyr's head gives way to an angel's head (Plate 63A), leading to a type of ware simulating Delft officinal pottery (Plate 63B). These later Franco-Belgian drug jars may be generally differentiated from the cognate pharmaceutical productions of Holland by the shape of the vessels and differences in colour, e.g. use of pale cerulean hues, sometimes with manganese-purple outlines, as opposed to the dark blue coloration of the Delft wares. Related to this heterogeneous class of drug vessels is a group of thickly potted jars and bottles decorated with motifs such as the satyr's head, coats of arms (Plate 64A), or the effigy of St. Michael, Patron Saint of Brussels, slaying the Demon (Plate 64B). The members of this class of ware, one of which bears the date 1680, were probably made at one of the potteries in existence in BRUSSELS in the last quarter of the seventeenth century.[12]

Pharmaceutical earthenware was made at DELFT at the latest in 1654 as shown by an ordinance issued in that year by the potters' guild, which required apprentices aspiring to the rank of craftsman to include a syrup jar among their diploma pieces.[13] Apothecary jars were also made at Haarlem[14] and possibly in other cities in Holland; however Delft was undoubtedly the main source of *apothekerspotten* in Holland, much as in England in the seventeenth and

---

[12] G. Dansaert, in *Les Anciennes Faïences de Bruxelles*, Brussels, 1922, p. 175, attributes the drug jars with St. Michael and the Demon to the factory of Corneille Mombaers.
[13] F. W. Hudig, *Delfter Fayence*, Berlin, 1929, p. 251.
[14] D. A. Wittop Koning, 'Haarlemse apothekerspotten', *Vrienden*, No. 36, 1964, pp. 23–5, 30.

Plate 63A   Theriac jar, painted in blue with manganese-purple outlines
             Probably BELGIUM, first quarter of 18th century. H. 19.5 cm (7.7 in).
             Inscription 'THERIAC.AND' (*Theriaca Andromachi*)
             Private ownership, on loan to Victoria and Albert Museum. See page 122

Plate 63B   Drug jar, painted in blue monochrome. Neck cut down
             HOLLAND, probably DELFT, first half of 18th century. H. 17 cm (6.7 in).
             Inscription 'C COCHLEAR.' (*Conserva cochleariae*)
             Oxford, Museum of the History of Science. See page 124

Plate 63C   Syrup jar, painted in blue monochrome
             HOLLAND, probably DELFT, beginning of 18th century. H. 22 cm
             (8.7 in). Inscription 'S PORTULACAE' (*Syrupus portulacae*)
             London, Royal College of Surgeons of England. See page 124

Plate 63D   Drug pot, painted in blue monochrome
             COPENHAGEN, Store Kongensgade factory, second quarter of 18th
             century. H. 10.5 cm (4.1 in). Inscription 'E ELEBOR: NIGR:' (*Extractum
             hellebori nigri*)
             *Copenhagen, Universitets Medicinsk Historiske Museum. See pages 126 and
             166*

eighteenth centuries pharmacists' needs for ceramic drug containers were met
mainly by the kilns of Southwark and Lambeth.

Many of the pharmaceutical wares of Delft carry the mark of the factory or
potter responsible for the production of the vessel. The marks, factories and
artists have been described in detail by Wittop Koning.[15] Potteries whose
marks occur on drug jars include the factories De porceleyne Schotel (The
Porcelain Dish), De Lampetkan (The Ewer), De twee Scheepjes (The Two
Little Ships), De drie vergulde Astonnen (The Three Golden Ashbarrels), De
Grieksche A (The Greek 'A') and De drie Klokken (The Three Bells). All
these factories were also important sources of non-pharmaceutical earthenware, but there is little stylistic affinity between the ornamental and officinal
wares of Delft. Whereas painters of non-pharmaceutical wares enlisted a wide
range of decorative themes—architectural compositions, subjects drawn from
mythology or the Bible, designs copied from Chinese or Japanese porcelain,
etc.—the painters of drug jars adhered to a more limited repertory of motifs, of
which the most important was the indented cartouche embellished with
peacocks, basket of fruit, winged head, tassels and swags of fruit or flowers
(Plates 63B,C). The decor was generally rendered in dark blue; manganese-
purple outlines are comparatively rare and probably indicative of a non-Delft
origin. In the eighteenth century there was a small production of jars with
peacock decor painted in a polychrome palette.[16]

Variations on the peacock design include substitution of angels or fishes for

[15] Wittop Koning, loc. cit. (note 9, above), pp. 141–58, 197–212. An account of marked Dutch
jars in the Wellcome Collection, and the factories associated with such marks is given in Crellin,
English and Dutch Medical Ceramics, p. 50 et seq.
[16] Crellin, *English and Dutch Medical Ceramics*, plate 2 (opp. p. 75).

Plate 64A   Drug jar, painted in pale blue monochrome. Coat of arms is believed to be
              that of Davy du Perron
              Probably BRUSSELS, last quarter of 17th century. H. 17 cm (6.7 in).
              Inscription 'E BENED. LAXAT.' (*Electuarium benedictae laxativae*)
              Bruges, Museum Gruuthuse. See page 122
Plate 64B   Drug jar, painted in blue monochrome
              Probably BRUSSELS, last quarter of 17th century. H. 17 cm (6.7 in).
              Inscription 'C.SALVIAE' (*Conserva salviae*)
              Sèvres, Musée National de Céramique. See page 122
Plate 64C   Ointment jar, painted in dark blue
              DELFT, c.1690. H. 18 cm (7.1 in). Inscription 'U MUND·SICCAT·'
              (*Unguentum mundificativum siccativum*)
              Basle, Collection Ciba-Geigy. See page 126
Plate 64D   Pyriform bottle, painted in blue monochrome
              DELFT, c.1690. H. 29 cm (11.4 in). Inscription 'V MELISSAE' (*Vinum
              melissae*)
              Copenhagen, Universitets Medicinsk Historiske Museum. See page 126

the peacocks,[17] and enrichment of the ornamentation with tendrils and stylised flowers on slender stems. Vessels with the last-named type of decor include albarelli and jars of baluster form (Plates 64C,D); on the evidence of a container in a Dutch private collection marked 'AK' they have been ascribed to Adrianus Koeks (or Kocx), a potter at the De Grieksche A factory.[18]

Towards the middle of the eighteenth century a range of new motifs was introduced, some of the designs being executed in polychrome. A subject particularly favoured by Delft pharmaceutical potters of this period was the deer, which occurs on jars with the marks of De porceleyne Schotel and the De drie Klokken factories (Plates 66A,C), as well as on unmarked wares (Plate 66B). Other designs of eighteenth-century date are formal garlands above an oval cartouche (Plate 65C), a plant believed to represent the medicinally important aloë (Plate 65A), female figures holding aloft banderoles above a flowery cartouche (Plate 65B) and the retort and staff of Asclepius (attributes of Chemistry and Medicine, respectively, borne by a pair of cherubs (Plate 65D).

The Delft type cartouche with decor of cherub's head, basket of fruit and festoons was widely copied in the eighteenth century by potters outside Holland. As already noted, it occurs on drug jars of Belgian manufacture; it is also found on some sets of pharmacy jars made in Denmark (Plate 63D), Germany[19] and Poland.[20] Equally a relationship exists between ornamental motifs on drug jars made in the Low Countries and ornamental patterns on pharmacy vessels of English manufacture, a relationship to which reference is made in the next chapter.

---

[17] Wittop Koning, loc. cit. (note 9, above), figs. 27 and 28.
[18] Wittop Koning, 'Apothekerspotten van Adrianus Kocx', *Vrienden*, No. 23, 1961, pp. 1–2, 20.
[19] G. Urdang and F. W. Nitardy, *The Squibb Ancient Pharmacy*, New York, 1940, pp. 94–5, No. 643; A. Klein, *Deutsche Fayencen im Hetjens-Museum*, Düsseldorf, 1962, Cat. No. 46.
[20] W. Roeske, 'Polnische keramische Apothekengefässe im Museum der Pharmazie in Krakau', *Veröffentlichungen der Internationalen Gesellschaft für Geschichte der Pharmazie*, vol. 38, 1972, pp. 231–9, fig. 2.

Plate 65A   Drug jar, painted in blue monochrome. Mark LPK
DELFT, De Lampetkan factory, end of 18th century. H. 19 cm (7.5 in).
Inscription 'C: MELISSAE' (*Conserva melissae*)
Basle, Collection Ciba-Geigy. See page 126

Plate 65B   Drug jar, painted in polychrome
DELFT, second half of 18th century. H. 17 cm (6.7 in). Inscription 's
ARCANUM DUB:' (*Sal arcanum duplicatum*)
Basle, Collection Ciba-Geigy. See page 126

Plate 65C   Syrup jar, painted in blue monochrome
DELFT, probably third quarter of 18th century. H. 20 cm (7.9 in).
Inscription 's PAPAV:ALB:' (*Syrupus papaveris albi*)
Amsterdam, Medisch-Pharmaceutisch Museum. See page 126

Plate 65D   Syrup jar, painted in blue monochrome
DELFT, probably third quarter of 18th century. H. 21 cm (8.3 in).
Inscription 's CARD:BENEDICT:' (*Syrupus cardui Benedicti*)
Amsterdam, Medisch-Pharmaceutisch Museum. See page 126

66A   Drug jar with brass cover, painted in blue. Mark P̣
DELFT, De porceleyne Schotel factory, probably middle of 18th century. H. 31 cm (12.2 in). Inscription 'E DIASCORD:FRAC:' (*Electuarium diascordium Fracastorii*)
Amsterdam, Medisch-Pharmaceutisch Museum. See page 126

66B   Drug jar, painted in green, red, brown, yellow and manganese-violet
DELFT, late 18th century. H. 18.5 cm (7.3 in). Inscription 'E DIASCORD:FR:'
Paris, Faculté de Pharmacie. See page 126

66C   Covered drug jar, painted in yellow and brown. Mark: 3 bells
DELFT, De drie Klokken factory, first half of 19th century. H. 22 cm (8.7 in). Inscription 'AXUNG: OXŸGENAT:'
Amsterdam, Medisch-Pharmaceutisch Museum. See page 126

G. Drug pot
    LONDON (probably LAMBETH), *c*.1720–5. H. 18 cm (7.1 in). Inscription
    'C:CORT:AUR:' (*Conditum cortices aurantiorum*, conserve of orange peel)
    London, Pharmaceutical Society of Great Britain. See page 136

H.   Albarello, porcelain
     CHINA, third quarter of 17th century. H. 24 cm (9.4 in). Inscription 'THER·ES
     merag.' (*Theriaca essentia meraca?*)
     London, British Museum. See page 176

Chapter 6
ENGLAND

Little is known of the containers used by apothecaries in England for storage of their wares before the second half of the sixteenth century. It is probable that medicines and spices were conserved in receptacles made of metal or wood, or in simple lead-glazed earthenware pots. Additionally, small quantities of albarelli and spouted jars were imported in the sixteenth century from Italy and the Netherlands for storage of drugs.

A documentary reference to what is almost certainly the first attempt at production in England of tin-enamelled pharmacy containers is to be found in John Stow's *Survey of the Cities of London and Westminster and the Borough of Southwark* (1755 ed.); the relevant passage reads,[1] 'About the year 1567, Jasper Andries[2] and Jacob Janson, Potters, came away from Antwerp, to avoid Persecution there, & settled themselves in Norwich; where they followed their Trade, making Gally Paving Tiles, and Vessels for Apothecaries and others, very artificially.' It appears that the enterprise at Norwich failed to prosper, or else that Andries and Janson judged that London would offer a more profitable outlet for their wares, for Stow's account continues, 'Anno 1570 they removed to London ... & desired by petition, from Queen Elizabeth, that they might have Liberty to follow their Trade in that City without Interruption. ...' It is believed that the Andries-Janson pottery was situated in the parish of Aldgate, and that it remained active until about 1625. The products of this early London workshop were ornamental dishes, mugs and uninscribed drug jars, sometimes of albarello shape, decorated with patterns of dashes, chevrons, interlacing curves, horizontal bands and similar designs (Plate 58c).[3] The decoration was generally executed in polychrome in

[1] Quoted e.g. by Anthony Ray, *English Delftware Pottery in the Robert Hall Warren Collection, Ashmolean Museum, Oxford*, London, 1968, p. 33.
[2] Jasper Andries was perhaps the son or grandson of Guido Andries of Castel Durante, to whom reference has been made in Chapter 5 (Honey, *European Ceramic Art: Dictionary*, pp. 39 and 44).
[3] Other examples of early uninscribed tin-glazed drug jars believed to be of English manufacture are given in C. H. Wylde, 'Old English drug and unguent pots found in excavations in London', *Burlington Magazine*, vol. 7, 1905, pp. 76–82; Agnes Lothian, 'Vessels for apothecaries: English

ENGLAND

ENGLAND

the Flemish manner, and the productions are not always distinguishable from contemporary wares made in the Netherlands. Similar drug vessels are also believed to have been made at a factory established early in the seventeenth century at Southwark on the South Bank of the Thames, and such wares may well have been among the 'gallypots' recorded as having been ordered in the first quarter of the century by the East India Company from 'the house in Southwarke where they bee made', for shipment to Japan and perhaps other Far Eastern countries.[4]

In the second quarter of the seventeenth century the tin-enamelled wares of the LONDON potteries began to acquire more distinctive characteristics, whilst vessels such as posset pots and wine flagons, often inscribed with the date of manufacture and name or initials of the owner, were added to the repertory of the potters.

Production of drug jars labelled with the name of the contents began in the middle of the seventeenth century, the earliest known dated specimen bearing the date 1652 (Plate 67A). The vessels were spouted jars for storage of liquids, and pots with straight or convex sides and everted neck, usually 'ribbed' above the base and below the shoulder, for holding solid drugs, ointments and electuaries. Pills (or pill-rolling mixture) were customarily contained in miniature pots, generally of ovoid form. Large jars of baluster shape, probably serving as objects of display in the pharmacy, are also known (Plates 69A,B).

---

delft drug jars', *Connoisseur Year Book*, 1953, pp. 113–21, fig. I; Crellin, *English and Dutch Medical Ceramics*, p. 14, and F. H. Garner and M. Archer, *English Delftware*, London, 1972, plates 2B and 2C.
[4] Court of Committee of the East India Company: Minutes of meetings held on 14 February 1614 and 14 November 1614. (I am grateful to Mr. A. J. Farrington, India Office Records, for providing this source.)

Plate 67A   Drug jar, painted in blue monochrome
LONDON, probably SOUTHWARK, dated 1652. H. 15 cm (5.9 in).
Inscription 'C.ANTHOS' (*Conserva anthos*)
London, British Museum. See pages 130 and 132

Plate 67B   Drug jar, painted in blue monochrome
LONDON, probably SOUTHWARK, c.1650–60. H. 16 cm (6.3 in).
Inscription 'DIACATHOL'
London, Royal College of Surgeons of England. See page 132

Plate 67C   Syrup jar, painted in blue monochrome
LONDON, probably LAMBETH, c.1700–20. H. 20.5 cm (8 in). Inscription 'S·TVSSILAGIN·' (*Syrupus tussilaginis*)
London, Royal College of Surgeons of England. See page 134

Plate 67D   Ointment jar, painted in pale blue
LONDON, dated 1679. H. 19.5 cm (7.7 in). Inscription 'V· ENVLAT·CV̄·☿' (*Unguentum enulatum cum mercurio*, compound ointment of elecampane and mercury)
Manchester, City Art Gallery. See page 134

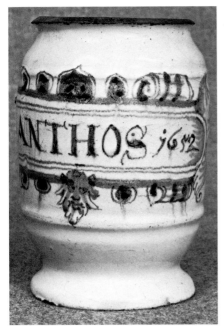

Albarelli or bottles, bearing the name of a drug, do not appear to have been
made in England.

The inscribed drug jars, like their unlabelled predecessors, are attributable
to the Thames-side potteries of SOUTHWARK and LAMBETH, the latter having
been founded in about 1665.[5] Potteries in the provinces, such as Bristol and
Brislington, which sprang up in the second half of the seventeenth century,
may have produced pharmaceutical earthenware, but with the exception of a
jar decorated with the figure of a liver bird (Plate 68D), and a small group of
related vessels, all of which were made in LIVERPOOL in the eighteenth century,
such productions have not been identified with certainty.

A number of decorative motifs were used for the ornamentation of labelled
tin-glazed drug jars; they achieved popularity at different periods. As shown
by the dates of manufacture, the earliest jars, which antedate the Great Fire of
1666, were painted with an elongated cartouche with rounded ends; the design
generally included formal scroll-work and a mask or satyr's head below the
inscription (Plates 67A,B), as on some jars of Netherlandish origin.[6] Additional
ornamentation was usually provided by a figure in profile at each end of the
label, which is thought to represent the head of a man smoking a pipe.[7] The

---

[5] From the close of the seventeenth century onwards tin-enamelled earthenware was also made
at two potteries at Vauxhall, to the south of Lambeth, and there is some evidence that one of
these potteries included pharmacy vessels among its products (Dennis Cockell, 'Some finds of
pottery at Vauxhall Cross, London', *Transactions of the English Ceramic Circle*, vol. 9, part 2,
1974, pp. 221–49).
[6] See page 118.
[7] Agnes Lothian, 'The pipe-smoking man on seventeenth century English delft drug jars',
Chemist and Druggist, vol. 163, 1955, pp. 566–8.

Plate 68A   Ointment jar, painted in blue
             LONDON, probably LAMBETH, c.1665–85. H. 18 cm (7.1 in). Inscription
             'V·E·SVCCIS·APERITIV' (*Unguentum ex succis aperitivis*)
             London, Royal College of Surgeons of England. See page 134
Plate 68B   Drug jar, painted in blue
             LONDON, probably LAMBETH, dated 1675. H. 17.5 cm (6.9 in).
             Inscription 'C·CICHORI' (*Conserva cichorii*)
             London, Royal College of Surgeons of England. See page 134
Plate 68C   Drug jar, painted in blue
             LONDON, c.1710–30. H. 17.5 cm (6.9 in). Inscription 'C:ROSAR:R:'
             (*Conserva rosarum rubrarum*)
             London, Pharmaceutical Society of Great Britain. See page 136
Plate 68D   Ointment jar, painted in blue
             Probably LIVERPOOL, c.1750. H. 19 cm (7.5 in). Inscription
             'U:BAS:NIGR·' (*Unguentum basilicum nigrum*)
             London, Royal College of Surgeons of England. See page 132
Plate 68E   Electuary jar, painted in blue
             LONDON, last quarter of 18th century. H. 18 cm (7.1 in). Inscription
             'ELECT:LENITIV:'
             London, Royal College of Surgeons of England. See page 136

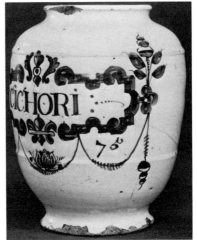

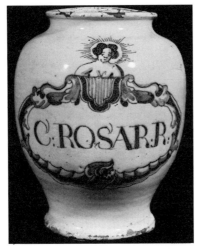

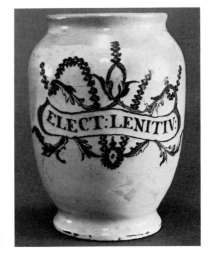

members of this class of pottery were almost invariably painted in blue monochrome; only a small number of vessels is known decorated in a polychrome palette.[8]

A type of ornament in vogue during the period *c.* 1658–1700 is the so-called 'ribbon label panel' design. In this motif, which owes little or nothing to foreign influence, the name of the drug is boldly inscribed on a ribbon scroll the ends of which are bisected and tapered to give the appearance of fluttering pennants. On many members of this class the label is surmounted by the head and shoulders of an angel with outspread wings (Plate 68A). On some post-Restoration jars the angel bears a distinct resemblance to the reigning monarch.[9] Variations on this design include the representation of a scallop below the cartouche,[10] and the substitution of a unicorn's head for the angel.[11] The 'Angel' design is also to be found on a rare Staffordshire slipware jar, dated 1692 and inscribed ':V:RVB:DESICC:', in the museum at Horsham in Sussex.[12] It is not known whether this specimen is a member of a series of drug jars, or a potter's isolated trial piece. Other jars of this period include pots with a cartouche outlined by a thick wavy line which incorporates an ornament resembling the heraldic lily (Plate 68B); this motif is sometimes referred to as the fleur-de-lis design.

The motif of festoons and cherub with pendant tassel below the cartouche, which was widely used on drug jars of the Low Countries in the second half of the seventeenth century and the eighteenth century, occurs also on English delftware, particularly on the so-called 'Merry Man' plates,[13] and on drug jars. Additional ornamentation is provided by song-birds at either end of the cartouche (Plates 67C, 69A) or, more rarely, by peacocks (Plate 67D), thus giving rise to the term 'bird design' for this class of ware.[14] On many members of this category the ornamentation includes the basket of fruit above the label which was a characteristic feature of drug jars made at Delft. As shown by inscribed dates, jars with the peacock motif began to be made in England about 1679, whereas Wittop Koning has put forward evidence showing that this motif had become established in Holland by 1665;[15] accordingly it is to be inferred that

---

[8] For a jar with polychrome ornamentation see G. E. Howard, *Early English Drug Jars*, London, 1931, plate II, No. 4 and p. 12; A. Lothian, 'English delftware in the Pharmaceutical Society's Collection', *Transactions of the English Ceramic Circle*, vol. 5, part 1, 1960, pp. 1–4, plate 4.
[9] Agnes Lothian, 'Angels in the design of seventeenth century English delft drug jars', *Chemist and Druggist*, vol. 163, 1955, pp. 732–6.
[10] Lothian, loc. cit. (note 8, above), plate 5b; Lothian, loc. cit. (note 9, above), figs. 13 and 14; (Sir) Victor Negus, *Artistic Possessions at the Royal College of Surgeons of England*, Edinburgh and London, 1967, p. 103.
[11] Lothian, loc. cit. (note 3; above), fig. XII.
[12] Cf. R. E. A. Drey, 'A dated slipware drug jar', *Pharmaceutical Historian*, vol. 5, 1975, No. 1.
[13] M. R. Parkinson, *The Incomparable Art: English Pottery from the Thomas Greg Collection*, Manchester, 1969, Cat. No. 66; Garner and Archer, loc. cit. (note 3, above), p. 16 and plate 51.
[14] Agnes Lothian, 'Bird designs on English drug jars', *Chemist and Druggist*, vol. 161, 1954, pp. 672–7.
[15] D. A. Wittop Koning, *Delftse Apothekerspotten*, Deventer, 1954, pp. 33 and 190.

69A Electuary jar of baluster shape, painted in blue LONDON, late 17th or early 18th century. H. 35 cm (13.8 in). Inscription 'E: DIASCORDIVM' (*Electuarium diascordium*) *London, Pharmaceutical Society of Great Britain. See pages 130 and 134*

69B Reverse of 69A

the English design was based on Delft antecedents. Although the decoration on inscribed English drug jars at times may have superficial resemblances to ornamentation on pharmaceutical wares from the Low Countries, shapes of English vessels are generally sufficiently distinctive to enable them to be readily separated from related Dutch or Belgian productions.

On a class of cognate jars cherubs with outspread wings appear in place of song-birds or peacocks. This so-called 'cherub design',[16] which often includes a scallop above the inscription, was executed in polychrome as well as in blue monochrome. The monochrome vessels span the greater part of the eighteenth century, whereas the polychrome wares appear to be confined to a set bearing the date 1723[17] and to some related jars which, although undated, were undoubtedly made at about the same period (Colour Plate G). Other designs assignable to the eighteenth century, found on several sets of jars, include the sun and sun-and-moon motifs,[18] scrolling foliage (Plate 68E) and the radiant head of Apollo, God of Healing (Plate 68C).

Manufacture of labelled tin-glazed earthenware drug jars continued to the end of the eighteenth century, when these productions began to be supplanted by creamware vessels generally devoid of decoration,[19] and by earthenware jars with transfer-printed ornamentation.[20]

Peculiar to English ceramic art are tiles with decoration painted in monochrome or polychrome, variously known as pill slabs, pill tiles or pharmaceutical tiles. The purpose to which these plaques were put has been the subject of debate which is still unresolved. It has been contended that the tiles were intended for rolling out pill mass into pills, or for making small quantities of ointment, but the circumstance that many tiles are elaborately decorated and have a non-functional shape argues against this hypothesis. Favoured shapes of tile were the heart (Plates 70A,B), the octagon of equal or unequal sides (Plates 70C,D) and the shield;[21] additionally one oval tile[22] has been recorded.

Decorative motifs on pharmacy tiles are the ribbon label (Plate 70A), which occurs also on drug jars, the royal arms[23] and the blazon of the Society of Apothecaries, a City Company which was formed in 1617 by Royal Charter

[16] Agnes Lothian, 'Cherub designs on English delft apothecary ware', *Chemist and Druggist*, vol. 165, 1956, pp. 608–13.
[17] For examples of dated polychrome jars with decor of cherubs see Lothian, loc. cit. (note 16, above), p. 608; Griselda Lewis, *A Collector's History of English Pottery*, London, 1969, fig. 70.
[18] Lothian, loc. cit. (note 3, above), figs XXXVIIIa and XL.
[19] Crellin, *English and Dutch Medical Ceramics*, figs. 211–24; L. G. Matthews, *Antiques of the Pharmacy*, London, 1971, plate 7.
[20] Crellin, *English and Dutch Medical Ceramics*, fig. 228.
[21] ibid., figs. 273–6; Garner and Archer, loc. cit. (note 3, above), plate 41.
[22] Ross E. Taggart, *The Frank P. and Harriet C. Burnap Collection of English Pottery in the William Rockhill Nelson Gallery*, Kansas City, Missouri, 1967, Cat. No. 90; L. G. Matthews, 'Apothecaries' pill tiles', *Transactions of the English Ceramic Circle*, vol. 7, part 3, 1970, pp. 200–9, plate 170c; G. A. Godden, *British Pottery: An Illustrated Guide*, London, 1974, fig. 29.
[23] Agnes Lothian, 'The armorial London delft of the Worshipful Society of Apothecaries', *The*

70A   Pharmaceutical tile, painted in blue
       LONDON, dated 1663. H. 27 cm (10.6 in); W. 27.5 cm (10.8 in)
       London, Pharmaceutical Society of Great Britain. See page 136

70B   Pharmaceutical tile, painted in blue
       LONDON, end of 17th century. H. 31 cm (12.2 in); W. 27 cm (10.6 in)
       London, Victoria and Albert Museum. See pages 136 and 139

70C   Pharmaceutical tile, painted in blue and manganese-purple
       LONDON or LIVERPOOL, middle of 18th century. H. 30 cm (11.8 in); W. 24 cm
       (9.4 in)
       London, Pharmaceutical Society of Great Britain. See pages 136 and 139

70D   Pharmaceutical tile, painted in light and dark blue
       Probably LONDON (LAMBETH), first quarter of 18th century. H. 26.5 cm
       (10.4 in); W. 27 cm (10.6 in)
       Bristol, City Art Gallery. See page 136

71   Armorial jug, decoration painted in blue, rim and foot in silver mounts
      LONDON, dated 1650. H. 25.5 cm (10 in)
      Cambridge, Fitzwilliam Museum (Glaisher Collection). See page 139

under the title The Worshipful Society of the Art and Mystery of the Apothecaries. The arms of the Society are a shield below mantling, depicting Apollo, armed with bow and arrow, slaying a mythical animal (variously designated as a serpent, and as Python, the dragon of Delphi), with a rhinoceros as crest and unicorns as supporters. On some eighteenth-century tiles a tree was placed on top of the rhinoceros (Plate 70C). According to belief the tree represents the Cedar of Lebanon, which was introduced into the Chelsea Physic Garden of the Apothecaries' Society in 1683. The motto of the Society of Apothecaries, 'Opiferque per orbem dicor', is taken from a passage in Ovid's *Metamorphoses*, in which Apollo discloses his identity to the nymph: 'Inventum medicina meum est, *opiferque per orbem dicor*, et herbarum subiecta potentia nobis' ('The art of medicine is my discovery. *I am called Help-Bringer throughout the World*, and all the potency of herbs is given unto me').[24]

Tiles emblazoned with these arms were in all probability displayed by members of the Society in their pharmacies to proclaim to the public their professional standing, and to assert their superior status over chemists and druggists, who did not have to undergo any formal training, and could not become members of the Society. On occasion the tile additionally bears the arms of the City of London (Plate 70B), an indication that the owner was a Freeman of the City.

The blazon of the Apothecaries' Society is also to be found on a number of jars exceptional both for their size and the quality of the painting. Like the armorial pharmaceutical tiles they are believed to have served as objects of display in the pharmacy. In addition to the heraldic bearings the vessels are embellished with a variety of decorative themes such as marine scenes (Plate 71), chinoiseries, mock gadroons and bird designs. Specimens inscribed with the year of manufacture range in date from 1647[25] to 1724.[26] Both a polychrome and a blue monochrome palette were used for the execution of the decoration.

Connoisseur, vol. 127, March 1951, pp. 21–6, fig. XVI; *Rev. Hist. Pharm.*, vol. 12, 1955–6, plate XXXIV (opp. p. 420).

[24] Agnes Lothian, 'Two centuries of dated drug jars', *Chemist and Druggist*, vol. 177, 1962, pp. 722–5; C. Wall, H. C. Cameron and E. Ashworth Underwood, *A History of the Worshipful Society of Apothecaries of London*, London, New York and Toronto, vol. 1, 1963, p. 404.

[25] Anon., *Pharmaceutical Journal*, vol. 172, 1954, p. 28; Lothian, loc. cit. (note 8, above), plate 1; Lothian, loc. cit. (note 24, above), p. 723; L. G. Matthews, *History of Pharmacy in Britain*, Edinburgh and London, 1962, frontispiece.

[26] Lothian, loc. cit. (note 14, above), figs. 5a and 5b.

Chapter 7

SPAIN AND PORTUGAL

Lustreware

MANISES, the great centre of manufacture of lustred earthenware, in the neighbourhood of the city of Valencia, to which reference has been made in Chapter 1, was the principal source of pharmaceutical pottery in Spain from the beginning of the fifteenth to the middle of the sixteenth century. Drug vessels, sometimes decorated with heraldic shields of clients, were supplied from the Hispano-Moresque potteries to court pharmacies, to monastic dispensaries and to urban apothecaries' shops in many parts of the Iberian peninsula. In addition to this domestic trade there were substantial shipments of pharmacy vessels and decorative wares from Manises to Italy and certain other countries in Western Europe, and further afield, to Egypt. Armorial shields on drug jars made for foreign customers, which have been recorded, include the royal arms of France[1] and the blazon of the province of Zeeland, in the Netherlands.[2]

Manufacture of lustred earthenware was not confined to the province of

---

[1] Alice W. Frothingham, *Lustreware of Spain*, New York, 1951, fig. 89.
[2] A. Van de Put, *Hispano-Moresque Ware of the Fifteenth Century. Supplementary Studies and Some Later Examples*, London, 1911, fig. 9.

Valencia. Hispano-Moresque potters at Manises were subject to periodic persecutions, and a number of them migrated northwards to Aragon, to Catalonia and to Narbonne in the province of Languedoc. At these places the expatriate potters established kilns and made lustred ornamental pottery which in many cases is barely distinguishable from wares made in Valencia province; only a small quantity of pharmaceutical lustreware appears however to have been made away from Manises (Plate 72C).

Following the loss of many of its ablest workmen the pottery industry at Manises in the second half of the sixteenth century entered into a period of decline. The execution of the decoration of the wares became perfunctory, whilst the noble yellow-brown ('golden') lustre which characterised the earlier Valencian wares gave place to a somewhat harsh reddish or copper-brown iridescence. In 1609–10 the remaining Hispano-Moresque artisans were expelled from Spanish soil; thereafter workmen of Christian descent took over manufacture of pottery at Manises, but the splendour of the fifteenth-century lustrewares was never recaptured. The later drug vessels of Manises include roughly fashioned pots of narrow diameter with curving sides (Plate 72A), and albarelli and spouted jars decorated with cursorily painted vine leaves or ivy leaves.

Early Non-Lustred Drug Jars

In addition to production of pharmaceutical lustreware mention must also be made of non-lustred officinal pottery made at various localities in Spain, and perhaps also in Portugal. The earliest of such wares, dating from about the end of the fourteenth century to the close of the fifteenth century, were painted in blue or green-and-purple colours, a palette which was also used for ornamentation of pottery of contemporary date made in Central and Southern Italy. Decorative motifs on these wares include vertically disposed panels of alternate colours,[3] lappet bands (Plate 3B), pseudo-Arabic inscriptions (Plate 3C), animals and palmettes.[4] These wares are assignable to Paterna and Manises in Valencia province, to Teruel in Aragon and to Seville in Andalusia, although other centres may also have been engaged in production of non-lustred drug jars. Towards the close of the fifteenth century and in the sixteenth century potters in Catalonia produced albarelli with decoration in dark blue, sometimes thickly applied, pigments (Plate 3D). Designs enlisted for the decoration of these vessels were stylised leaves and roughly sketched arabesque-like patterns, motifs which were probably derived from Valencian wares of an earlier period.

TALAVERA, in Castile province, was another major source of decorative and useful pottery, including pharmaceutical earthenware. The earliest pro-

---

[3] Juan Ainaud de Lasarte, *Ars Hispaniae*, vol. 10 (*Cerámica y Vidrio*), Madrid, 1952, fig. 631; Balbina Martínez Caviró, *Catálogo de Cerámica Española*, Madrid, 1968, fig. 125.
[4] *World Ceramics*, p. 140, fig. 395; Martínez Caviró, loc. cit. (note 3, above), figs. 41–49.

73A Jar of baluster shape, painted in polychrome TALAVERA, third quarter of 16th century. H. 28.5 cm (11.2 in)
Destroyed in Schlossmuseum, Berlin, during Second World War. See page 144

73B Double-handled jar (*cántaro*), painted in blue with touches of yellow, grey and brown TALAVERA, first quarter of 17th century. H. 49 cm (19.3 in). Inscription 'AQ·CICHOREAE' (*Aqua cichorii*) *Madrid, Museo Arqueológico Nacional. See page 146*

73C Albarello, painted in blue and yellow, with details in grey-green and orange TALAVERA, first quarter of 17th century. H. 30.5 cm (12 in). Inscription 'MIXAE' *New York, Hispanic Society of America. See page 146*

ductions from this locality, dating from about the middle of the sixteenth century, were tile panels, dishes and storage vessels painted in polychrome or blue monochrome with human figures, animals, hunting scenes and other subjects. Italian and Flemish potters are known to have worked at Talavera during the formative period, and the influence of Italy and Antwerp can be discerned on many of the wares from this centre.

The first drug vessels assignable to Talavera date from about 1565; they are uninscribed jars of globular or barrel form decorated with *ferronnerie* motifs, and emblazoned with the gridiron of St. Laurence and the Lion of St. Jerome, insignia of the royal monastery of San Lorenzo del Escorial, for whose pharmacy they were made (Plate 73A). Other drug jars of early date from the Talavera kilns are albarelli with decor of formal foliage painted in blue and ochre cross-strokes (Plate 72D), an ornamental design which occurs also extensively on non-pharmaceutical pottery from this locality.[5]

Later Non-Lustred Drug Jars

The later pharmaceutical wares of the Iberian peninsula stem from kilns in Talavera, Catalonia, Aragon, Seville (Triana), Alcora, Lisbon, Coimbra, Viana Darque, and possibly other localities. These productions cannot always be assigned to a particular source; in particular Aragonese drug jars are not readily distinguishable from apothecary jars of Catalonian manufacture (Plates 76A,B); similarly there is an element of uncertainty regarding the origin of some wares decorated with debased Bérain ornamentation (Plate 79B), or with polychrome baroque scrolling (Plate 75D), and these wares have been variously given to Alcora, Talavera and Catalonia.

Shapes of vessels of the later Iberian period were principally albarelli and jars of baluster or globular form; some sets of drug jars of barrel form are also known (Plate 74A).[6] Spouted jars, such as were used in other European countries for storage of oils and syrups, do not appear to have been produced in Spain or Portugal after about 1650. Decorative motifs on drug jars, as on tableware and display pieces, were principally floral patterns, foliage, animals and coats of arms. Drug jars bearing an artist's signature or a potter's mark are almost unknown, and wares inscribed with the date of manufacture appear to be confined to a small group of jars of Portuguese origin.[7]

TALAVERA remained a source of drug jars of distinction throughout the seventeenth and eighteenth centuries. A considerable part of the output of the

[5] e.g. see Alice W. Frothingham, *Talavera Pottery with a Catalogue of the Collection of the Hispanic Society of America*, New York, 1944, figs. 14, 15, 99; Honey, *European Ceramic Art: Illustrated Survey*, plate 74B.

[6] A barrel-shaped drug jar with the arms of the royal monastery of Guadalupe is illustrated by Guillermo Folch Jou in 'La colección de botes de farmacia en el Museo de la Farmacia Hispana', *Boletin de la Sociedad Española de Historia de la Farmacia*, No. 66, 1966, pp. 51–77, fig. 391.

[7] José Queirós, *Cerâmica Portuguesa*, 2nd ed., Lisbon, 1948, vol. 1, fig. 192; Reynaldo Dos Santos, *Faiança Portuguesa*, Séc. XVI e XVII, Oporto, 1960, figs. 69, 73, 74; Lisbon, Biblioteca Nacional, *Exposição de Faianças Portuguesas de Farmácia*, Lisbon, 1972, plates 12 and 31 (Cat. Nos. 4 and 24).

74A   Drug jar, decoration painted in blue,
inscription in brown
TALAVERA, second half of 17th
century. H. 26 cm (10.2 in). Inscription
'IVIVBAE' (*Jujubae*, jujube berries)
Madrid, Museo Arqueológico Nacional.
See page 144
74B   Albarello, painted in blue
monochrome
TALAVERA, late 17th
century. H. 30 cm (11.8 in)
New York, Hispanic Society of
America. See page 146
74C Albarello, painted in blue, inscription
in manganese-purple
TALAVERA, late 17th or early 18th
century.
Inscription 'R.PETROSELINI' (*Radix*
petroselini)
London, Wellcome Institute of the
History of Medicine. See page 146

kilns was destined for monastic pharmacies, as shown by heraldic shields of monasteries and religious orders. Probably the earliest drug jars from Talavera inscribed with the name of the contents are albarelli and large two-handled jars (*cántaros*) for storage of medicated waters, made for the pharmacy of the monastery of El Escorial. In addition to the drug name the vessels carry the monastic insigna; the remainder of the surface is covered with a speckled pattern such as might have been applied by means of a sponge (*decoración al esponjado*) (Plates 73B,C). These jars, which date from the first half of the seventeenth century, were presumably a replacement for the uninscribed vessels of *c*.1565 to which reference has been made earlier (Plate 73A). Other armorial drug jars, with few exceptions decorated in blue monochrome, bear the arms of Leon and Castile (Plate 75B), or of a religious order such as the Augustinian Order (Plate 74C), the Carmelite Order (Plate 75A), or the Order of Our Lady of Mercy (Mercedarians) (Plate 74B). On many of the apothecary vessels from Talavera the drug name is characteristically displayed on a rectangular panel bordered by leafy scroll-work (Plates 74B,C, 75C).

Stylistically related to the pharmacy jars of Talavera is a group of albarelli made at Triana, a suburb of SEVILLE. These wares, which date from the last quarter of the seventeenth century to the close of the eighteenth century, have been described in some detail by Alice Frothingham.[8] Ornamental themes are mainly coats of arms of monasteries (Plate 79D) or of a religious order. Additionally potters at Seville were responsible for a series of albarelli with polychrome ornamentation of hunters, hounds and their quarries, each subject gracefully framed in a cinquefoil arch.[9]

---

[8] Frothingham, loc. cit. (note 5, above), pp. 91–3, 160–6.
[9] Frothingham, loc. cit. (note 5, above), figs. 144 and 145; Folch Jou, loc. cit. (note 6, above), fig. 781.

Plate 75A   Albarello, painted in dark blue, inscription in yellow and manganese-purple
                 Possibly ALCORA, but more probably TALAVERA, 18th century. Inscription 's.BERBER' (*Semen berberidis*, barberry seeds)
                 Madrid, Museo de la Farmacia Hispana. See page 146

Plate 75B   Albarello, painted in blue monochrome
                 TALAVERA, 18th century. H. 25 cm (9.8 in). Inscription 's.CARTAM.' (*Semen carthami*)
                 Madrid, Museo Arqueológico Nacional. See page 146

Plate 75C   Albarello, painted in blue monochrome
                 TALAVERA, 18th century. Inscription 'R. SATYRII.' (*Radix satyrii*)
                 Madrid, Museo Arqueológico Nacional. See page 146

Plate 75D   Albarello, displaying badge (*tau* cross) of Order of St. Anthony, decoration painted in polychrome
                 TALAVERA or ALCORA, middle of 18th century. H. 32.5 cm (12.8 in). Inscription 'Tart.Albi.'
                 Paris, Collection Monsieur L. Cotinat. See page 144

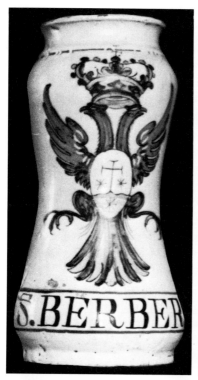

The influence of Italy which characterised some of the early productions from Talavera is also discernible on some pharmaceutical wares of seventeenth-century date made in the province of CATALONIA. These jars were decorated in polychrome tones with stylised petals, medallion portraits and wreaths of foliage (Plate 76C) in the manner of drug jars made in the sixteenth century at Castel Durante and Faenza. The later productions from Catalonia were embellished with subjects such as stylised flowers on coiling stems (Plate 77A), or with animals, figures or buildings traced with a broad brush (Plate 76D). Other decorative motifs favoured by Catalonian potters were patterns of curlicues (Plate 79A) and roughly executed lambrequin ornaments (Plate 77B). Another ornamental design found on many sets of Catalonian apothecary vessels is a ribbon and bow arranged to form an oval cartouche (Plates 77C,D).

Pharmaceutical pottery of note was also made at ALCORA, to the north of the city of Valencia, where a factory was founded in 1727 by the ninth Count of Aranda. Operations at this workshop were entrusted during the first ten years of its existence to Joseph Olerys and Edouard Roux, artist-potters formerly working at Marseilles and Moustiers, in the south of France. Roux resigned his position at Alcora in 1735, and two years later Olerys returned to France; thereafter the factory came under the control of native Spanish potters who for some years continued to work in the style of Moustiers.

The earliest drug jars from Alcora, believed to date from about 1745, are decorated in blue monochrome with motifs such as delicately drawn foliated scrolls and diaper patterns which occur on ornamental wares from Moustiers as well as on drug jars from Alcora. However, whereas at Moustiers the dominant ornamental themes were narrative subjects, chinoiseries and arabesques, the principal subjects employed for the ornamentation of Alcora pharmacy jars were grinning masks or menacing heads of monsters grotesquely juxtaposed to winged cherubs (Plates 78A,B,C).[10] It has been suggested that the expressions

---

[10] For other examples of these exceptional jars see Francisco de P. Bofill, *Cerámica Española*, Barcelona, 1942, pl. LI; Manuel Escrivá de Romaní y de la Quintana, Conde de Casal, *Historia de la Cerámica de Alcora*, 2nd ed., Madrid, 1945, plates XXVI and XXIX; Ainaud de Lasarte,

---

Plate 76A   Albarello, painted in blue monochrome
             ARAGON or CATALONIA, 18th century. H. 27 cm (10.6 in). Inscription
             'Lign.Sant.' (*Lignum santali*)
             Madrid, Museo Arqueológico Nacional. See page 144
Plate 76B   Reverse of 76A
Plate 76C   Albarello, painted in yellow, blue and green
             CATALONIA, middle of 17th century. Inscription 'Se.citrulli.' (*Semen citrulli*)
             Madrid, Museo Arqueológico Nacional. See page 148
Plate 76D   Albarello, painted in dark blue
             CATALONIA, first half of 18th century. H. 23.5 cm (9.2 in). Inscription
             'Balsam UniversAl.'
             Paris, Faculté de Pharmacie. See page 148

on the faces and masks were intended to portray in graphic form the effects of the respective drugs on the patient, or that the menacing expressions were intended to frighten away evil spirits. Although such explanations are ingenious it should be borne in mind that masks and monsters have been part of the repertory of the decorative artist since antiquity, and their presence on pharmacy jars probably has no special significance.

After the middle of the eighteenth century the influence of Moustiers at Alcora disappeared. The later apothecary vessels of Alcora were decorated in a polychrome palette, with subjects such as naturalistically painted flowers (Plate 79C) and portraits in medallions.[11]

The pharmaceutical pottery of PORTUGAL is attributable principally to the kilns of Lisbon and Coimbra. Some Portuguese drug jars were made in the sixteenth century, as shown by an albarello bearing the date 1589,[12] but by far the greatest number of the pharmacy vessels from Portugal date from the middle of the seventeenth to the close of the eighteenth century. Decorative subjects include human figures, floral motifs and geometric patterns; one series of albarelli carries a braid-like design.[13] Drug jars are also known with heraldic insignia, such as the coat of arms of Portugal (Plate 79E) or the emblem of the Oratory of St. Philip Neri.[14]

The tradition of embellishing pharmacies with decorated ceramic jars inscribed with names of medicaments continues to the present day. Drug jars

---

loc. cit. (note 3, above), p. 288, fig. 774; Ramón Jordi González, *Cerámica Farmacéutica en el Museo de Arte de Cataluña*, Barcelona (Colegio Oficial de Farmacéuticos), 1971; R. E. A. Drey, 'Pots de pharmacie d'Alcora vers 1745', *Rev. Hist. Pharm.*, vol. 23, 1976, pp. 93–6.
[11] Folch Jou, loc. cit. (note 6, above), No. 383.
[12] Queirós, loc. cit. (note 7, above), vol. 1, p. 34, fig. 15.
[13] P. Julien, 'L'histoire de la pharmacie au Congrès de la F.I.P. à Lisbonne', *Rev. Hist. Pharm.*, vol. 21, 1972–3, plate LIII (opp. p. 282). A jar from this series is in the Victoria and Albert Museum (Accession No. C.63–1910).
[14] Julien, loc. cit. (note 13, above).

Plate 77A	Albarello, painted in blue
	CATALONIA, 18th century. H. 28 cm (11 in.). Inscription 'Aurū Pigmē' (*Auripigmentum*)
	Present ownership unknown. See page 148
Plate 77B	Albarello, painted in blue
	CATALONIA, middle of 18th century. H. 28.5 cm (11.2 in). Inscription 'S. Anisi.' (*Semen anisi*)
	Basle, Collection F. Hoffmann-La Roche & Co. See page 148
Plate 77C	Albarello, painted in blue, yellow and brown, outlines traced in black
	CATALONIA, middle of 18th century. H. 27.5 cm (10.8 in). Inscription 'S. Psÿlÿ' (*Semen psyllii*)
	London, Victoria and Albert Museum. See page 148
Plate 77D	Globular jar, painted in blue, yellow, brown and green
	CATALONIA, second half of 18th century. H. 27 cm (10.6 in). Inscription 'Flor. Sambuc.' (*Flores sambuci*).
	Heidelberg, Deutsches Apothekenmuseum. See page 148

78A   Globular jar, painted in blue
ALCORA, c.1740–50
H. 24 cm (9.4 in)
Inscription 'Diversae radices' (Assorted roots)
Madrid, Museo de la Farmacia Hispana. See page 148

78B   Albarello, painted in blue
ALCORA, c. 1740–50
H. 29.5 cm (11.6 in).
Inscription 'R.Zedoariae.' (*Radix zedoariae*)
Basle, Collection F. Hoffmann-La Roche & Co. See page 148

78C   Albarello, painted in blue
ALCORA, c.1740–50
H. 29.5 cm (11.6 in).
Inscription 'S.Papav.rub.' (*Semen papaveris rubri*)
Sèvres, Musée National de Céramique. See page 148

79A — Albarello, painted in blue
Probably CATALONIA, 18th century. H. 24 cm
(9.4 in). Inscription 'Galange'
Paris, Faculté de Pharmacie. See page 148

79B — Albarello, decoration painted in blue, inscription in black
CATALONIA or ALCORA, 18th century. H. 29 cm
(11.4 in). Inscription 'Sem. Melonis.'
Paris, Faculté de Pharmacie. See page 144

79C — Albarello, painted in yellow, blue, green and brown
Probably ALCORA, second half of 18th century.
Inscription 'S· Napi·' (*Semen napi*)
Madrid, Museo Arqueológico Nacional. See page 150

79D — Albarello, displaying emblem of Monastery of
Sahagún, decoration painted in yellow, blue,
green and brown
Probably SEVILLE, 18th century. H. 26 cm
(10.2 in). Inscription 'FAR. SECAL.' (*Farina secalis*)
Author's collection. See page 146

79E — Albarello, emblazoned with arms of Portugal,
decoration painted in blue and manganese-purple
LISBON, middle of 17th century. H. 23 cm (9 in)
London, Victoria and Albert Museum, See page 150

for display in pharmacies are currently made at potteries in the Iberian peninsula, in Italy,[15] in Holland,[16] in France,[17] and probably in other countries also. The modern jars, although incorporating ornamental themes in use in earlier centuries, are generally readily distinguished from their antecedents by major differences in shape and decoration. A notable exception is a large group of albarelli and vessels of baluster form painted with motifs which were current at Talavera in the second half of the sixteenth century and in the seventeenth century—*ferronnerie* patterns, coats of arms of the monasteries of El Escorial, Guadalupe and others; additionally they are often inscribed with names of priors or abbots of such monasteries. A number of such jars have entered public collections, or appear periodically on the art market, where they are described as antique Talavera pottery, but the somewhat cursory brushwork and certain inconsistencies (e.g. elongated drug name panels with square or pointed ends, names of unusual drugs) and the circumstance that as recently as 1963 no examples of this class of ware were known in Spain[18] suggests that they are of twentieth-century date.

[15] e.g. see Alessandro Ragionieri, *Un Centro Internazionale di Ceramiche da Farmacia a Sesto Fiorentino*, Sesto Fiorentino, 1973.
[16] e.g. see D. A. Wittop Koning, *Art and Pharmacy*, Deventer, vol. II, 1958, figs. E and F (pp. 6 and 7) and plate 42.
[17] e.g. see L. Cotinat, 'La S.H.P. en Val-de-Loire: Malicorne', *Rev. Hist. Pharm.*, vol. 24, 1977, pp. 179–180.
[18] Guillermo Folch Jou, *Boletin de la Sociedad Española de Historia de la Farmacia*, No. 56, 1963, pp. 171 and 172.

Chapter 8

GERMANY AND AUSTRIA

The development of the ceramic industry in Germany and Austria during the Renaissance followed a different course from that in Italy, France and the Southern Netherlands. Whereas the Renaissance potters of the latter countries were primarily engaged in production of tin-enamelled earthenware the efforts of artisans in Germany and Austria were chiefly directed to the making of lead-glazed pottery (*Hafner*-ware) and stoneware. The stoneware industry, which was centred at Cologne, Raeren, Siegburg and the Westerwald in the Rhineland produced mainly jugs and tankards. The *Hafner* (lead-glaze potters), whose kilns were located mainly in Southern Germany, Austria and the Tyrol, specialised in manufacture of tiles for stoves. In the second or third decade of the sixteenth century a number of *Hafner* began to make tin-glazed earthenware dishes and other articles to meet the increasing demands for this class of ware which hitherto had to be imported from Italy.

The maiolica objects of this formative period include a group of pharmacy jars, the earliest recorded specimen being a portrait albarello dated 1544, devoid of drug name, painted in manganese-purple, cobalt-blue and copper-green (Plate 80A). The shape of the vessel, the delicate tracery and the ornamentation at the shoulder and base are evidently derived from a model of Italian, perhaps Faenza origin, but the portraiture is essentially Germanic in character, the subject having probably been taken from an engraving or a woodcut by a German artist. In the second half of the sixteenth century there was a transition to a predominantly blue palette, whilst the name of the drug was occasionally displayed on the walls of the vessel (Plate 80B). Decorative designs on the small number of specimens that have survived[1] are patterns of stylised foliage on coiling stems; on occasion the blazon of the owner is featured. These later wares are noticeably free from foreign influence; thus the

---

[1] Other drug vessels of sixteenth-century date are illustrated in H. Kohlhaussen, 'Kleine Beiträge zur deutschen Renaissance-Fayence', *Keramos*, No. 10, 1960, pp. 98–106; in Kohlhaussen *et al.*, *Alte Apothekengefässe*, p. 25; and in K. Strauss, 'Ein süddeutscher Apothekerfayencetopf vom Jahre 1591', *Keramik-Freunde der Schweiz*, No. 70, 1966, pp. 3–5, figs. 1 and 2.

covered cylindrical armorial jar from the court pharmacy at Sulzbach shown in Plates 81A and 81B has virtually no counterpart in the sixteenth-century productions of any other country.

The sites of manufacture of the pharmaceutical maiolica of Germany and Austria have not been established with certainty; it is thought that the kilns were located in Franconia, at places such as Nuremberg, and possibly also in Swabia and Brixen (Bressanone) in the Tyrol.

The above pharmacy jars were no more than occasional articles of potters whose staple products were tiles and tableware; they were reserved for the personal pharmacies of a few select noblemen. Owners of urban *Apotheken* generally had recourse to more modest receptacles for storage of drugs — unglazed or lead-glazed pots, or vessels made of stoneware, metal, wood or glass, although not infrequently these lesser vessels also possessed considerable artistic merit. Stoneware jars were generally decorated in relief, the finest examples being pots of cylindrical form[2] and albarelli made at RAEREN in the vicinity of Aachen at the close of the sixteenth century by Jan Emens Mennicken, Jan Baldems Mennicken and others. The vessels have a grey body, usually with patches of glaze stained blue. The ornamentation comprises motifs such as gadroons (Plate 80D) or a ruff-like pattern; the initials of the potter and the date of manufacture of the mould are also sometimes incorporated into the design (Plate 80C). Additional features are coats of arms or a rectangular panel bearing a motto in Low German or Dutch (Plate 80C);

[2] e.g. see Kohlhaussen *et al.*, *Alte Apothekengefässe*, p. 42; D. A. Wittop Koning, 'Raerener Apothekengefässe', *Veröffentlichungen der Internationalen Gesellschaft für Geschichte der Pharmazie*, vol. 36, 1970, pp. 185–95, figs. 2 and 5.

Plate 80A   Albarello, painted in blue, green and manganese-violet
SOUTHERN GERMANY, possibly SWABIA (Ulm), dated 1544. H. 17.5 cm (6.9 in)
Ulm, Ulmer Museum. See page 155

Plate 80B   Pharmacy flask, painted in blue and yellow. Coat of arms is believed to be that of Ziegler. Pewter cover and mounts
SOUTHERN GERMANY, possibly SWABIA, *c*.1560. H. 13.5 cm (5.3 in). Inscription 'S· DE· MENTHA' (*Syrupus de mentha*)
Stuttgart, Württembergisches Landesmuseum. See page 155

Plate 80C   Storage jar, grey and blue stoneware. Mark Y.E.M.
RAEREN, workshop of Jan Emens Mennicken, dated 1591. H. 12.5 cm (4.9 in). Inscription 'SLANGEN·BLOET·YS·GUDT·FENNEIN' (*Slangenbloed is een goed venijn*, serpent blood is a good venom)
Heidelberg, Deutsches Apothekenmuseum. See page 156

Plate 80D   Storage jar of albarello shape, grey and blue stoneware
RAEREN, workshop of Jan Baldems Mennicken, *c*.1600. H. 18 cm (7.1 in)
Amsterdam, Rijksmuseum. See page 156

81A   Covered cylindrical jar, painted in blue monochrome with arms of the Count Palatine Ottheinrich von Zweibrücken-Sulzbach and his wife Dorothea Maria von Württemberg
SOUTHERN GERMANY, possibly FRANCONIA, dated 1583. H. 22 cm (8.7 in)
Nuremberg, Germanisches Nationalmuseum. See page 156

81B   Reverse of 81A.

82A   Covered bottle, foot in
pewter mount, painted in
blue with arms of
Elector of Saxony
KREUSSEN, workshop of
monogrammist LS, dated
1618. H. 24 cm (9.4 in)
*Nuremberg, Germanisches
Nationalmuseum. See page
160*

82B   Spouted jar, painted in blue
KREUSSEN, *c.*1620. H.
21 cm (8.3 in)
*Nuremberg, Germanisches
Nationalmuseum. See page
160*

82C   Albarello, painted in blue
KREUSSEN, first half of
17th century. H. 31 cm
(12.2 in)
*Basle, Collection F.
Hoffmann-La Roche & Co.
See page 160*

on occasion the panel was left blank, so providing a space in which a label could be affixed (Plate 80D).

After the close of the sixteenth century the potteries of KREUSSEN near Bayreuth, in Southern Germany, took up manufacture of tin-glazed earthenware drug jars. The staple products of the Kreussen kilns were uninscribed albarelli and spouted jars with blue decoration of spirals, stylised leaves and other motifs (Plate 82B,C). Many of these containers were exported to Northern Germany and to Denmark, and perhaps elsewhere in Europe. In addition to these 'spiral wares', as the Kreussen drug jars are sometimes known, there was a production of four-sided armorial flasks dated 1618 with decor of heads of cherubs in relief and monogram 'HVCZS' ('Herzog Vnd Churfürst Zu Sachsen') (Plate 82A). These containers were commissioned by the Elector (Kurfürst) of Saxony, reputedly for the court pharmacy at Dresden. On the evidence of the letters 'L·S' or the monogram '$\mathcal{L}$'[3] which appear on the side of some of the flasks, the wares are thought to be the work of Leonhard Schmidt or Lorenz Speckner, leading potters at Kreussen in the first half of the seventeenth century.

Production of spouted jars and albarelli at Kreussen continued into the second half of the seventeenth century, some of the later specimens bearing the date of manufacture.[4]

---

[3] W. Stengel, 'Studien zur Geschichte der Deutschen Renaissance-Fayencen', *Mitteilungen aus dem Germanischen Nationalmuseum*, 1911, pp. 20–105, fig. 67; R. Stettiner, 'Der Fayencemeister L.S. und seine Werkstätte', *Der Cicerone*, vol. 15, 1923, pp. 47–62, fig. 3; K. Strauss, 'Seltene Deutsche Fayencen in ausländischen Museen', *Keramos*, No. 57, 1972, pp. 31–45, fig. 2.
[4] Examples of dated Kreussen albarelli and spouted jars are given in Honey, *European Ceramic Art: Illustrated Survey*, plate 73C, and in Kohlhaussen *et al.*, *Alte Apothekengefässe*, p. 33.

Plate 83A   Albarello, painted in blue, yellow, ochre and manganese-violet
              Probably NUREMBERG, 18th century. H. 27 cm (10.6 in)
              Düsseldorf, Hetjens-Museum. See page 162

Plate 83B   Pharmacy jar, inscribed with monogram FWR (Friedrich Wilhelm Rex), decoration in blue monochrome
              BERLIN, *c.*1720, probably painted by Gerhard Wolbeer. H. 15 cm (5.9 in)
              Hamburg, Museum für Kunst und Gewerbe. See page 164

Plate 83C   Pharmacy jar, displaying arms of Saxony and monograms of Christian Duke of Saxony-Weissenfels and his wife Louise-Christine, decoration painted in blue monochrome
              DRESDEN, BERLIN, or HANAU, dated 1716. H. 16 cm (6.3 in)
              Paris, Musée des Arts Décoratifs. See page 164

Plate 83D   Syrup jar, emblazoned with arms of Electorate of Saxony and Kingdom of Poland, decoration painted in blue monochrome
              DRESDEN, workshop of Peter Eggebrecht, dated 1718. H. 30 cm (11.8 in). Inscription 'SYR:VIOLAR:'
              New York, Metropolitan Museum of Art. See page 164

At the end of the seventeenth century the primacy of Kreussen as a source of ceramic drug jars passed to other factories in Germany and Austria. Prominent among these were the potteries of DRESDEN, BERLIN, FULDA, NUREMBERG (Plate 83A), MÜNDEN (Plate 84F), SCHREZHEIM (Plate 84D), KELSTERBACH (Plate 84B), HANAU[5] and the porcelain factory at VIENNA.

German eighteenth-century apothecary jars can only rarely be related to decorative faience of known manufacture, and trustworthy factory marks are normally absent. Consequently the attribution of a given drug vessel to a particular potter or factory is often a matter of conjecture.

Shapes of vessel of the eighteenth century were the cylindrical pot with everted neck, either with or without foot, for storage of solid drugs and ointments (Plates 84A,F), and the spouted jar (Plate 83D) and pear-shaped vase (Plate 84E) for liquid medicaments. In addition to these strictly functional forms there were also small productions of other shapes of vessel, including the albarello of classical form (Plate 83A) and the Delft-type pot with waist defined by indentation (Plate 83B). The ornamentation of these wares comprised generally sprigs of foliage, or a simple wreath, or scroll-work surrounding the inscription. Sometimes the decoration included the emblem of the pharmacy for which the jar was made, e.g. a swan designating a *Schwan-Apotheke* (Plate

---

[5] E. Zeh, *Hanauer Fayence*, Marburg, 1913, pp. 164–5.

Plate 84A   Drug jar, painted in blue
     Probably HANAU or FULDA, second half of 18th century. H. 11 cm (4.3 in). Inscription 'LAUD· OPIAT: COMPL·'
     Heidelberg, Deutsches Apothekenmuseum. See page 162

Plate 84B   Drug jar, painted in blue
     Probably KELSTERBACH, second half of 18th century. H. 16 cm (6.3 in). Inscription 'AX: VULPIS:' (*Axungia vulpis*)
     Heidelberg, Deutsches Apothekenmuseum. See page 162

Plate 84C   Drug jar, painted in blue, outlines and inscription in black
     Probably FULDA, middle of 18th century. H. 8.5 cm (3.4 in). Inscription 'BALS: CINNAMOM:'
     London, private collection. See page 164

Plate 84D   Drug jar, painted in blue with manganese-purple outlines
     Probably SCHREZHEIM, second half of 18th century. Inscription 'OL· LILIOR ALB' (*Oleum liliorum alborum*)
     Stuttgart, Württembergisches Landesmuseum. See page 162

Plate 84E   Drug jar, painted in blue, yellow, brown and black
     Probably HANAU, 18th century. H. 20 cm (7.9 in). Inscription 'SYR:DIASENN'
     Nyon (Switzerland), Musée au Château. See page 162

Plate 84F   Drug jar, decoration painted in blue, inscription in black
     MÜNDEN (HANOVER), 18th century. H. 18 cm (7.1 in). Inscription 'CORT:AURANT: FLAV:' (*Cortex aurantiorum flavorum*)
     Sèvres, Musée National de Céramique. See page 162

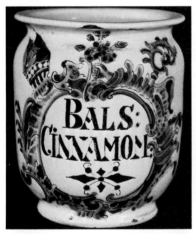

84A), or the head of an angel indicative of an *Engels-Apotheke* (Plate 84B). Among the more notable services of this type is a group of pots with blue *rocaille* cartouche incorporating a mitre and crozier, outlined in manganese-purple or black (Plate 84C), believed to have been made at Fulda in about 1760 for the *Schloss-Apotheke* in that city.

Sets of drug jars were commissioned in the eighteenth century not only for urban pharmacies but also for the dispensaries of the nobility. Vessels from royal or ducal pharmacies of which specimens have survived were made at Berlin by Gerhard Wolbeer for the pharmacy of Frederic William I of Prussia (reigned 1713–40) (Plate 83B), at Dresden or Hanau or Berlin for the *Apotheke* of the Duke of Sachsen-Weissenfels at Weissenfels-an-der-Saale (Plate 83C), and at Dresden by Peter Eggebrecht for the Court of Augustus II, Elector of Saxony and King of Poland (Plate 83D). These sets of jars sometimes numbered one hundred or more pieces; thus the service made in 1718 for the pharmacy of Augustus II originally comprised 182 individual jars, further additions being made by Augustus III in 1734.[6]

Finally reference must be made to porcelain apothecary jars of Austrian and German manufacture. The earliest such set known to us was made about 1725 at the factory of Claudius Innocentius du Paquier in Vienna (Plate 57B). The ornamentation may have been copied from faience drug jars of seventeenth-century date, thus accounting for the 'interesting combination of the heavy cartouches, suggestive of the monumental mason, and the spidery scroll-work'.[7] Other porcelain jars of Viennese manufacture include a series of covered cylindrical pots dating from about 1760, decorated in polychrome with a lion's head and scrolling cartouche; the set was made for an Austrian *Löwen-Apotheke*.[8] In the nineteenth century porcelain was used increasingly as material for drug jars, both in Germany and in Austria, in conformity with similar developments in France.

---

[6] G. Urdang and F. W. Nitardy, *The Squibb Ancient Pharmacy*, New York, 1940, p. 92, No. 639.
[7] J. F. Hayward, *Viennese Porcelain of the du Paquier Period*, London, 1952, p. 55.
[8] E. Leisching, *Kunst und Kunsthandwerk*, vol. 19, 1916, p. 195; J. Antall and G. Szebellédy, *Pictures from the History of Medicine: The Semmelweis Medical Historical Museum, Budapest*, Budapest, 1973, p. 109.

Chapter 9

OTHER WESTERN EUROPEAN COUNTRIES: SWITZERLAND, DENMARK, SWEDEN

Switzerland

The evolution of the pottery industry in Switzerland closely followed that of Southern Germany and the Tyrol. The products of the early Renaissance, made at places such as Lucerne and Winterthur, were lead-glazed stove tiles, dishes and drinking vessels (*Hafner*-ware). Towards the middle of the sixteenth century the maiolica technique of painting in high-temperature colours on a stanniferous glaze began to be adopted by the *Hafner*, and richly-decorated heraldic dishes and commemorative pieces were added to the repertory of the potters.

In the second half of the sixteenth century an artisan named Ludwig Pfau became master-potter at WINTERTHUR, and under his direction this factory assumed a leading position in Switzerland. The dominance of Winterthur was maintained by Pfau's descendants, who controlled the factory until well into the eighteenth century. Records show that in the middle of the seventeenth century some forty craftsmen were engaged in the manufacture of pottery at Winterthur. The wares of the workshop are characterised by boldly-painted designs executed in a polychrome palette, in which manganese-purple is distinctive.

Pharmacy vessels began to be made at Winterthur about the middle of the seventeenth century; shapes of vessel were covered jars of markedly tapering form (Plates 85A,B,C), pots of double-ogee profile (Plates 86A,B) and syrup jars with spouts of square or hexagonal cross-section (Plate 86C). One signed spouted jar has been recorded; it bears the name of Abraham Pfau (1637–91) and the date 1674.[1] Decorative motifs were large leaves on coiled stems, stylised flowers, cattle, birds (Plate 86D) and angels playing musical instruments or engaged in children's games (Plate 86C). Some jars bear the

[1] A. Nisoli, 'Winterthurer Apotheker-Fayencen', *Schweizerische Apotheker-Zeitung*, vol. 108, 1970, pp. 611–20, fig. 2a.

effigies of the Apostles, each with the symbol of his calling or other attribute (Plates 85A,B,C). A complete set of such jars is in the Museum zu Allerheiligen at Schaffhausen.[2]

The later drug jars of Winterthur were decorated in blue monochrome,[3] the wares perhaps emanating from the workshop of David Sulzer. In the middle of the eighteenth century, due to competition from other factories, the pottery industry at Winterthur gradually declined, and pharmacists turned to Germany and Eastern France for ceramic drug containers. Additionally, it is believed that small quantities of apothecary jars were made in the eighteenth century at localities such as Schooren, near Zurich, at Beromünster and at Lenzburg, but these wares have not been identified with certainty.[4]

Denmark and Sweden

The first pharmaceutical ceramic wares attributable to Scandinavia are believed to have been vessels with blue monochrome decoration made in the third decade of the eighteenth century at the Store Kongensgade factory in COPENHAGEN. Before that date pharmacists' needs for drug containers were met by vessels imported from Germany, particularly from Kreussen, and from Delft and elsewhere in the Low Countries. These imported drug containers were to influence the pharmaceutical productions of Denmark. Thus the ornamentation of the basket of fruit, cherub's head, festoons and tassels on the members of a drug jar service made at the Store Kongensgade factory for the *Svane Apotek* (Swan Pharmacy) at Aalborg in Jutland (Plate 63D), was clearly copied from an apothecary jar of Delft manufacture; similarly the shape of the drug pots illustrated in Plates 87A and 87B is derived from vessels of German origin.

Many of the drug vessels of Denmark carry the royal crown above the cartouche (Plates 87A,B,C) in recognition of the fact that the grant of the tenure of a pharmacy was a royal prerogative. On occasion the monogram of the reigning monarch (Plate 87C) or the name of the owner of the pharmacy[5] was also featured on the jar.

The pharmaceutical productions from Store Kongensgade are generally identifiable by the mark of Johan Ernst Pfau,[6] manager of the factory from 1727 to 1749, or by some distinctive trait in their ornamentation. A number of Danish drug jars are known however which are either unmarked or devoid of characteristic features indicative of their origin. Such wares have been attributed on somewhat tenuous evidence to the Østerbro factory (1764–9)

[2] H. Stafski, *Aus Alten Apotheken*, 4th ed., Munich, 1967, plate 29.
[3] Nisoli, loc. cit. (note 1, above), fig. 25.
[4] B. Reber, *Considérations sur ma Collection d'Antiquités au Point de Vue de l'Histoire de la Médecine, la Pharmacie et les Sciences Naturelles*, Geneva, 1905, pp. 46–9; H. E. Thomann, 'Die "Roche"-Apotheken-Fayencen-Sammlung', *Keramik-Freunde der Schweiz*, Nos. 58–9, 1962.
[5] A. Øigaard, *Fajancefabriken i Store Kongensgade*, Copenhagen, 1936, plate LXX; Dannesboe Andersen, *Gammelt Dansk Apoteksinventar*, Copenhagen, 1944, pp. 221, 223.
[6] Øigaard, loc. cit. (note 5, above), plates LXVII–LXXIII.

85A Covered cylindrical jar, painted in manganese-violet, blue, yellow and green WINTERTHUR, middle of 17th century. H. 15.5 cm (6.1 in) *Zurich, Schweizerisches Landesmuseum. See pages 165 and 166*

85B, 85C Pair of covered jars, painted in polychrome WINTERTHUR, end of 17th century. H. of each 19 cm (7.5 in) *Basle, Collection F. Hoffmann-La Roche & Co. See pages 165 and 166*

(Plate 87B) and to the Vesterbro factory (1787 onwards), both in Copenhagen, and to Kastrup, a short distance south-east of Copenhagen, on the island of Amager (*c*.1755–1814).[7]

In Sweden the potteries of MARIEBERG and RÖRSTRAND[8] in the second half of the eighteenth century made small quantities of drug containers, mostly decorated in blue monochrome. The Marieberg productions include a set of jars made for the Serafimer Hospital in Stockholm (Plate 87D); the vessels bear the emblem of this hospital.

Towards the close of the eighteenth century the ascendancy in manufacture of apothecary jars passed to the Royal Porcelain Factory in COPENHAGEN, which had been a source of tableware and decorative wares of distinction since its foundation by Frantz Heinrich Müller in 1775. Some thirteen sets of porcelain jars, made for various pharmacies between 1785 and 1821, have been listed by Andersen.[9] The earliest of these sets was a large service of 330 vessels with blue monochrome decoration of a garland and ribbon;[10] the set was made in 1785 for the pharmacy at Christianshavn, on the outskirts of Copenhagen, which Müller acquired in that year. Vessels of later date from the Royal Porcelain Factory include jars with ornamentation of sprays of foliage, and jars with braid-like decoration (Plate 87E) made for the *Løve-apoteket* (Lion Pharmacy) in Copenhagen.

---

[7] Kai Uldall, *Gammel Dansk Fajence fra Fabriker i Kongeriget og Hertugdømmerne*, 2nd ed., Copenhagen, 1967; Dannesboe Andersen, loc. cit. (note 5, above), pp. 205, 215, 217, 241, 243, 257.

[8] Margareta Modig, 'Svensk farmacihistorie', *Farmaceutisk Tidende*, vol. 84, 1974, p. 135.

[9] Dannesboe Andersen, loc. cit. (note 5, above), pp. 28–9.

[10] Dannesboe Andersen, loc. cit. (note 5, above), p. 289.

Plate 86A   Ointment jar, painted in yellow, pale blue, pale green, manganese-purple and black
WINTERTHUR, second half of 17th century. H. 16 cm (6.3 in). Inscription 'VNG· POPVLEON.' (*Unguentum populeum*)
London, Victoria and Albert Museum. See page 165

Plate 86B   Reverse of 86A

Plate 86C   Spouted jar, painted in polychrome
WINTERTHUR, second half of 17th century. H. 20.5 cm (8 in). Inscription 'ROB DE·RIBES·'
Basle, Collection F. Hoffmann–La Roche & Co. See page 165

Plate 86D   Spouted jar, painted in polychrome
WINTERTHUR, second half of 17th century. H. 20.5 cm (8 in). Inscription 'SYR· ROSAR :SICCAR·' (*Syrupus rosarum siccarum*)
Zurich, Schweizerisches Landesmuseum. See page 165

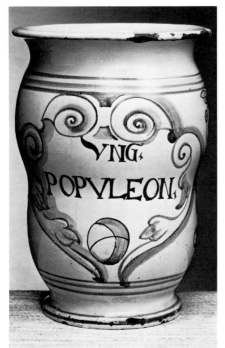

Plate 87A   Drug jar, painted in blue monochrome
             COPENHAGEN, Store Kongensgade factory, c.1740. H. 11 cm (4.3 in).
             Inscription 'EXTRACT: LIQVIRIT:'
             Copenhagen, Universitets Medicinsk Historiske Museum. See page 166
Plate 87B   Drug jar, painted in blue monochrome
             COPENHAGEN, possibly Østerbro factory, c. 1765. H. 16 cm (6.3 in).
             Inscription 'CONSERV: COCHLEAR:'
             *Copenhagen, Universitets Medicinsk Historiske Museum. See pages 166 and
             168*
Plate 87C   Spouted jar, displaying monogram of Christian VI of Denmark and
             Norway, decoration painted in blue monochrome
             COPENHAGEN, Store Kongensgade factory, c.1730–40. H. 19 cm (7.5 in)
             Copenhagen, Universitets Medicinsk Historiske Museum. See page 166
Plate 87D   Drug jar, displaying emblem of Serafimer Hospital, Stockholm,
             decoration painted in blue monochrome
             MARIEBERG, c.1760. H. 13.5 cm (5.3 in). Inscription 'P:S:STAPH:AGR:'
             (Probably *pulvis simplex staphisagriae*, simple powder of stavesacre)
             London, Victoria and Albert Museum. See page 168
Plate 87E   Porcelain syrup jar, painted in blue monochrome. Mark: three wavy lines
             COPENHAGEN, Royal Porcelain Factory, c.1800. H. 20.5 cm (8 in).
             Inscription 'Sÿrup mÿrtillor.' (*Syrupus myrtillorum*)
             Copenhagen, Universitets Medicinsk Historiske Museum. See page 168

Chapter 10

PHARMACEUTICAL CERAMIC WARES FROM CHINA

Use of drugs in China for treatment of disease had its origin at an early period in the country's history. There is evidence that already in the third millennium a system of therapy existed, based on administration of drugs of vegetable origin, among which the antimalarial agent *Ch'ang Shan* (root of the plant *Dichroa febrifuga*) and the anti-asthmatic herb *Ma Huang* (member of the genus *Ephedra*) held a prominent place.

Documentary accounts of Chinese pharmacopoeial practice made their appearance during the Han Dynasty. The first detailed compilation of the materia medica of China was entitled *Shen Nung Pên Tshao Ching* ('Pharmacopoeia of the Heavenly Husbandman'); it was written in the first or second century A.D. and described several hundred medicinal agents of vegetable, animal and mineral origin.[1] This work was followed by other pharmacopoeial treatises, some of which were produced under imperial auspices. The most important of these were the *Hsin Hsiu Pên Tshao* ('Newly Reorganised Pharmacopoeia'; T'ang Dynasty), the *Pên Tshao Thu Ching* ('Illustrated Pharmaceutical Natural History'; Sung Dynasty) and the numerous successive editions of the *Ching Shih Chêng Lei Pei Chi Pên Tshao* ('Classified and Consolidated Armamentarium of Pharmaceutical Natural History').

There is thus a considerable body of knowledge of the medicaments used in China for the healing of the sick, but very little information is available on the containers employed for storage of drugs. It is to be presumed that ceramic vessels, which had been made in China since neolithic times, served for this purpose, although no pre-Ming storage jars inscribed in Chinese characters with names of drugs appear to have been recorded. Uncertainty exists even in regard to ceramic vessels made during the Ming Dynasty. Thus it is a matter of

[1] Pierre Huard and Ming Wong, *La Médecine Chinoise au Cours des Siècles*, Paris, 1959; Joseph Needham and Lu Gwei-Djen, 'Chinese medicine', in *Medicine and Culture*, ed. F. N. L. Poynter, London, 1969, pp. 255–84; Joseph Needham, *Science and Civilisation in China*, vol. 5, part II, Cambridge, 1974.

88   Porcelain jar of albarello shape, decorated in underglaze blue
      CHINA, early 15th century. H. 21 cm (8.3 in)
      Washington, Freer Gallery of Art. See page 176

89A Spouted porcelain jar, painted
in underglaze blue
CHINA, late 16th or early 17th
century. H. 26 cm (10.2 in).
Inscription 'S.RHODOM.'
*New York, Mr. and Mrs. R. Y.
Mottahedeh. See page 176*

89B Armorial porecelain pharmacy
jar, polychrome decoration in
enamel colours of the *famille
verte*
CHINA, end of 17th century.
H. 18 cm (7.1 in)
*London, British Museum. See
page 176*

90A Porcelain drug jar, painted in red, blue, yellow, green, white and black
CHINA, *c.*1725–40.
H. 45 cm (17.7 in).
Inscription 'Aq·
Portulac·'
Leyden, Rijksmuseum voor de Geschiedenis der Natuurwetenschappen.
See page 176

90B Side view of 90A

conjecture whether a rare fifteenth-century albarello (the shape of vessel traditionally associated in the Near East and in Europe with storage of herbs and spices), now in the Freer Gallery of Art (Plate 88), served for storage of a drug, or whether a spouted jar from 1575–1620 inscribed with the unidentified name 's.RHODOM.', in the Mottahedeh Collection (Plate 89A), at any time held a syrup or other medicament. It is only in the second half of the seventeenth century that there was a production of ceramic containers whose inscriptions proclaim that they were intended for storage of drugs. Even these later jars are objects of some rarity, and virtually nothing is known of their history, except that in common with other Chinese porcelain wares destined for export they were made in the potteries of Ching-tê-Chên, in the province of Kiangsi.

An extensive search has revealed two series of jars with identifiable pharmaceutical inscriptions. The first series, made in the reign of the Emperor K'ang Hsi, comprises albarelli whose upper and lower portions exhibit a convex curvature.[2] The jars are painted in underglaze blue colours with decoration of peonies, animals and Oriental faces (Colour Plate H). The fluency of the composition is in marked contrast to the awkwardness of the inscription; the contorted lettering

CONS·cals·fiṅul·

and indiscriminate use of majuscule and minuscule characters (Colour Plate H) attest to the artist's lack of familiarity with Western script.

The second series, of which only one vessel, in the Museum of the History of Science in Leyden, appears to have survived, dates from c.1725–40 (reign of Yung Chêng or Ch'ien Lung). This specimen is of baluster form and decorated in polychrome colours. The nearly indecipherable inscription 'Aq. Portulac.'[3] is displayed both on the front and on the reverse of the jar (Plate 90A), whilst on either side there is a representation of cranes, symbol of longevity, in flight among stylised clouds (Plate 90B).

One set of drug jars, the members of which are devoid of pharmaceutical inscription, is also known. The vessels carry the Russian Imperial arms; they are of K'ang Hsi date and are richly decorated in polychrome enamel colours. Shapes of containers are the cylindrical pot (Plate 89B) and the covered syrup jar.[4] The vessels, which were made for the pharmacy of Peter the Great at St. Petersburg, are of particular interest in that they are the earliest known porcelain apothecary jars displaying a coat of arms.

[2] Four members of the series have been traced; they bear the inscriptions 'THER.ES merag' (British Museum), 'ELECT·IND' (Victoria and Albert Museum), 'CONS·cass·fistul·' (City Museum, Stoke-on-Trent) and 'Diacarth.' (Private Collection, U.S.A.).
[3] André Kret, 'Un vase de pharmacie en Chine de Commande', Rev. Hist. Pharm., vol. 17, 1964–5, pp. 441–4.
[4] Michel Beurdeley, Porcelain of the East India Companies, London, 1962, p. 125.

GLOSSARY
of the More Important Terms used in Apothecary Jar Inscriptions

GLOSSARY
of the More Important Terms used in Apothecary Jar Inscriptions

Introduction

A knowledge of the meaning of inscriptions on pharmacy jars is desirable, not only for the inherent interest of the drug names, but also because inscriptions on jars of known date afford to the social and pharmaceutical historian a means of establishing at what period in history a particular medicament or confection enjoyed popularity. However, in the absence of access to contemporary pharmacopoeias, dispensatories and *antidotaria* the interpretation of pharmaceutical inscriptions often presents difficulties.

The glossary which follows has been compiled to provide a guide to the more commonly encountered terms which appear in drug jar inscriptions. It is to be hoped that the compilation will be of assistance to museum officials with pharmacy jars in their keeping, to private collectors with ceramic drug vessels in their possession, and to others.

The glossary lists names of *simpliciae* (drugs of vegetable, animal or mineral origin), names of *compositae* (medicinal preparations containing one or more therapeutically active ingredient),[1] and certain words such as physicians' names which were sometimes appended to compound drug names to denote the authorship of a particular formula (*cf.* Plates 50B and 66A). Where no indication is given to the contrary it is to be taken that the term explained is rendered in Latin or in pseudo-Latin, e.g. *flos* (flower), *sambucus* (elder-tree). The usual rules of Latin declension apply to such terms, e.g. *syrupus florum sambuci* (syrup of elder flowers).

Plants Yielding Drugs, Spices, Resins, Colouring Agents, etc
In the case of Latin or pseudo-Latin names of vegetable drugs the following information is given wherever possible: (a) common name of the plant from which the drug, spice, etc. was obtained, (b) probable botanical name of plant, (c) part or parts of plant used (herb,[2] flower, fruit, seeds, leaves, root, bark,

---

[1] Also termed compounded drugs, formulated products, or polypharmaceuticals.
[2] The word 'herb' is intended to signify that the whole plant, or aerial parts of the plant, were used.

resinous secretion, etc.). It must be stressed however that officinal practice in different countries and at different periods in history showed variations in regard to parts of plants used.

For plant names and certain other terms rendered in languages other than Latin or pseudo-Latin (e.g. *nenufaro, nerprun*) only the common name and, where appropriate, the Latin or pseudo-Latin equivalents are given, so as to avoid unnecessary reiteration of botanical names and parts of plants used.

Compound Drug Names

In order to conserve space no attempt has been made to list and interpret individually the numerous formulated drugs which have been in use in past centuries. The meaning of such names will however be readily derived from the respective generic and specific names. Thus the entries *trochiscus*, *unguentum* and *althaea* will provide the meaning of the inscriptions *trochisci althaeae* (marsh-mallow lozenges) and *unguentum althaeae* or *unguentum de althaea* (marsh-mallow ointment). 'Specialty' products are normally listed under the name which would be unabbreviated in the inscription. Thus *Philonium Romanum* and *Confectio de hyacintho*, customarily abbreviated to *Philonium R.* and *C. hyacintho*, appear under *Philonium (Romanum)* and *Hyacintho, confectio de*, respectively. Cross-references are provided where necessary.

Interpretation of Drug Jar Inscriptions

In the transcription and interpretation of drug jar inscriptions allowance must be made (i) for possible variations or errors in spelling, e.g. 'teifera magna' for *Trifera magna* (Plate 19C), 'A·FNOCCHIO' for *A. finocchio* (Plate 21A); (ii) for use of unorthodox abbreviations, e.g. 'TIRICA·M·G' for *Theriaca magna* (Plate 59C); and (iii) for coalescence of words, e.g. 'ra·dacoro' for *Radice di acoro* (Plate 9B), 'Estr. Degeieure' for *Extrait de genièvre* (Plate 45A). Common orthographical variants, examples of which are given in the Glossary, include the use of *s* for *z*, *i* for *j* or *y*, *f* for *ph*, *e* for *ae* or *oe*, *v* for *u*, and vice versa.

Various devices were used by drug jar painters to accommodate lengthy names within the cartouche; examples of such expedients include the reduction of certain letters to minuscule size, as in the inscription 'C°L°QVINTIDA' (*coloquintida*) (Plate 6A), and the use of a bar over a letter to denote the omission of one or more following letters; e.g. 'M. Violatū' for *M. violatum* (Plate 44B); 'colloq̂tida' for *coloquintida* (Plate 16A). On one series of jars of Dutch or Belgian manufacture, where the artist was unable to accommodate the drug name within the confines of the cartouche, the terminal part of the inscription appears on the underside of the vessels.[3]

Occasionally an inscription is encountered which is unidentifiable, either

---

[3] D. A. Wittop Koning, (a) 'Gemerkte "Delftse" Apothekerspotten', *Vrienden*, No. 34, 1964, pp. 8–9 and 40; (b) 'Singulière série de marques sous des piluliers en Delft', *Rev. Hist. Pharm.*, vol. 18, 1966–7, pp. 39–40.

91   Cabinet de Pharmacie of the old Hôpital de la Charité, Lyons, 17th century
     Now in Musée Historique des Hospices Civils, Lyons. See page 82.

because it is rendered in a vernacular whose meaning has been lost, or is the
subject of a major orthographical error, or because the drug name is the
invention of a particular pharmacist, and is not recorded in any pharmacopoeia, dispensatory or antidotary. Examples of unidentified inscriptions are
the drug names 'Cons. di Grugnial' (Rackham, *Catalogue VAM*, No. 1267),
'Bals. Cameroni.' (Plate 49D) and 'SYᴼ·DI·ANTUF' (Plate 8A); the latter term has
been the subject of debate.[4]

Synonyms
Not infrequently a given plant, mineral substance or pharmaceutical
preparation was known by two or more names, which had their origin at
different periods of history. Thus rosemary was referred to by the names of

[4] *Rev. Hist. Pharm.*, vol. 17, 1964–5, pp. 60 and 148.

rosmarinus and *anthos*; comfrey was usually termed *symphytum* (Plate 42A) but was also known as *consolida*, and the herb elecampane was known variously as *enula*, *enula campana* and *helenium*. Examples of synonyms for mineral compounds are the names *mercurius*, *argentum vivum* and *hydrargyrum*, all of which denote the element mercury, *panacea mercurii rubra* and *arcanum corallinum* which signify red mercuric oxide, and *arcanum duplicatum*, *sal duplicatum*, *sal de duobus*, *sal polychrestum (Glaseri)*, *tartarum vitriolatum* and *kalium sulphuricum*, which were alternative names for the compound now known as potassium sulphate. Formulated products endowed with dual names may be exemplified by reference to Ointment of the Apostles (*unguentum Apostolorum* and *unguentum dodecapharmacum*), and to Ophthalmic Pills (*pilulae lucis majores* and *pilulae opticae*).

Glossary

2 Radicibus, syrupus de   See *duabus radicibus, syrupus de*

5 Radicibus, syrupus de; 5que radicibus, syrupus de   See *quinque radicibus, syrupus de*

☿ Symbol for the element mercury (as in *unguentum enulatum cum mercurio* (Plate 67D))

♄ Symbol for the element sulphur

♈ Symbol denoting the word *contra*, against (e.g. Plate 28C)

A.   At beginning of inscription: *acqua; adeps; aqua; axungia.* At end of inscription: *agaricus* (as in *pilulae de hiera cum a.*); *alba*, etc.; *amara*, etc. (as in *oleum amygdalarum a.*); *Andromachus* (as in *theriaca A.*); *apium* (as in *unguentum mundificativum de a.*); *aureus*

Abete (Italian); **abezzo** (Italian); **abies**   Member of the genus *Abies* (Fir-tree). Twigs and resin used

Abrotanum   Southernwood (*Artemisia abrotanum*). Leaves used

Absinthii, sal   See *sal absinthii*

Absinthium; absintio (Italian)   Wormwood, Absinth (*Artemisia absin-thium*). Leaves and flowering tops used

Acacia   Inspissated juice of the unripe fruit of certain species of *Acacia* and *Mimosa*

Acacia Germanica; acacia nostras   Inspissated juice of the unripe sloe

Acaciae, gummi   Gum acacia, gum Arabic. Dried exudation from stem and branches of certain species of *Acacia*

Acetatus, syrupus   Syrup of vinegar

Acetosa   Sorrel (*Rumex acetosa*). Leaves and root used

Acetosella   See *luiula*

Acetosus, syrupus   Syrup of vinegar

Acetum   Vinegar

Ache (French)   Smallage (cf. *apium*)

Aconitum   Aconite, Wolf's-bane (*Aconitum napellus*). Root used

Acoro (Italian); **acorus**   Term applied to the rhizome of the Sweet Flag (*Acorus calamus*) and to the Galingale

Acqua (Italian)   Water

Adeps   Fat, grease, lard

Adeps lana   Wool fat, lanolin

Adianthum; adiantum   Name applied to certain ferns, e.g. True Maidenhair (*Adiantum capillus-Veneris*)

Adragante, gomme (French)   Gum tragacanth (cf. *tragacantha*)

Aegyptiacum, unguentum   Egyptian Ointment. Made from basic copper acetate, vinegar and honey. Used in treatment of ulcers

Aërophorus laxantis, pulvis   Effervescent laxative powder, Seidlitz powder

Aerugo   Verdigris, basic copper acetate. Sometimes denotes copper oxide

Aes   Copper

Aethiops Martialis   Ethiops Martial, black iron oxide

Aethiops mineralis   Ethiops mineral, black mercuric oxide

Agallochum   See *aloes, lignum*

Agaricus   Larch agaric (*Polyporus officinalis*)

Ageratum   Maudlin (*Achillea ageratum*). Herb used

Aggregativae, pilulae   Purgative pills[5] made from aloes, scammony, larch agaric, colocynth, turpeth root, rhubarb, myrobalans and other ingredients. Used for relief of headaches and gastric pains

Agnocasto (Italian); **agnus castus**   Chaste-tree (*Vitex agnus castus*). Fruit used

Agresta   Unripe grape

Agrimonia   Agrimony (*Agrimonia eupatoria*). Herb used

Agrippae Regis, unguentum   Ointment made from squill, iris rhizome, bryony root, dwarf elder root, male fern rhizome, wax and other ingredients. Used in treatment of tumours and of dropsy. Named after Herod Agrippa I, King of Judaea, for whom the ointment was supposedly prescribed

Agro (Italian)   (1) Sour-tasting, unripe. (2) Juice of a bitter fruit

Agro di limone (Italian)   Lemon juice

Alabastrinum, unguentum; alabastro, unguentum de   Ointment made from powdered alabaster, chamomile flowers, rose petals, rose oil, white wax and other ingredients. Used as an emollient

---

[5] The plethora of purgatives and emetics (*catartico imperiale, confectio Hamech, electuarium diacatholicon, electuarium diaphoenicum, electuarium Episcopi, electuarium hydragogum, electuarium Indum* (*majus* and *minus*), *electuarium lenitivum, extractum panchymagogum, hiera Logod, hiera picra, pilulae cocciae, pilulae de duobus, pilulae de tribus, pilulae Indae ex Hali, pilulae Rudii, pilulae sine quibus esse nolo, pulvis Cornachinus, syrupus de tribus*, etc.) prescribed by the physician of former times had its origin in the 'Hippocratic theory that the first requirement of

Alabastrum Alabaster

Alandali, trochisci See *alhandali, trochisci*

Alba; album, etc. White

Albi Rhasis, trochisci Lozenges made from white lead and other ingredients

Album refrigerans, ceratum See *refrigerans Galeni, ceratum*

Album, unguentum Ointment made from white lead, white wax, egg white, oil of roses and rose water. Used for treatment of burns

Alcermes, confectio See *alkermes, confectio*

Alces Elk

Alchechengi (Italian) Winter Cherry (cf. *alkekengi*)

Alchemilla Lady's Mantle (*Alchemilla vulgaris*). Herb used

Alchermes, confectio See *alkermes, confectio*

Alephanginae, pilulae Scented pills, made from aloes, aloë-wood, cinnamon, nutmeg, cloves, myrrh, rose petals and other ingredients. Used in treatment of epilepsy, vertigo, migraine and melancholy

Alessandrino, elettuario (Italian) Electuary having purgative action, named after Alessandro Petronio, physician to Pope Gregory XIII, who formulated the preparation

Alexandrina, aurea See *aurea Alexandrina*

Alexandrinum, julapium See *regius, syrupus*

Alexipharmacum Antidote against a poison

Alhandali, trochisci Colocynth lozenges

Alkekengi Winter Cherry (*Physalis alkekengi*). Berries used

Alkermes, confectio Polypharmaceutical preparation named after the kermes insect, one of its ingredients

Alliaria Jack-by-the-hedge (*Sisymbrium alliaria*). Herb used

Allium Garlic

Allume (Italian) Alum

Aloe Aloes. Substance having purgative action, obtained by evaporating the liquid which exudes from the cut leaves of various species of the genus *Aloë*

Aloe, lignum See *aloes, lignum*

Aloephanginae, pilulae See *alephanginae, pilulae*

Aloes, lignum Aloë-wood, Eagle-wood, Agalloch. Resinous wood of an East Indian thymelaeaceous tree (*Aquilaria agallocha*)

Aloe Socotrina Aloes obtained from the island of Socotra

Alquermes, confectio See *alkermes, confectio*

Althaea Marshmallow (*Althaea officinalis*). Root used

Alumen Alum, potassium aluminium sulphate

Amande (French); **amandola** (Italian) Almond (cf. *amygdala; mandorla*)

Amara; amarum, etc. Bitter-tasting

---

medical treatment has to be the purification of the body from illness-producing humours' (Kremers and Urdang, *History of Pharmacy*, pp. 13–14).

Ambra citrina   Amber (resin)

Ambra grisea   Ambergris

Ambusta, unguentum ad   Anti-burn ointment

Amec, confectio; Amech, confectio   See *Hamech, confectio*

Amidala (Italian)   Almond

Amido (Italian)   Starch

Amigdala   See *amygdala*

Ammi   Member of genus *Ammi* (Bishop's-weed). Seeds used

Ammoniacum, gummi   Ammoniacum, gum ammoniac. Gum resin exuded from stem of the plant *Dorema ammoniacum.*

Ammoniacum, sal   Sal-ammoniac; ammonium chloride

Amomum   Term applied to certain zingiberaceous plants, including the species which yield cardamoms and Grains of Paradise

Amygdala amara   Bitter almond

Amygdala dulcis   Sweet almond

Amylum   Starch

Anacardium   Cashew-tree (*Anacardium occidentale*). Nuts (anacards, cashew nuts) used

Anagallis   Term applied to the Common Pimpernel (*Anagallis arvensis*) and possibly other plants, e.g. the Water Speedwell (*Veronica anagallis-aquatica*)

Anas; anatra (Italian)   Duck

Anchusa   Name denoting the Common Alkanet (*Anchusa officinalis*) and certain related plants. Root and herb used. (Cf. *buglossum*)

Andromachi, theriaca   Theriac prepared according to the formula of Andromachus

Andromachus   Roman physician (first century A.D.), originator of a variety of *mithridatium* and of theriac

Anethum; aneto (Italian)   Anet, Dill (*Anethum graveolens*). Herb and seeds used

Anetra (Italian)   Duck

Angelica   Angelica (*Angelica archangelica*). Root used

Animale Dippelii, oleum   Dippel's Animal Oil, bone-oil. Oily preparation derived from hartshorn. Named after J. C. Dippel (1673–1734), a German physician who introduced the product into medicine

Anime, gummi   Gum animé. Resin obtained from *Hymenaea courbaril* and certain other trees

Anisum   Anise (*Pimpinella anisum*). Fruit (aniseed) used

Anisum estrellatum; anisum stellatum   Star Anise (*Illicium verum*). Fruit used

Anitra (Italian)   Duck

Anodynum   Anodyne, medicament for relief of pain

Anonis   Member of genus *Ononis* (Rest-harrow). Herb and root used

Anser   Goose

Anthora   Name applied to an unidentified mountainous plant, allied to

Wolf's-bane (cf. *aconitum*). Root used

Anthos   See *rosmarinus*

Antidotum haemagogum; antidotum hemagogum   Emmenagogic preparation made from root of long birthwort, root of elecampane, pellitory of Spain, seeds of rue, lupins, myrrh and other ingredients

Antihecticum Poterii   A preparation, used for treatment of hectic fever and certain other conditions, made by heating a mixture of antimony, tin and nitre. Named after Pierre Potier (Petrus Poterius), a French chemist of the seventeenth century

Antimonium diaphoreticum   Diaphoretic antimony. Medicinal preparation made by heating a mixture of antimony and nitre

Antipestilentiales, pilulae   See *pestilentiales, pilulae*

Antirrhinum   Plant of genus *Antirrhinum* (Snapdragon)

Aper   Wild boar

Aperientes, quinque radices   The five aperient roots (roots of fennel, smallage, parsley, asparagus and butcher's broom)

Aperientis   Aperient, laxative

Apii mundificativum   See *mundificativum (de apio), unguentum*

Apis   Bee

Apium   Smallage, Wild Celery (*Apium graveolens*). Root and seeds used

Apium dulce   Celery

Apostolicum, unguentum; Apostolorum, unguentum   (*Unguentum dodecapharmacum*). Ointment of the Apostles, named after the twelve ingredients from which it was prepared, viz. myrrh, frankincense, bdellium, galbanum, opopanax, rosin, turpentine, gum ammoniac, root of long birthwort, verdigris, litharge and white wax. Used in treatment of wounds and ulcers

Apozema   Decoction, infusion

Appio (Italian)   Smallage (cf. *apium*)

Aqua   (1) Water. (2) Medicated water, aromatic water. Usually obtained by aqueous distillation of a plant, or an appropriate part of a plant

Aqua vitae   Alcohol, brandy

Aquifolium   Holly (*Ilex aquifolium*). Leaves used

Arabicum, gummi   Gum Arabic, gum acacia

Arabicus, costus   See *costus*

Aragon, unguentum   See *arogon, unguentum*

Arantium   See *aurantium*

Arbor Vitae   Tree of Life. A shrub or tree of the genus *Thuja*

Arcaei, balsamum; Arcaei, linimentum; Arcaei, unguentum   Ointment made from gum elemi, lard and turpentine; named after its originator, Francesco Arcaeus, a Spanish physician (1493–1567)

Arcanum corallinum   Crude red mercuric oxide

Arcanum duplicatum   'The Double Secret'. Residue from the evaporation or distillation of a mixture of saltpetre and vitriol; crude potassium sulphate

Arcei, balsamum   See *Arcaei, balsamum*

Ardea   Heron

Aregon, unguentum   See *arogon, unguentum*

Argentina   Silver Weed, Wild Tansy, Goose Tansy, Goose Grass (*Potentilla anserina*). Herb used

Argentum   Silver

Argentum vivum   Mercury, quicksilver

Aristolochia longa   Long Birthwort. Root used

Aristolochia rotunda   Round Birthwort. Root used

Armel (Italian)   Wild Rue (cf. *harmala*)

Armeniacae, gummi   Apricot gum. Dried gummy exudation from the trunk and branches of the apricot tree

Armeniacum   Gum ammoniac (cf. *ammoniacum, gummi*). Sometimes denotes the apricot

Armeniacum, sal   See *sal Armeniacum*

Arnica   Arnica, Mountain Tobacco (*Arnica montana*). Rhizome and flowers used

Arogon, unguentum (derived from Greek ἀρήγω = to help, to succour)   Ointment made from rosemary, marjoram, sage leaves, bay-laurel leaves, bryony root, frankincense, oil of bay-laurel berries, bear's grease and other ingredients. Used as a nerve restorative

Aromaticum, vinum   See *Hippocraticum, vinum*

Arsenicum   Arsenic

Artanita   See *arthanita*

Artemisia   Mugwort (*Artemisia vulgaris*). Herb used

Arthanita   Sowbread (*Cyclamen europaeum*). Tuberous rootstock used

Arthemisia   See *artemisia*

Arum   Lords-and-ladies (*Arum maculatum*). Rhizome used

Arundo   Reed

Asafetida; asafoetida   Asafoetida. Resinous gum obtained from the rhizome and root of *Ferula assafoetida* and certain other species of *Ferula*.

Asarum   Asarabacca, Hazelwort (*Asarum europaeum*). Rhizome, roots and leaves used

Asenzio   See *assenzio*

Asfalto (Italian)   Bitumen of Judaea (cf. *asphaltus*)

Aspalathi, lignum; aspalathum; aspalato (Italian)   Rosewood

Aspalto (Italian)   Bitumen of Judaea (cf. *asphaltus*)

Asparagus   Asparagus. Seeds and root used

Asperula   Woodruff (*Asperula odorata*). Herb used

Asphaltus   Bitumen of Judaea. Bituminous matter found on surface of Dead Sea. Used as an emollient

Aspidium   See *filix*

Asplenium   See *ceterach*

Assafoetida   See *asafoetida*

Assentio (Italian); **assenzio** (Italian)   Wormwood (cf. *absinthium*)

Athanasia magna (from Greek ἀθανασία, immortality)   Elixir made from opium, poppy seeds, *costus* root, spikenard, saffron, myrrh and other ingredients. Used as an analgesic and hypnotic

Atramentum   1. Alchemical term for copper sulphate and ferrous sulphate. 2. Atrament. Black pigment used in preparation of ink. 3. Ink

Atriplex   Member of genus *Atriplex*, especially *Atriplex hortensis* (Garden Orach, Mountain Spinach). Leaves used

Aurantium   Orange (fruit)

Aurea Alexandrina   Polypharmaceutical preparation made from gold leaf, silver leaf, pearls, powdered ivory, red coral, mandrake root, opium, myrrh and other ingredients

Aureum, unguentum   'The Golden Ointment'. Salve made from saffron, olive oil, yellow wax, frankincense, colophony and other resins. Used as a vulnerary

Aureus, pulvis   Face powder prepared from gold leaf, iron oxide, galingale, cinnamon and aniseed

Auripigmentum   Orpiment; arsenic trisulphide

Aurum potabile   'Potable Gold' (term probably of alchemical origin). Name applied to certain metallic preparations of golden or yellow colour

Aveline (French); **avellana**   Hazelnut

Avicenna   Ibn Sina (A.D. 980–1037), celebrated Arab physician. Author of a comprehensive treatise on medicine, translated into Latin under the title *Canon Medicinae Avicennae*

Avorio (Italian)   Ivory

Axungia   Grease, fat, lard

Axungia oxygenata   Oleaginous matter obtained by treating pork fat with nitric acid

B.   At beginning of inscription: *bacca; balsamum; baume*. At end of inscription: *bianco; blanc*

Bacca; baie (French)   Berry

Balaustium   Wild Pomegranate-tree. Flowers (balaustines) used

Balsamicae Mortonii, pilulae   Anti-tussive pills made from Balsam of Peru, sublimate of benzoin, gum ammoniac, saffron and other ingredients

Balsamicus, syrupus   Syrup of Balsam of Tolu

Balsamina   Balsam-apple. Fruit of tree *Momordica balsamina*

Balsamum   Balsam, balm. Aromatic resinous substance

Balsamum sulphuris   Balsam of Sulphur. Medicinal preparation for treatment of ulcers, made by heating flowers of sulphur in olive oil

Bardana   Burdock (*Arctium lappa*). Root and seeds used

Basilicon, unguentum; basilicum, unguentum (from Greek βασιλικόν, royal)   Ointment made from wax, pitch, olive oil, myrrh, frankincense and other resins. Used to promote healing of wounds

Baume (French)   Balsam, balm

Bdellium, gummi   Bdellium resin. Gum resin obtained from certain trees or shrubs of the genus *Balsamodendron* and *Commiphora*

Beccabunga   Brook-lime (*Veronica beccabunga*) and certain other species of *Veronica*. Herb used

Beccheri, pilulae   See *Becheri, pilulae*

Becchiche, pillole (Italian)   See *bechicae, pilulae*

Becher   Johann Joachim Becher, celebrated German physician and chemist (1635–82)

Becher, pilules de (French); **Becheri, pilulae**   Alterative pills composed of aloes, rhubarb, myrrh and other ingredients

Bechicae, pilulae; bechicae, trochisci; bechiche, pillole (Italian) (from Greek βήξ, a cough)   Anti-tussive pills or lozenges, made from iris rhizome and other ingredients

Bechio (Italian)   Coltsfoot (cf. *tussilago*)

Béchiques, pilules (French)   See *bechicae, pilulae*

Bechium   Coltsfoot (cf. *tussilago*)

Been album; behen album   White Behen. Plant of uncertain identity, believed to be the composite plant *Centaurea behen*; probably also applied to the caryophyllaceous plants *Silene inflata* (Bladder Campion) and *Silene armeria*

Belgimi (Italian); **belgioini** (Italian)   Benzoin (cf *benzoinum*)

Belladonna   Belladonna, Deadly Nightshade (*Atropa belladonna*). Leaves and root used

Bellericus, myrobalanus   See *myrobalanus bellericus*

Belloste, pilules de (French); **Bellostii, pilulae**   Pills made from mercury, aloes, scammony, rhubarb, black pepper and honey; used in treatment of skin disorders. Named after their inventor, Augustin Belloste (*c*.1650–1730), a French surgeon

Benedetta (Italian); **Benedicta, herba**   Common Avens, Herb Bennet (*Geum urbanum*). Herb and root used

Benedicta laxativa   Laxative electuary made from turpeth root, *hermodactylus*, gromwell and other ingredients

Benedictum, unguentum   Ointment made from mercury, litharge, white lead, frankincense and lard

Bengioino (Italian); **bengivo** (Italian); **benzoinum**   Benzoin, gum benzoin, gum Benjamin. Resin obtained from *Styrax benzoin* and certain other trees of the genus *Styrax*

Berberis   Common Barberry (*Berberis vulgaris*). Bark, berries and seeds used

Betonica; bettonica (Italian)   Wood Betony (*Stachys betonica*). Herb used

Betula   Birch-tree. Bark and leaves used

Bezoar   Calculus found in the stomach or intestines of certain animals

Bezoardicum minerale   A substance obtained by the action of nitric acid on antimony trichloride

Biacca (Italian)   Ceruse, white lead

Bianco (Italian)   White

Bichiche, pillole   See *bechiche, pillole*

Bisantiis, syrupus de; Bisantino, siropo (Italian)   See *Byzantiis, syrupus de*

Bistorta   Bistort, Snakeweed, Adderwort (*Polygonum bistorta*). Rhizome used

Bitumen Judaicum   See *asphaltus*

Bituro (Italian); **biturro** (Italian)   Butter

Bizantiis, syrupus de   See *Byzantiis, syrupus de*

Blanc (French)   White

Blatta Bysantia   Shell of *Murex inflatus* and certain other molluscs

Bolus   Bole. Fine earthy or unctuous clay, obtained from Armenia (*bolus Armenus*), from the isle of Lemnos (*terra Lemnia*) and from other parts of Europe and Asia. Used internally as a remedy for gastro-intestinal disorders, and externally for application to wounds. The material was sometimes pressed into cylindrical tablets and stamped with an appropriate device, and consequently was also known as *terra sigillata*

Bombax   Cotton-plant. Seeds and cotton used

Bombyx   Silkworm

Bontius   Latinised form of Jacob de Bondt, Dutch physician and Inspector of Surgery in the Dutch East Indies (1598–1631)

Borace (Italian)   Borax

Boragine (Italian); **borago; borrago**   Common Borage (*Borago officinalis*). Herb and flower used

Bos   Ox

Bourrache (French)   Borage (cf. *borago*)

Brassica   Cabbage

Brionia   See *bryonia*

Bruciato (Italian); **brugiato** (Italian)   Burnt, calcined

Brunella   See *prunella*

Bruscus   See *ruscus*

Bryonia   Common Bryony (*Bryonia dioica*). Root used

Bufo   Toad

Buglossa (Italian); **buglossum**   Bugloss. Term denoting the Common Alkanet, *Anchusa officinalis*, and certain other members of the family *Boraginaceae*. Leaves, flowers and root used

Burgundica, pix   See *pix Burgundica*

Bursa pastoris   Shepherd's Purse (*Capsella bursa pastoris*). Herb used

Butyrum   Butter

Bysantia, blatta   See *blatta Bysantia*

Byzantiis, syrupus de   Syrup made from bugloss, endive, smallage, hops and sugar. Used in treatment of liver disorders

92   Pharmacy, Hôtel-Dieu, Tournus, Saône-et-Loire, France. *See page 82*

C.   At beginning, or in middle of inscription: *compositum; conditum; confectio; confezione; conserva; corteccia; cortex; costus* (as in *c. Arabicus*); *cum*. At end of inscription: *compositum; composto*

C.A.   *cum agarico*

CC.   *cornu cervi*

C.R.   *cum rhabarbaro, cum rheo* (e.g. *syrupus rosarum C.R.*, syrup of roses with rhubarb)

Cachecticus, syrupus   Syrup made from senna, larch agaric, polypody rhizome, leaves of agrimony and maidenhair, safflower seeds, cinnamon and other ingredients. Used in treatment of cachexy

Cadmia   A metallic preparation, especially impure zinc oxide

Caeruleum, unguentum   'The Blue Ointment'. Unguent made from mercury, hog's lard and turpentine. Used as an anti-venereal agent

Calamentum   See *calamintha*

Calamina; calaminaris lapis   Calamine, basic zinc carbonate

Calamintha   Common Calamint (*Calamintha officinalis*), and certain other members of the genus *Calamintha*. Flowering herb used

Calamo (Italian); **calamus**; **calamus aromaticus**   Calamus. Aromatic plant of Eastern origin but of uncertain identity, in use already in biblical times (cf. Exodus, xxx, 23). Perhaps a member of the genus *Andropogon*

Calcatrepola; **calcitrapa**   Caltrop, Star-thistle (*Centaurea calcitrapa*). Herb used

Calendula   Garden Marigold (*Calendula officinalis*). Flowers used

Calx   Lime, quicklime

Calybeatae, pilulae   See *chalybeatae, pilulae*

Camaemelum; camomilla (Italian)   See *chamomilla*

Campechense, lignum   Logwood. Heartwood of the tree *Haematoxylon campechianum*

Camphora   Camphor

Camphorata   A herb having a camphoraceous aroma, e.g. the plant *Camphorosma Monspeliaca*

Canada, baume du (French); **Canadense, balsamum**   Canada Balsam, Canada Turpentine. Resin obtained from the Balsam Fir, *Abies balsamea*

Cancer   Crab

Canella   Canella, white cinnamon. Bark of the Wild Cinnamon, *Canella alba*

Canfora (Italian)   Camphor

Cannabis   Cannabis, Hemp (*Cannabis sativa*)

Cannella   See *canella*

Cantharides   Dried Spanish Fly

Caphura   Camphor

Capillus Veneris   True Maidenhair, Venus Hair (*Adiantum capillus-Veneris*). Dried fronds used

Capparis   Capers. Flower-buds of the shrub *Capparis spinosa*

Capretto (Italian)   Kid (young of goat)

Carabe   Amber

Caranna, gummi   Gum resin obtained from a South American resiniferous tree

Cardamomum   Cardamom. Seed-capsules of the plant *Elettaria carda-momum*

Cardiaca, confectio   Polypharmaceutical preparation made from rosemary, juniper berries, saffron and other ingredients. Used as a cordial

Carduus Benedictus   Blessed Thistle, Holy Thistle (*Cnicus Benedictus*). Flowering tops used

Carduus Marianus   Our Lady's Milk Thistle (*Silybum Marianum*). Fruit used

Carduus Sanctus   See *carduus Benedictus*

Carduus stellatus   See *calcitrapa*

Carica   Dried fig

Cariocostinum, electuarium   See *caryocostinum, electuarium*

Cariophylli   See *caryophylli*

Carlina   Carline Thistle (*Carlina acaulis*). Root used

Carneolus; carneolus, lapis   Cornelian

Carpobalsamum   Fruit of the tree *Commiphora opobalsamum* and of certain other balsamiferous trees (cf. *opobalsamum*; *xylobalsamum*)

Carthamus   Safflower, Bastard Saffron, Saffron Thistle (*Carthamus tinctorius*). Seeds used

Carvum   Caraway. Dried ripe fruits of the plant *Carum carvi*

Caryocostinum, electuarium   Purgative electuary made from cloves, *costus* root, scammony and other ingredients. Used in treatment of gout and bilious attacks

Caryophyllata   See *Benedicta, herba*

Caryophylli   Cloves. Dried flower-buds of the tree *Caryophyllus aromaticus*

Cascarilla   Cascarilla. Bark of the tree *Croton eluteria*

Caseus   Cheese

Cassia; cassia fistularis   Cassia. Pulp obtained from pods of the tree *Cassia fistula*

Cassia lignea   Cassia cinnamon, cassia bark. Bark of the tree *Cinnamomum cassia*

Castor; castoreo (Italian); **castorio** (Italian)   Castor, castoreum. Substance having an empyreumatic odour, obtained from the beaver

Cataplasma   Cataplasm, poultice

Catartico imperiale   See *imperiale, catartico*

Catechu   Catechu. Substance having astringent action, obtained from *Acacia catechu* and certain other Eastern trees and shrubs

Catellus   Little dog, puppy

Catharticus Glauberi, sal; catharticus, sal   See *sal catharticus Glauberi*

Catholicon; catholicum, electuarium   See *diacatholicon, electuarium*

Cauda equina   See *equisetum*

Caulibus, lohoch de   *Lohoch* made from red cabbage juice, sugar and honey. Used in treatment of ailments of the chest

Caulis   Red cabbage

Cavallo (Italian)   Horse

Cavretto (Italian)   Kid (young of goat)

Cedro (Italian)   Citron (fruit). Sometimes denotes the lemon

Celidonia (Italian)   Greater Celandine (cf. *chelidonium majus*)

Centaurium minus   Common Century (*Erythraea centaurium*). Dried flowering tops used

Centinodium   See *polygonum*

Cepa   Onion

Cephalicum   Drug for relief of headache

Cera   Wax, beeswax

Cerasum   Cherry

Cérat de Galien (French)   See *refrigerans Galeni, ceratum*

Ceratum   Cerate. Ointment compounded from a wax, an oil and other ingredients

Ceratum epuloticum   See *epuloticum, ceratum*

Ceratum Galeni; ceratum refrigerans Galeni   See *refrigerans Galeni, ceratum*

Ceratum stomachale; ceratum stomachicum   See *stomachale, ceratum*

Cerefolium   Chervil (*Anthriscus cerefolium*). Herb used

Ceroneum, emplastrum   Poultice made from litharge, fenugreek, myrrh, yellow wax and other ingredients. Used as an emollient and in treatment of muscular pain

Ceroto (Italian); **cerotto** (Italian)   Poultice, plaster

Ceruleum, unguentum   See *caeruleum, unguentum*

Cerussa   Ceruse, white lead, basic lead carbonate

Cervus   Stag

Ceterach   Name denoting the Common Spleenwort (*Asplenium ceterach*) and possibly certain other ferns

Chaerefolium   See *cerefolium*

Chalibeatae, pilulae   See *chalybeatae, pilulae*

Chalibeatus, syrupus   See *chalybeatus, syrupus*

Chalibées, pilules (French); **chalybeatae, pilulae**   Purgative pills, prepared from iron oxide, aloes, saffron and other ingredients

Chalybeatus, syrupus   Syrup containing iron oxide and other ingredients. Used in treatment of anaemia and dropsy

Chamaedrys   Common Germander, Wall Germander (*Teucrium chamaedrys*). Herb used

Chamaemelum; chamaemilla   See *chamomilla*

Chamaepitys   Ground Pine, Gout Ivy (*Ajuga chamaepitys*). Leaves used

Chamomilla   Term applied to the Roman Chamomile (*Anthemis nobilis*), the German Chamomile (*Matricaria chamomilla*) and possibly other members of the family *Compositae*

Chardon Bénit (French)   Blessed Thistle (cf. *carduus Benedictus*)

Charyophylli   See *caryophylli*

Chebulus, myrobalanus   See *myrobalanus chebulus*

Cheiri   Wallflower (*Cheiranthus cheiri*). Flowers used

Chelidonium majus   Greater Celandine (*Chelidonium majus*). Leaves and root used

Chelidonium minus   Lesser Celandine, Pilewort (*Ranunculus ficaria*). Leaves and root used

Cherefolium   See *cerefolium*

Chermes   See *kermes*

Chicorée (French)   Chicory, Succory (cf. *cichorium*)

China   China, China root. Rhizome of the plant *Smilax China*

China chinae; chinae cortex   See *Peruvianus, cortex*

Cholagogum, electuarium   Purgative electuary for treatment of disorders of the bile

Cicer   Chich, Chick-pea (*Cicer arietinum*). Seeds used

Cicerbita See *sonchus*

Cichorium; cicorea (Italian); **cicoria** (Italian) Chicory, Succory (*Cichorium intybus*). Root, leaves, flowers and seeds used

Cicuta Hemlock (*Conium maculatum*). Leaves used

Cidonia See *cydonia*

Cidro (Italian) See *cedro*

Ciguë (French) Hemlock (cf. *cicuta*)

Cilidonia See *celidonia*

Cina (Italian) China root (cf. *China*)

Cinae, semen See *santonicum*

Cinara Artichoke

Cinchona See *Peruvianus, cortex*

Cinnabaris Cinnabar, red mercuric sulphide

Cinnamomum Cinnamon, Ceylon cinnamon. Inner bark of the tree *Cinnamomum zeylanicum*

Cinoglossa (Italian) Hound's Tongue (cf. *cynoglossum*)

Cinorrhodon; cinosbatos See *cynorrhodon; cynosbatos*

Cinquefoglio (Italian) Cinquefoil (cf. *pentaphyllum*)

Cinque radici, sciroppo di (Italian) See *quinque radicibus, syrupus de*

Cipero (Italian) Galingale (cf. *cyperus*)

Cipheos, trochisci See *cyphi, trochisci*

Citonium See *cydonium*

Citrace (Italian); **citraggine** (Italian); **citrago** Balm, Lemon-balm (cf. *melissa*)

Citreum, unguentum Ointment made from lemons, white coral, frankincense and other ingredients. Used for removal of skin blemishes

Citrin (French) Lemon-coloured

Citrinum, unguentum Ointment of mercuric nitrate. Used as an escharotic agent

Citrinus, myrobalanus See *myrobalanus citrinus*

Citron (French) Citron, lemon

Citrullus Water-melon (*Citrullus vulgaris*). Seeds used

Citrum; citrus Lemon, citron

Cocciae, pilulae Purgative pills composed of aloes, scammony, colocynth and other ingredients

Coccinilla Cochineal

Cochiae, pilulae See *cocciae, pilulae*

Cochinilla Cochineal

Cochlearia Scurvy-grass (*Cochlearia officinalis*). Herb used

Codium Poppy-head

Coeruleum, unguentum See *caeruleum, unguentum*

Coing (French) Quince (cf. *cydonium*)

Cola See *kola*

Colagogum, electuarium See *cholagogum, electuarium*

Colcothar   Colcothar, ferric oxide

Collyrium   Collyrium, eye-salve, eye-lotion

Colocynthis   Coloquintida, Colocynth, Bitter-apple (*Citrullus colocynthis*). Dried pulp of fruit used

Colophonia   Colophony, rosin. Resinous residue obtained from distillation of turpentine

Coloquinta (Italian); **coloquintida** (Italian)   Colocynth (cf. *colocynthis*)

Comino (Italian)   Cumin, caraway (cf. *cyminum; carvum*)

Comitissae, unguentum   Ointment made from medlars, bilberries and other ingredients; reputedly named after the Contessa di Vadra (fifteenth century), for whom it was prescribed

Composito; compositum; composto (Italian)   Compound, compounded, composite (as opposed to *simplex*)

Comtissae, unguentum   See *Comitissae, unguentum*

Condito (Italian); **conditum**   Sweetmeat made by boiling sliced fruit, fruit rinds, etc. with sugar and water, followed by straining and evaporation of the mixture. Crystallised fruit, candied fruit

Confectio; confezione (Italian)   Syrupy preparation, made from powdered drugs, honey and other ingredients

Conserva   Preparation made from finely cut herbs or flowers and sugar

Consolida; consoude (French)   Comfrey (cf. *symphytum*)

Contessa, unguentum   See *Comitissae, unguentum*

Contra pestem, pilulae   Anti-pestilential pills

Contrayerva   Contrayerva (*Dorstenia contrayerva*). Root used

Copahu, balsamum; copaivae, balsamum   Copaiba. Oleo-resin obtained from the trunk of certain trees of the genus *Copaifera*

Copal   Copal. Hard, translucent resin furnished by various tropical trees

Corallina   Coralline, Sea-moss (*Corallina officinalis*)

Corallium (album; rubrum)   (White; red) coral

Cordialis, syrupus   Syrup having tonic properties; made from saffron, cloves, ambergris and other ingredients

Coriandrum   Coriander

Cornachinus, pulvis   Purgative preparation, made from scammony, cream of tartar and *antimonium diaphoreticum*. Named after Marco Cornacchini, Professor of Medicine at Pisa

Corne de cerf (French); **cornu cervi**   Stag's horn, hartshorn

Corteccia (Italian); **cortex**   Bark, peel, rind

Cortex aurantiorum   Orange peel

Cortex citri   Lemon peel, citron peel

Cortex Peruviana; cortex Peruvianus   See *Peruvianus, cortex*

Cortex quercus   Oak bark

Corylus   Hazelnut

Costino, olio (Italian); **costinum, oleum**   Liniment made from *costus* root, sweet marjoram, cassia bark, white wine and olive oil

Costo (Italian); **costus**; **costus Arabicus** A plant native in the East, believed to be *Saussurea lappa (Compositae)*, formerly known as *Aucklandia costus.*[6] Root used

Cotogno (Italian); **cotonea** Quince-tree (cf. *cydonia*)

Cotyledon major See *umbilicus Veneris*

Cremor tartari Cream of tartar, potassium hydrogen tartrate

Crespino (Italian) Common Barberry (cf. *berberis*)

Creta Chalk

Crocus 1. Saffron. Dried stigmas of the plant *Crocus sativus*. 2. A powder obtained by calcination of a metal

Crocus Martis; crocus Martis aperiens Red iron oxide, ferric oxide

Crocus Saturni Lead oxide

Crocus Veneris Copper oxide

Crosta di pane, empiastro di (Italian) See *crusta panis, emplastrum de*

Crudus Crude, unrefined

Crusta panis, emplastrum de Poultice made from bread crusts, red coral, mastic, oil of quinces and other ingredients

Cubeba Cubeb. Dried unripe fruits of the shrub *Piper cubeba*

Cucumis Cucumber (*Cucumus sativus*). Seeds used

Cucurbita Member of the gourd family, especially the Pumpkin (*Cucurbita pepo*). Seeds used

Cum With (preposition)

Cuminum See *cyminum*

Cuniculus Rabbit

Cupressus Cypress-tree (*Cupressus sempervirens*). Wood and nuts used

Cuprum Copper

Curcuma Turmeric (*Curcuma longa*). Rhizome used

Cuscuta; cuscutha Plant of the genus *Cuscuta* (Dodder). Herb used

Cyanus Cornflower (*Centaurea cyanus*). Flowers used

Cydonia Quince-tree. Fruit and seeds used

Cydonium Quince (fruit)

Cyminum Cumin (*Cuminum cyminum*). Fruit used

Cynae, semen See *santonicum*

Cynara See *cinara*

Cynoglossum Hound's-tongue (*Cynoglossum officinale*). Root used

Cynorrhodon; cynosbatos The Dog-rose (*Rosa canina*) and other wild roses. Fruit (hip) used

Cyperus Plant of the genus *Cyperus*, e.g. *Cyperus longus* (English Galingale). Root used

Cyphi, trochisci Aromatic lozenges made from cinnamon, myrrh,

---

[6] M. C. Cooke, 'Costus', *Pharmaceutical Journal*, 21 July 1877, pp. 41–4; F. A. Flückiger, 'Note on Costus', ibid., 18 August 1877, p. 121; Sir R. N. Chopra, *Indigenous Drugs of India*, 2nd ed., Calcutta, 1958, pp. 402–7.

bdellium resin, cassia bark, spikenard, galingale and other ingredients. Used as a remedy against rheumatism and pestilence

Cypressus See *cupressus*

D. At beginning, or in middle of inscription: *de; decoctum; di.* At end of inscription: *Damocratis* (as in *Mithridatium D.*); *double; dulcium* (as in *oleum amygdalarum d.*); *duplicatum*

Dactylus Date (fruit)

Damocrates Servilius Damocrates, Roman physician (first century A.D.). Originator of a variety of *Mithridatium* and of theriac

Damocratis, confectio; Damocratis, Mithridatium See *Mithridatium*

Daucus Carrot

Decoctio; decoctum Preparation made by boiling one or more vegetable drugs with water, followed by straining

Defensivum, unguentum Ointment made from dragon's blood (*sanguis draconis*), Armenian bole, rose oil, vinegar and wax. Used in treatment of inflammations

Democratis, confectio; Democratis, Mithridatium See *Mithridatium*

Dens Tooth

Dens leonis See *taraxacum*

Dentifricus, pulvis Tooth-cleaning powder, made from powdered pumice, white coral, cuttle-bone, iris rhizome and mastic

Desiccativum, unguentum See *rubrum desiccativum, unguentum*

Despumatum, mel See *mel despumatum*

Dia Prefix indicating 'made from'. Thus *diacassia* or *diachassia*, a preparation made from cassia pulp and other ingredients; *diacodion* or *diacodium*, a medicament made from poppy-heads and other ingredients; *diacorum*, a preparation whose principal ingredient was sweet flag rhizome; *diacrocum* (Italian *diacrocoma*), a medicament containing saffron; *diaireos* (made from iris rhizome); *dialacca* (made from lac); *dialthaea* (made from marsh-mallow root); *diambra* (made from ambergris); *diamoron* (made from mulberries); *diamoschum* (made from musk); *dianthos* (made from rosemary); *diaprunus* (made from dried plums); *diasaturnus* (made from lead acetate); *diascordium* (made from water germander); *diasena* or *diasenna* (made from senna leaves or pods); *diatrion sandalon* or *diatrium santalorum* (made from white, yellow and red sandalwood, and other ingredients)

Diacatholicon, electuarium; diacatholicum, electuarium Purgative electuary made from senna leaves, tamarind pulp, cassia pulp, polypody rhizome, seeds of cucumber and fennel, rhubarb, liquorice and other ingredients

Diacnicum, syrupus Syrup prepared from seeds of the saffron thistle and other ingredients

Diacridium See *diagridium*

Diafoenicum, electuarium See *diaphoenicum, electuarium*

Diagridium Mucilage made by triturating powdered scammony with a fruit juice

Diaphoenicum, electuarium Electuary having purgative action, compounded from dates, scammony, turpeth root and other ingredients. Used in treatment of lethargy, dropsy, paralysis and certain other ailments

Diaphoreticum, electuarium Electuary having sudorific properties, prepared from contrayerva root, nitre and syrup of orange peel

Diaphoreticum minerale See *antimonium diaphoreticum*

Diarhodon Medicinal preparation having tonic action; made from red rose petals and other ingredients

Diatessaron, theriaca See *theriaca diatessaron*

Diatrionpipereon; diatrium piperon, pulvis Powder made from three kinds of pepper, and from ginger, thyme and aniseed. Used as a digestive agent

Dictamnus albus White Dittany (*Dictamnus albus*). Root used

Dictamnus Creticus Dittany of Crete, Dittany of Candy (*Origanum dictamnus*). Leaves used

Difensivum, unguentum See *defensivum, unguentum*

Digestivo, unguento (Italian); **digestivum, unguentum** Ointment made from white wax, turpentine and rose oil or olive oil; used in treatment of suppurative inflammation

Digitalis Foxglove (*Digitalis purpurea*). Leaves used

Dioscorides Greek physician and botanist (*c*.A.D. 50–100), author of works on materia medica and of a herbal

Dippelii, oleum animale See *animale Dippelii, oleum*

Dipsacus Plant of the genus *Dipsacus* (Teasel), especially *Dipsacus sylvestris* (Wild Teasel). Herb used

Diptamnus albus See *dictamnus albus*

Distillatus Distilled

Dittamo (Italian) White Dittany (cf. *dictamnus albus*)

Dodecapharmacum, unguentum See *Apostolorum, unguentum*

Dolce (Italian) Sweet-tasting

Doronicum Leopard's-bane (*Doronicum pardalianches*). Herb and root used

Draconis, sanguis See *sanguis draconis*

Dracunculus Tarragon (*Artemisia dracunculus*). Herb used

Dragante (Italian) Gum tragacanth (cf. *tragacantha*)

Duabus radicibus, syrupus de Syrup prepared from roots of fennel and of parsley

Dulcamara Bittersweet, Woody Nightshade (*Solanum dulcamara*)

Dulcis Sweet-tasting

Duobus, pilulae de Purgative pills, prepared from colocynth and scammony

Duobus, sal de See *arcanum duplicatum*

Duobus radicibus, syrupus de   See *duabus radicibus, syrupus de*
Duplicatum   Double
Dya   See *dia*

E.   *Eau; electuarium; elettuario; elixir; empiastro; emplastrum; erba; essentia; extractum*

Eau (French)   Water
Ebulus   Dwarf Elder, Danewort (*Sambucus ebulus*). Herb and root used
Ebur   Ivory
Eclegma   Sweet, semi-fluid medicine, intended to be licked off the spoon
Écorce (French)   Bark, peel, rind
Edera (Italian)   Ivy, Ground-ivy (cf. *hedera*)
Egittiaco, unguento (Italian); **Egyptiacum, unguentum**   See *Aegyptiacum, unguentum*
Elaterium   Elaterium. Sediment which deposits in the juice of the Squirting Cucumber (*Ecballium elaterium*)
Electuarium   Electuary. Medicinal preparation of honey-like consistency, made by mixing powdered herbs or other drugs with a sweetening agent
Elemi   Gum elemi. Resin furnished by various exotic trees, e.g. *Canarium commune, Icica icicariba*
Elescoph, electuarium   See *Episcopi, electuarium*
Elettuario (Italian)   Electuary (cf. *electuarium*)
Elixir   Elixir, in the sense of a tincture (cf. *tinctura; paregoricum, elixir*)
Elleboro (Italian)   Hellebore (cf. *helleborus*)
Emagogum, antidotum   See *antidotum haemagogum*
Emblicus, myrobalanus   See *myrobalanus emblicus*
Emmaenagogicae, pilulae; emmenagogae, pilulae   Emmenagogic pills, made from birthwort, saffron, myrrh and other ingredients
Empiastro (Italian); **emplastrum**   Plaster, Poultice, cataplasm
Endivia   Endive (*Cichorium endivia*). Root and leaves used
Enula; enula campana   Elecampane (*Inula helenium*). Rhizome used
Enulatum, unguentum   Ointment made from elecampane rhizome, oil of wormwood, turpentine and lard. Used in treatment of skin disorders
Enulatum cum mercurio, unguentum   The preceding ointment, admixed with mercury
Epatica   See *hepatica*
Episcopi, electuarium   'The Bishop's electuary'. Purgative electuary, made from scammony, turpeth root, polypody rhizome and other ingredients
Epispasticum, emplastrum   Vesicatory poultice, made from cantharides and other ingredients
Epithema   Epithem, fomentation
Epithymus; epitimo (Italian)   Thyme Dodder, Epithyme (*Cuscuta epithymum*). Herb used

93   Pharmacy, Hôtel-Dieu, Louhans, Saône-et-Loire, France. *See pages 29 and 82*

Epuloticum, ceratum   Ointment for treatment of wounds, made from
calamine, olive oil and wax
Equisetum   Common Horsetail (*Equisetum arvense*). Dried green stems
used
Equus   Horse
Erba (Italian)   Herb
Eringium   See *eryngium*
Ermodattilo (Italian)   Hermodactyl (cf. *hermodactylus*)
Eruca   Garden Rocket (*Eruca sativa*). Seeds used
Eryngium   Eryngo, Sea Holly (*Eryngium maritimum*). Root used
Erysimum   Hedge Mustard (*Erysimum officinale*). Herb used
Esipo (Italian)   Wool fat, lanolin
Essentia   1. Essential oil. Oil obtained from a plant, or part of a plant, by
distillation, expression or otherwise. 2. Essence. Alcoholic solution of one or
more essential oils and other aromatic substances
Esula   Leafy Spurge (*Euphorbia esula*), and possibly other members of the
genus *Euphorbia*. Root used
Ethiops (Martialis; mineralis)   See *aethiops (Martialis; mineralis)*

Euforbium   See *euphorbium*

Eufragia (Italian); **eufrasia** (Italian)   Eyebright (cf. *euphrasia*)

Eupatorio (Italian); **eupatorium**   Probably Hemp Agrimony (*Eupatorium cannabinum*). Herb used

Euphorbium   Euphorbium. Dried latex obtained from the stem of *Euphorbia resinifera* and other species of *Euphorbia*

Euphragia; euphrasia   Euphrasy, Eyebright (*Euphrasia officinalis*). Leaves used

Excestrense, oleum   Exeter Oil. Liniment made from various herbs, olive oil and wine

Extractum   Extract

F.   At beginning, or in middle of inscription: *farina*; *fel*; *feuilles*; *fiori*; *fleurs*; *flores*; *foglie*; *folia*. At end of inscription: *Fernelius*; *fina*; *flavum*; *Fracastoro*

Faba   Bean

Faetidae, pilulae   See *foetidae, pilulae*

Farfara (Italian); **farfaro** (Italian)   Coltsfoot (cf. *tussilago*)

Farina   Flour

Febrifugus   Febrifuge

Febris   Fever

Fel; fele (Italian)   Gall, bile

Feles; felis   Cat

Fellandrium   See *phellandrium*

Fel tauri; fel taurinum   Ox-gall

Feniculum   See *foeniculum*

Fenocchio (Italian); **fenouil** (French)   Fennel (cf. *foeniculum*)

Fenugraecum   See *foenugraecum*

Fernelius   Jean Fernel (1497–1558). Renowned physician and Professor of Medicine at the University of Paris. Author of *Universa Medicina*, a treatise on physiology, pathology and therapeutics

Fetidae, pilulae   See *foetidae, pilulae*

Feuille (French)   Leaf

Ficus   Fig

Fiel (French); **fiele** (Italian)   Gall, bile

Fieno greco (Italian)   Fenugreek (cf. *foenugraecum*)

Filix; filix mas   Male Fern (*Dryopteris filix-mas*). Rhizome used

Filonio (Italian); **Filonium**   See *Philonium*

Filosofi, olio de (Italian)   Oil of bricks (cf. *philosophorum, oleum*)

Fina; fino (Italian)   Fine, choice (as in *mostarda fina*)

Finocchio (Italian)   Fennel (cf. *foeniculum*)

Fiore (Italian)   Flower

Flava, flavum, etc.   Yellow

Fleurs (French); **flores**   In botanical sense: Flowers (of plant). In chemical sense: A sublimate, e.g. *flores benzoini*, a substance obtained by sublimation of gum benzoin; *flores sulphuris*, flowers of sulphur, sublimed sulphur

Flores tunicae   See *tunicae, flores*

Flos   Flower

Foeniculum   Fennel (*Foeniculum vulgare*). Leaves, root and fruit used

Foenugraecum   Fenugreek (*Trigonella foenum graecum*). Seeds used

Foetidae, pilulae   Pills made from gum asafoetida and other ingredients

Foglia (Italian); **folium**   Leaf

Frac. (Abbreviation)   1. *Fracastoro* (q.v.).   2. *Fractura* (fracture), as in *emplastrum pro fracturis*

Fracastorius; Fracastoro   Girolamo Fracastoro (1484–1553). Italian physician, biologist, geologist, physicist and astronomer; noted for investigations into the nature of syphilis and other contagious diseases. Formulated *diascordium*, an electuary to which panacea-like virtues were attributed

Fragaria   Wild Strawberry (*Fragaria vesca*). Root, leaves and fruit used

Frassino (Italian); **fraxinus**   Ash tree. Bark, leaves and seeds used

Fructus   Fruit

Fuligo   Soot

Fumaria; fumeterre (French); **fumosterno** (Italian)   Common Fumitory (*Fumaria officinalis*). Herb used

Fuscum, unguentum   'The Dark Ointment'. Salve prepared from pine tar, frankincense, mastic, wax and other ingredients. Used in treatment of ulcers

G.   At beginning of inscription: *gomme; grasso; gummi*. At end of inscription: *Galeni; Galeno; Galien*

Gaïac (French)   Guaiacum wood (cf. *guaiaci, lignum*)

Galam, beurre de (French)   Galam Butter. Fatty matter obtained from the seeds of *Butyrospermum Parkii* and certain other *Sapotaceae*

Galanga   Galingale. Rhizome of certain Eastern plants, in particular *Alpinia officinarum* and *Kaempferia galanga*

Galbanum   Galbanum. Gum resin furnished by *Ferula galbaniflua* and certain other species of *Ferula*

Galega   Goat's Rue (cf. *ruta capraria*)

Galeni, ceratum; Galien, cérat de (French)   See *refrigerans Galeni, ceratum*

Galeno (Italian); **Galenus; Galien** (French)   Galen of Pergamon (A.D. 130–201), one of the most celebrated physicians and surgeons of Classical Antiquity. Noted for his writings on anatomy, pathology, surgery, hygiene and materia medica, and for his exposition of the humoral doctrine, according to which disease is to be regarded as a state of imbalance of the four humours of the body (blood, phlegm, yellow bile, black bile), imbalance which may be redressed by the administration of an appropriate drug

Galliae moschatae, trochisci   Lozenges composed of aloë-wood, musk, ambergris, gum tragacanth and rose water. Used as a restorative

Gallina Hen

Gambogium Gamboge. Gum resin obtained from trees of the genus *Garcinia*

Garance (French) Madder (cf. *rubia tinctorum*)

Garofano (Italian) Clove (cf. *caryophylli*). Sometimes denotes also the Clove-gillyflower (cf. *tunicae, flores*)

Garou (French) Spurge-flax (cf. *thymelaea*)

Gayac (French) See *gaïac*

Gemmae populi Poplar buds

Gengero (Italian); **gengiovo** (Italian) Ginger (cf. *zingiber*)

Genièvre (French) Juniper (cf. *juniperus*)

Genista Common Broom (*Cytisus scoparius*). Leaves, flowers and seeds used

Gentiana Yellow Gentian (*Gentiana lutea*), and certain other species of the genus *Gentiana*. Root used

Geum See *Benedicta, herba*

Giacintina, confezione (Italian) See *hyacintho, confectio de*

Giacinto (Italian) Jacinth (gem)

Gialappa (Italian) Jalap (cf. *jalapium*)

Giallo (Italian) Yellow

Giglio (Italian) Lily (cf. *lilium*)

Ginepro (Italian) Juniper (cf. *juniperus*)

Ginestra (Italian) Broom (cf. *genista*)

Gingembre (French) Ginger (cf. *zingiber*)

Ginseng Ginseng. Root of the plant *Panax ginseng*

Giuggiola (Italian); **giugiuba** (Italian) Jujube. Fruit of the Jujube-tree, cf. *jujuba*

Giulebbe (Italian); **giuleppo** (Italian) Julep

Giusquiamo (Italian) Henbane (cf. *hyoscyamus*)

Glauberi, sal catharticus See *sal catharticus Glauberi*

Glechomatis hederacea See *hedera terrestris*

Glycyrrhiza Liquorice (*Glycyrrhiza glabra*). Root used

Gomme (French) Gum, gum resin

Graisse (French) Fat, grease

Gramen; gramigna (Italian) Couch-grass (*Agropyrum repens*). Rhizome used

Grana Paradisi Grains of Paradise. Seeds of *Aframomum meleguetta*

Granata; granata malus Pomegranate-tree (*Punica granatum*). Rind of fruit, bark of stem and bark of root used

Granatum Pomegranate (fruit)

Granatus Garnet (gem)

Granum Grain, seed

Grasso (Italian) Fat, grease

Gratia Dei Term applied to Herb-Robert (*Geranium Robertianum*),

Meadow Crane's-bill (*Geranium pratense*) and certain other plants. Herb used

Gratiola   Hedge-hyssop (*Gratiola officinalis*). Herb used

Grossularia   Gooseberry Bush. Fruit used

Guaiaci, lignum   Guaiacum wood, Pockwood. Heartwood of *Guaiacum officinale* and *Guaiacum sanctum*

Gummi   Gum, gum resin

Gummi ammoniacum   See *ammoniacum, gummi*

Gummi Arabicum   See *Arabicum, gummi*

Gummi Armeniacae   See *Armeniacae, gummi*

Gummi asafoetidae   See *asafoetida*

Gummi copal   See *copal*

Gummi euphorbii   See *euphorbium*

Gummi hederae   See *hederae, gummi*

Gummi sarcocollae   See *sarcocolla*

Gummi tacamahaca   See *tacamahaca, gummi*

Gummi tragacanthum   See *tragacantha*

Guteta, pulvis de   See *gutteta, pulvis de*

Gutta   Drop

Gutta gamba   See *gambogium*

Gutteta, pulvis de   Anti-epileptic preparation, made from root of peony and root of valerian. Sometimes other ingredients (root of white dittany, oak mistletoe, etc.) were also present

H.   *Herba; huile*

Haedera   See *hedera*

Haemagogum, antidotum   See *antidotum haemagogum*

Haematites, lapis   Bloodstone

Hamamelis   Witch Hazel (*Hamamelis Virginiana*). Leaves used

Hamech, confectio; Hamech, confezione (Italian)   Purgative preparation, reputedly named after an Arab physician of the name of Hamech. Compounded from colocynth, scammony, agaric, senna leaves, rhubarb, myrobalans and other ingredients

Harmala; harmel   Wild Rue, Syrian Rue (*Peganum harmala*). Seeds used

Hedera arborea   Ivy (*Hedera helix*). Leaves used

Hederae, gummi   Dried latex obtained from the Ivy plant (*Hedera helix*)

Hedera terrestris   Ground-ivy (*Glechoma hederacea*). Herb used

Hedychroi, trochisci   Strongly scented anti-pestilential lozenges. Made from saffron, cassia bark, cinnamon, myrrh, opobalsam, asarabacca root, *costus* root, spikenard and other ingredients.[7]

Helenium   See *enula*

---

[7] Aromatic mixtures of this type served as fillings for pomanders to protect the wearer against infection.

Helleborus albus   White Hellebore (*Veratrum album*). Rhizome and root used

Helleborus niger   Black Hellebore, Christmas Rose (*Helleborus niger*). Rhizome and root used

Helminthochorton   Corsican Moss. The alga *Alsidium helminthochorton*, found in the Mediterranean

Hemagogum, antidotum   See *antidotum haemagogum*

Hematites, lapis   See *haematites, lapis*

Hepatica   Hepatica, Liverwort (*Anemone hepatica*). Herb used

Herba; herbe (French)   Herb

Hermodactylus   Hermodactyl. Botanical drug of uncertain identity, obtained from the East; believed to be the corm of a species of *Colchicum*, perhaps *Colchicum variegatum*[8]

Hiacintho, confectio de   See *hyacintho, confectio de*

Hiera diacolocynthidos   Purgative electuary whose principal constituent was colocynth

Hiera Logadii; hiera Logod   Electuary having purgative action. Made from colocynth, aloes, agaric, scammony, squill, polypody rhizome and other ingredients. Supposedly named after Logadius, physician at Memphis

Hiera picra (from Greek ἱερά, sacred, and πικρά, bitter)   Purgative electuary composed of Socotra aloes, saffron, cinnamon and other ingredients

Hiosciamus   See *hyoscyamus*

Hipericum   See *hypericum*

Hippocrates   Celebrated Greek physician (*c*.460–370 B.C.); author of works on medicine which formed the basis of a collection of treatises known as the Hippocratic Collection. Among writings ascribed to Hippocrates or his disciples are the Physician's Oath and the famous aphorism, 'Life is short, and the art (of medicine) is long; the occasion fleeting, experience deceitful and judgment difficult.'

   In his teachings Hippocrates stressed the importance of hygiene and a balanced diet for maintenance of health. With the exception of purgation (see page 183, note 5), he placed less reliance than his predecessors on use of drugs in treatment of sickness, believing that nature provided its own cures

Hippocraticum, vinum   Hippocras. Wine flavoured with cinnamon, cloves and other spices

Hippopotamus   Hippopotamus. Teeth used in manufacture of dentures

Hircus   Goat

Hirudo   Leech

Hirundo   Swallow

Hissopo humida   See *oesypus humida*

---

[8] Cf. M. C. Cooke, 'Hermodactyls', *Pharmaceutical Journal*, 1 April 1871, pp. 784–5; E. Perrot, M. Mascré, J. Régnier, P. Crété and R. Weitz, *Matières Premières Usuelles du Règne Végétal*, Paris, 1943–4, vol. 1, p. 626.

Hissopus See *hyssopus*

Histerica, aqua; histericae, pilulae, etc. See *hysterica, aqua; hystericae pilulae,* etc.

Hoedera See *hedera*

Homo Man

Hordeum Barley

Huile (French) Oil

Hyacintho, confectio de Polypharmaceutical preparation, named after the jacinth, one of its ingredients

Hyacinthus 1. (Also *hyacinthus gemma; hyacinthus lapis*) Jacinth (precious stone). 2. (Also *hyacinthus Anglicus*) Wild Hyacinth, Wood Hyacinth, Bluebell (*Scilla nutans*). Root used

Hydragogum, electuarium Purgative electuary. Used in the treatment of dropsy and sciatica

Hydrargyrum Quicksilver, mercury

Hydromel Liquor consisting of honey and water, which on fermentation yields mead

Hydropicae, pilulae Purgative pills. Used as a remedy against dropsy

Hyera picra See *hiera picra*

Hyoscyamus Henbane (*Hyoscyamus niger*). Leaves, root and seeds used

Hypericum St. John's Wort (*Hypericum perforatum*). Flowering tops, leaves and seeds used

Hypocistis Hypocist. Inspissated juice of the parasitic plant *Cytinus hypocistis*

Hyssopus Hyssop (*Hyssopus officinalis*). Leaves and flowering tops used

Hyssopus humida See *oesypus humida*

Hysterica, aqua; hystericae, pilulae; hystericum, electuarium; hystericus, pulvis Medicated water (pills; electuary; powder) used in treatment of uterine disorders

I. *Impiastro; infusum*

Iacobaea See *jacobaea*

Ialapium See *jalapium*

Ibiscus See *althaea*

Ichthyocolla (from Greek ἰχθυς, fish, and κόλλα, glue) 1. A fish (especially the sturgeon) yielding isinglass. 2. Isinglass

Iera (diacolocynthidos; Logod; picra) See *hiera (diacolocynthidos; Logod; picra)*

Imperatoria Masterwort (*Peucedanum Ostruthium*). Rhizome used

Imperiale, catartico (Italian) Purgative electuary, made from scammony, cardamom seeds, cinnamon and other ingredients

Imperialis, aqua Aromatic liquid obtained by distillation of a mixture of water and white wine spiced with cinnamon, cloves, nutmeg, lemon peel and other ingredients. Used as a tonic, and in treatment of gastric disorders

Impiastro (Italian)   Plaster, poultice

Indae ex Hali, pilulae   Purgative pills composed of agaric, colocynth, Indian myrobalans, Indian spikenard and other ingredients

Indicum   Indigo (dye)

Indicus, myrobalanus   See *myrobalanus Indicus*

Indivia (Italian)   Endive (cf. *endivia*)

Indum, folium   Indian leaf (cf. *malabathrum*)

Indum majus, electuarium; Indum minus, electuarium   Purgative electuaries, made from turpeth root, scammony, cardamom seeds, cinnamon and other ingredients

Infrigidans Galeni, unguentum   See *refrigerans Galeni, ceratum*

Infusum   Infusion

Intybus   See *endivia*

Iohannis de Vigo, emplastrum   See *Vigo, emplastrum de*

Ipecacuanha   Ipecacuanha (*Cephaëlis ipecacuanha*). Root used

Iride (Italian)   Iris

Irino, olio (Italian)   Liniment made from iris rhizome and olive oil or sesame oil

Irios (Italian); **iris; irride** (Italian)   Iris, Orris (*Iris Florentina, Iris Germanica* and possibly other members of the genus *Iris*). Rhizome used

Isopo (Italian)   Hyssop (cf. *hyssopus*)

Isopus humida   Wool fat, lanolin

Issopo (Italian)   Hyssop (cf. *hyssopus*)

Iuglans   See *juglans*

Iuiuba   See *jujuba*

Iulep   See *julep*

Iuniperus   See *juniperus*

Iusquiano (Italian)   Henbane (cf. *hyoscyamus*)

Iustini, electuarium   Electuary made from elecampane rhizome, pennyroyal leaves, juniper berries, lovage and other ingredients

Iva (Italian); **iva arthetica; iva arthritica**   Ground Pine (cf. *chamaepitys*)

Jacea   Wild Pansy (*Viola tricolor*). Plant used

Jacobaea   Ragwort, St. James's Wort (*Senecio Jacobaea*). Leaves used

Jalapium   Jalap. Tubercles of *Ipomoea purga* and some other convolvulaceous plants; also the resin furnished by the tubercles

Jera picra   See *hiera picra*

Johannis de Vigo, emplastrum   See *Vigo, emplastrum de*

Juglans   Walnut-tree (*Juglans regia*). Nuts and leaves used

Jujuba   Jujube-tree (*Zizyphus vulgaris*). Fruit used

Julep   Julep. Sweet pleasant-tasting drink, generally prepared from a syrup and an aromatic water

Juniperus   Common Juniper (*Juniperus communis*). Fruit and wood used

Jusquiame (French)   Henbane (cf. *hyoscyamus*)

Justini, electuarium   See *Iustini, electuarium*

94   Pharmacy, Hôpital Saint-Jacques, Besançon, France. *See page 82*

Kalium sulphuricum   Potassium sulphate (term chiefly in use in nineteenth century)

Karabe   See *carabe*

Keiri   See *cheiri*

Kermes   Kermes. Red dye-stuff consisting of the dried bodies of the Scarlet Grain insect

Kermes mineralis   Kermes mineral, sulphurated antimony. Red powder consisting of a mixture of sulphides of antimony

Kina kina   Cinchona bark (cf. *Peruvianus, cortex*).

Kola; kolae, nuces   Cola nuts. Seeds of certain trees of the genus *Cola*

L.   At beginning, or in middle of inscription: *lapis; lattuario; lignum; lilium; linimentum; lohoch*. At end of inscription: *lauri; lénitif; lenitivum*

Labdanum   See *ladanum*

Labrusca   Fox Grape (*Vitis labrusca*)

Lacca   Lac. Resinous substance secreted by the lac insect

Lacerta   Lizard

Lac sulphuris   Precipitated sulphur

Lactuca   Garden Lettuce (*Lactuca sativa*) and certain other species of *Lactuca*. Leaves, seeds and latex used

Lactucarium   Lettuce-opium, concentrated or dried latex of *lactuca* (q.v.)

Ladanum   Gum resin exuded from leaves of plants of the genus *Cistus*

Laetificans, electuarium (from the Latin *laetificare*, to gladden)   Electuary having tonic properties

Lambrusca   See *labrusca*

Lamium   Member of the genus *Lamium* (Dead-nettle). Flowers used

Lapathum   Member of the genus *Rumex* (Dock), especially *Rumex hydrolapathum* (Water Dock)

Lapis   Stone (in sense of precious stone, gem)

Lapis calaminaris   Calamine

Lapis haematites   Bloodstone

Lapis lazuli   Lapis lazuli

Lappa   See *bardana*

Larix   Larch. Resin (Venice Turpentine) used

Later   Brick, tile

Lateribus, oleum e; lateritium philosophorum, oleum   See *philosophorum, oleum*

Lattuario (Italian)   Electuary

Lattuca (Italian)   Lettuce (cf. *lactuca*)

Lattucario (Italian)   Lettuce-opium (cf. *lactucarium*)

Lattuga (Italian); **latuca** (Italian)   Lettuce (cf. *lactuca*)

Laudanum   A preparation containing opium, e.g. alcoholic tincture of opium

Lauri, baccae   Bay-laurel berries

Laurier (French)   Bay-laurel (cf. *laurus*)

Laurinum, oleum   Oil of bay-laurel berries

Lauro (Italian)   Bay-tree, Bay-laurel (cf. *laurus*)

Lauro, bacche di (Italian)   Bay-laurel berries

Laurus   Bay-tree, Bay-laurel (*Laurus nobilis*). Leaves and berries used

Lavandula; lavendula   Lavender, especially Spike Lavender (*Lavandula latifolia*). Flowers and leaves used

Laxativus   Laxative

Legno (Italian)   Wood

Lénitif fin (French); **lenitivo elettuario** (Italian); **lenitivum, electuarium**   Electuary having mild purgative action. Made from senna, tamarind pulp, prunes, polypody rhizome, liquorice and other ingredients

Lentiscus   Lentisk, Mastic-tree (*Pistacia lentiscus*). Resin used. (Cf. *mastiche*)

Leo   Lion

Lepus   Hare

Letificans, electuarium   See *laetificans, electuarium*

Leucoium   See *cheiri*

Levisticum   Lovage (*Levisticum officinale*). Herb, root and seeds used

Lichen Islandicus   Iceland Moss, Iceland Lichen (*Cetraria Islandica*)

Lignum   Wood

Lignum aloes   See *aloes, lignum*

Lignum aspalathi   See *aspalathi, lignum*

Lignum campechense   See *campechense, lignum*

Lignum guaiaci   See *guaiaci, lignum*

Lignum nephriticum   See *nephriticum, lignum*

Lignum rhodii   See *rhodii, lignum*

Lignum Sanctum   See *guaiaci, lignum*

Lignum sandali; lignum santali   See *santalum*

Lignum vitae   See *guaiaci, lignum*

Ligusticum   See *levisticum*

Lilium   Lily

Lilium album   White Lily, Madonna Lily (*Lilium candidum*). Flowers and root used

Lilium convallium   Lily of the Valley (*Convallaria majalis*). Flowers, leaves and root used

Limatura   Iron filings

Limone (Italian); **limonum**   Lemon, citron or other fruit of the genus *Citrus*

Linaria   Toadflax (*Linaria vulgaris*). Herb used

Linctus   Linctus. Syrupy medicament having anti-tussive or pectoral properties

Lingua avis   Seeds of the Ash tree

Lingua cervina   See *scolopendrium*

Linimentum   Liniment

Linitivum, electuarium   See *lenitivum, electuarium*

Linosa (Italian); **linum**   Common Flax (*Linum usitatissimum*). Seeds (linseed) used

Liquiritia; liquirizia (Italian)   Liquorice (cf. *glycyrrhiza*)

Lithargyrum   Litharge, lead monoxide

Lithontripticum, electuarium; lithontripticus, pulvis   Lithontriptic electuary, lithontriptic powder. Medicament for elimination of urinary calculi

Lithospermum   Common Gromwell (*Lithospermum officinale*). Seeds used

Locatelli, balsamum   Ointment formulated by Lodovico Locatelli (d. 1657), an Italian physician. Made from red sandalwood, olive oil, pine resin and other ingredients. Used for treatment of ulcers

Locco (Italian); **loch** (Italian)   See *lohoch*

Logod, hiera   See *hiera Logod*

Lohoch   Medicament of honey-like consistency, for licking up with the tongue

Lombrico (Italian)   Earthworm

Longue vie, sirop de (French) 'Syrup of long life'. Made from borage, bugloss, iris rhizome, gentian root and the plant *mercurialis*

Looch See *lohoch*

Lucatelli, balsamum See *Locatelli, balsamum*

Lucis majores, pilulae Pills for treatment of ophthalmic disorders

Lucius Pike (fish)

Luiula; lujula Wood-sorrel (*Oxalis acetosella*). Herb used

Lumbricus Earthworm

Lunaria Name probably denoting the fern Moonwort (*Botrychium lunaria*)

Lupinus Lupin (*Lupinus albus* and other members of the genus *Lupinus*). Seeds used

Lupulus The Hop plant (*Humulus lupulus*)

Lupus Wolf

Lutea, luteum, etc. Yellow

M. At the beginning of inscription: *medulla; mel; miel; mirobalano; mistura; Mithridatium; miva; mixtura; myrobalanus*. At end of inscription: *magistralis; magna; Mesuë; mondo; Mortonii; mundificativum; Mynsicht*

M.P. *Massa pilularum* (q.v.)

Macis Mace. Dried outer covering of the nutmeg

Macri, pilulae Stomachic pills made from aloes, sweet marjoram leaves and other ingredients. Named after Aemilius Macer (first century B.C.), Roman author, whose writings include poems on drugs (*Theriaca, De Herbis*)

Macropiper Long Pepper (*Piper longum*)

Madreselva (Italian) Honeysuckle

Madreselva, unguento di (Italian) Ointment whose chief ingredient was honeysuckle leaves

Maggiorana (Italian) Sweet Marjoram (cf. *majorana*)

Magisterium Magistery. Mineral substance obtained by precipitation of a metal from an acid solution, e.g. *magisterium bismuthi*, Magistery of Bismuth, bismuth oxychloride

Magistralis Term attached to medicaments which were formulated by a physician for a particular case

Magna; magnum, etc. Great

Majorana Sweet Marjoram (*Origanum majorana*). Leaves and flowering tops used

Malabathrum Indian leaf. Aromatic leaf of a species of the genus *Cinnamomum*

Malum Apple

Malum armeniacum Apricot

Malum aureum Orange (fruit)

Malum citreum Citron, lemon

Malum cotoneum Quince

Malum granatum Pomegranate

Malum persicum Peach

Malum punicum Pomegranate

Malum sylvestris Crab-apple

Malus A fruit-bearing tree, e.g. *malus armeniaca* (the apricot-tree), *malus aurantia* (the orange tree), *malus cydonia* (the quince-tree), *malus persica* (the peach-tree)

Malva Common Mallow (*Malva sylvestris*). Flowers, leaves and root used

Mandorla (Italian) Almond

Mandragora Mandrake (*Mandragora officinarum*). Leaves and root used

Manna; manne (French) Sugary juice exuded from the bark of the Manna Ash (*Fraxinus ornus*)

Margarita Pearl

Marjorana See *majorana*

Marmor Marble

Maro (Italian) Cat Thyme (cf. *marum*)

Marrubium White Horehound (*Marrubium vulgare*). Leaves and flowering tops used

Martiales, pilulae See *chalybeatae, pilulae*

Martianum, unguentum; Martiatum, unguentum Ointment made from bay-laurel leaves, sweet basil, sweet marjoram, sage, rue, olive oil, wax and other ingredients. Used for relief of sciatic pains

Martis limatura praeparata Powdered iron oxide prepared by exposing iron filings to action of moisture

Marum Name applied to the labiate plants *Thymus mastichina* (Herb Mastich) and *Teucrium marum* (Cat Thyme). Herb used

Massa pilularum Pill mass; mixture of drugs and excipients from which pills were rolled[9]

Mastiche Mastic. Gum resin exuded from the bark of the tree *Pistacia lentiscus*

Mastichinum, oleum Liniment made by heating mastic in a mixture of rose oil and wine

Matico Matico. Shrub (*Piper angustifolium*), native in South America. Leaves used

Matricale (Italian); **matricaria** Term applied to the plant Feverfew (*Chrysanthemum parthenium*), and possibly certain other members of the family *Compositae*. Herb used

Matthaei, pilulae Matthews's Pills. Pills marketed by Richard Matthews in imitation of *Pilulae Starkei*, q.v.

Mechoacana Mechoacan. The plant *Ipomoea jalapa*. Root used

Meconium Evaporated juice of the Opium Poppy. Opium

Medulla Bone marrow

Medulla cruris bovis Ox-bone marrow

[9] Cf. L. G. Matthews, *History of Pharmacy in Britain*, Edinburgh and London, 1962, p. 300; G. E. Trease, *Pharmacy in History*, London, 1964, p. 234.

Mel Honey

Mel depuratum; mel despumatum Purified honey, clarified honey

Melilotus Common Melilot (*Melilotus officinalis*). Leaves and flowers used

Melissa Balm, Lemon-balm (*Melissa officinalis*). Leaves used

Mel mercuriale 'Honey of Mercury'. Decoction of the plant *mercurialis* and honey

Mel Narbonense (Name derived from Narbonne, in the Languedoc district.) Honey with distinctive aromatic scent, produced in the south of France

Mel nenupharinum Honey of Water-lilies. Decoction of water-lily flowers and honey

Melo Melon (*Cucumis melo*). Seeds used

Mel rosatum Honey of Roses. Decoction of rose petals and honey

Mel violaceum; mel violatum Honey of Violets

Menianthes See *trifolium palustre*

Mentha Peppermint (*Mentha piperita*), Spearmint (*Mentha spicata*) and certain other members of the genus *Mentha*. Herb or leaves used

Menyanthes See *trifolium palustre*

Mercuriale, mel See *mel mercuriale*

Mercuriale, unguentum Ointment of mercury (cf. *caeruleum, unguentum; enulatum cum mercurio, unguentum; Neapolitanum quadruplicatum mercurio, unguentum; Neapolitanum simplex, unguentum*)

Mercuriales, pilulae Mercurial pills (cf. *Bellostii, pilulae*)

Mercurialis A plant of the genus *Mercurialis*, especially *Mercurialis annua* (Annual Mercury), and *Mercurialis perennis* (Dog's Mercury). Herb used

Mercurio (Italian); **mercurius** Mercury, quicksilver

Mercurius corallinus Red oxide of mercury (cf. *arcanum corallinum*)

Mercurius dulcis Calomel, mercurous chloride

Mespilus Common Medlar (*Mespilus Germanica*). Fruit and seeds used

Mesuë A figure in medieval medicine, possibly fictitious, to whom are ascribed various medical writings, including the *Grabadin*, one of the earliest collections of materia medica to be arranged in pharmacopoeial form

Metridatum See *Mithridatium*

Meum Spignel, Baldmoney (*Meum athamanticum*). Root used

Mezereon Mezereon (*Daphne mezereum*). Bark used

Micleta, electuarium Polypharmaceutical preparation. Used for arrestment of haemorrhages

Midolla (Italian) Bone marrow

Miel (French) Honey

Miel de Narbonne (French) See *mel Narbonense*

Miele (Italian) Honey

Milium Millet (*Panicum miliaceum*). Seeds used

Milium solis See *lithospermum*

Millefolium Yarrow, Milfoil (*Achillea millefolium*). Leaves and flowering tops used

95   Pharmacy, Hospice Condé, Chantilly. *See pages 82 and 100*

Minium   Red lead oxide, triplumbic tetroxide
Mirabile, sal   See *sal catharticus Glauberi*
Mirobalano (Italian)   Myrobalan (cf. *myrobalanus*)
Mirra (Italian); **mirrha** (Italian)   Myrrh (cf. *myrrha*)
Mirtillo (Italian)   Bilberry, Whortleberry (cf. *myrtillus*)
Mirto (Italian)   Common Myrtle (cf. *myrtus*)
Mistura   Mixture. Potion containing two or more medicinal constituents
**Mithridatium; Mithridatium Andromachi; Mithridatium Democ-
ratis; Mithridatum; Mitridato** (Italian)   Mithridate. Polypharma-
ceutical preparation allied to *theriaca* (q.v.), devised by Mithridates, King of

Pontus (131–64 B.C.) as an antidote against poisons; subsequently modified by Andromachus and by Damocrates

Miva   Jelly, jam, preserve (especially quince jam)

Mixa   See *sebesten*

Mixtura   See *mistura*

Moerbei (Dutch)   Mulberry

Mondificatif, onguent (French)   See *mundificativum, unguentum*

Mondificatif d'ache, onguent (French)   Ointment whose principal ingredient was smallage (cf. *mundificativum de apio, unguentum*)

Mondo (Italian)   Peeled, purified

Mora (Italian)   Mulberry

Morsus diaboli   Devil's-bit (*Scabiosa succisa*). Leaves, flowers and root used

Morton, pilules de (French); **Mortonii, pilulae**   See *balsamicae Mortonii, pilulae*

Morus   Mulberry-tree (*Morus nigra*). Fruit and bark of root used

Moscata, noce   See *noce moscata*

Moschata, nux   See *nux moschata*

Moschatae, trochisci galliae   See *galliae moschatae, trochisci*

Moschus   Musk, deer musk

Mostarda (Italian)   Mustard (cf. *sinapi*)

Moxa   Moxa. Downy covering of leaves of various wormwoods of Eastern Asia, especially *Artemisia moxa*, used for burning on skin in treatment of gout, etc. (moxibustion)

Mucago; mucilago   Mucilage

Mundificativum, unguentum (From Latin *mundus,* clean) Ointment for cleansing of wounds, whose chief ingredient was smallage (*unguentum mundificativum de apio*), or a resin (*unguentum mundificativum de resina*)

Mus   Mouse, rat

Mus agrestis, Mus rusticus   Field-mouse

Mus alpinus; mus montanus   Marmot

Mynsicht   Adrianus van Mynsicht (1603–38), German physician and chemist. Introduced tartar emetic into medical practice

Myristica, nux   See *nux myristica*

Myrobalanus bellericus   Belleric Myrobalan, Bastard Myrobalan (*Terminalia bellerica*). Fruit used

Myrobalanus chebulus   Chebulic Myrobalan (*Terminalia chebula*). Fruit used

Myrobalanus citrinus   Yellow Myrobalan (*Terminalia citrina*). Fruit used

Myrobalanus emblicus   Emblic Myrobalan (*Phyllanthus emblica*). Fruit used

Myrobalanus Indicus   Indian Myrobalan (variety of Chebulic Myrobalan; cf. *myrobalanus chebulus*). Fruit used

Myrrha   Myrrh. Gum resin furnished by *Commiphora myrrha* and certain other species of *Commiphora*

Myrrhis   Sweet Cicely (*Myrrhis odorata*). Herb and seeds used

Myrtillus   Bilberry, Whortleberry (*Vaccinium myrtillus*). Fruit and leaves used

Myrtinus, syrupus   Syrup made from myrtle berries, pomegranates, medlars, quince juice and other ingredients

Myrtus   Common Myrtle (*Myrtus communis*). Leaves and berries used

Myva   See *miva*

Myxa   See *sebesten*

N.   At end of inscription: *nero; Nicolai; Nicolao; niger*

Napolitain quadruple de mercure, onguent (French) See *Neapolitanum quadruplicatum mercurio, unguentum*

Napolitain simple, onguent (French)   See *Neapolitanum simplex, unguentum*

Napus   Rape (*Brassica napus*). Seeds used

Narancia (Italian)   Orange (fruit)

Narancio (Italian)   Orange-tree

Narbonense, mel; Narbonne, miel de (French)   See *mel Narbonense*

Nardinum, oleum   Liniment made by heating spikenard in a mixture of wine and sesame oil or olive oil. Used in treatment of palsy and of nervous conditions

Nardus   Nard, Spikenard. Term applied to 'various valerianaceous plants and to balsamic substances obtained from them'[10]

Nardus Celtica   Celtic Spikenard. Probably the root of the plant *Valeriana Celtica*

Nardus Indica   Indian Spikenard. Root of the Eastern valerianaceous plant *Nardostachys jatamansi*

Nasturtium aquaticum   Water-cress (*Nasturtium officinale*). Herb used

Nasturtium hortense   Garden-cress (*Lepidium sativum*). Leaves and seeds used

Natrium sulphuricum   Sodium sulphate (term chiefly in use in nineteenth century)

Neapolitanum quadruplitacum mercurio, unguentum   (term derived from *mal de Naples*, ancient French name for syphilis)   Mercurial ointment used in treatment of venereal disease

Neapolitanum simplex, unguentum   Mercurial ointment used as a parasiticidal agent

Nenufaro (Italian)   Water-lily (cf. *nymphaea*)

Nepeta   Cat-mint, cat-nip (*Nepeta cataria*). Herb used

Nephriticum, lignum   Nephritic wood. Wood allied to sandalwood, an infusion of which was used in treatment of kidney disease

Nero (Italian)   Black

Nerprun (French)   Buckthorn (cf. *rhamnus*)

[10] R. G. Todd (ed.), *The Extra Pharmacopoeia (Martindale)*, London, 25th ed., 1967, p. 1536.

Nervinum, unguentum   Ointment for fortifying the nerves

Nicolai, requies   See *requies Nicolai*

Nicolao; Nicolas; Nicolaus; Nicolo (Italian)   1. Nicolaus Myrepsus, physician who practised in the thirteenth century at Byzantium; formulated *requies magna* (lit. The Great Repose), an opiate which was in use until the close of the eighteenth century. 2. Nicolaus Salernitanus (Nicholas of Salerno); presumed author of the *Antidotarium Nicolai*, a dispensatory which enjoyed a high reputation in the Middle Ages

Nicotiana   Tobacco-plant (*Nicotiana tabacum*). Leaves used

Nigella   Fennel-flower (*Nigella sativa*). Seeds used

Niger; nigra, etc.   Black

Nimphaea   See *nymphaea.*

Ninfea (Italian)   White Water-lily (cf. *nymphaea*)

Nitri, sal; nitrum   Term applied to certain compounds of sodium and potassium, e.g. soda, potash, saltpetre, or a mixture of these[11]

Nitrum vitriolatum   Sulphate of potassium or sodium

Noce (Italian)   Nut, walnut

Noce moscata (Italian); **moce muscata** (Italian)   Nutmeg

Noir (French)   Black

Noli me tangere   The plant Touch-me-not, Yellow Balsam (*Impatiens noli tangere*). Herb used

Nuces   Nuts

Nucleus pini   See *pini, nucleus*

Nutritum, unguentum   See *triapharmacum, unguentum*

Nux   Nut

Nux colae   Cola nut (cf. *kola*)

Nux cupressi   Galbulus. Fruit of the Cypress

Nux juglans   Walnut

Nux moschata; nux myristica   Nutmeg

Nux vomica   Nux vomica. Seeds of the tree *Strychnos nux-vomica*

Nymphaea   White Water-lily (*Nymphaea alba*). Flowers and root used

O.   At beginning of inscription: *oleum; olio; onguent; opiatum.* At end of inscription: *opium* (as in *collyrium album cum o.*)

Oca (Italian)   Goose

Ocimum   Sweet Basil (*Ocymum basilicum*). Herb and seeds used

Oculis, unguentum de tutia pro   See *tutia pro oculis, unguentum de*

Ocymum   See *ocimum*

Oeillet (French)   Clove-scented Pink (cf. *tunicae, flores*)

Oesipus; oesypus; oesypus humida   Wool fat, lanolin

Oglio   See *olio*

---

[11] M. P. Crosland, *Historical Studies in the Language of Chemistry*, London, Melbourne and Toronto, 1962, p. 106.

Olea   Olive-tree (*Olea europaea*). Leaves, fruit, and oil expressed from fruit used

Oleum   Oil, olive oil

Olibani, gummi; olibanum   Olibanum, Frankincense, Thus. Oleo-resin furnished by trees of the genus *Boswellia*

Olio (Italian)   Oil, olive oil

Omphacinum, oleum   Oil expressed from unripe olives

Omphacium   Juice pressed from unripe grapes

Onguent (French)   Ointment

Ononis   See *anonis*

Ophthalmicum, unguentum   Zinc oxide ointment. Used for treatment of inflammations and certain other disorders of the eye (cf. *tutia pro oculis, unguentum de*)

Opiata Salomonis   Polypharmaceutical electuary. Used in treatment of infectious diseases and of helminitic infestations

Opiatum   Opiate

Opio (Italian); **opium**   Opium

Opobalsamum   Opobalsam, Balm of Gilead, Balm of Mecca. Oleo-resin obtained from the tree *Commiphora opobalsamum*

Opodeldoc   Soap liniment, used in treatment of sprains and bruises

Opopanax   Opopanax. Gum resin furnished by the root of *Opopanax chironium*

Oppio (Italian)   Opium

Opticae, pilulae   See *lucis majores, pilulae*

Optima, optimum, etc.   Of the best quality

Orchis   See *satyrium*

Ordeum   See *hordeum*

Origano (Italian); **origanum**   Wild Marjoram (*Origanum vulgare*). Leaves and flowering tops used

Origanum Creticum   See *dictamnus Creticus*

Oriza   See *oryza*

Orobanche   Broomrape, Chokeweed (member of genus *Orobanche*)

Orobo (Italian); **orobus**   Term probably denoting the Tuberous Pea (*Lathyrus macrorrhizus*)

Orso (Italian)   Bear

Ortica (Italian)   Nettle (cf. *urtica*)

Orviétan (French); **Orvietanum**   Electuary used as an antidote against poisons, as a prophylactic agent against pestilence, as a remedy against smallpox and as a tonic. Name supposedly derived from Christophoro Contugi of Orvieto, who formulated the preparation

Oryza   Rice

Orzo (Italian)   Barley

Os   Bone

Os cordis cervi   Stag's heart bone

Osipo (Italian)   Wool fat

Ossa sepiae   Cuttle-bone

Osso (Italian)   Bone

Ovis   Sheep, ewe

Ovo, electuarium de   Antipestilential electuary, made from eggs and other ingredients

Oximel   See *oxymel*

Oxitriphyllon   See *luiula*

Oxizaccara (Italian)   See *oxysacchara*

Oxyacantha   Hawthorn, Whitethorn (*Crataegus oxyacantha*). Berries, leaves and flowers used

Oxycroceum, emplastrum   Poultice made from saffron, yellow wax, vinegar, myrrh, frankincense, mastic and other resins. Used for relief of muscular pains

Oxymel   Oxymel. Potion prepared by evaporating to a syrupy consistency a mixture of clarified honey and vinegar

Oxymel scilliticum   Oxymel of Squills. Anti-tussive preparation made by evaporating to a syrupy consistency a mixture of clarified honey and a vinegary extract of squills

Oxymel simplex   See *oxymel*

Oxysacchara; oxysaccharum   A product obtained by evaporating a mixture of sugar and vinegar, sometimes with the addition of pomegranate juice, to a syrupy consistency

Oxytriphyllon   Wood-sorrel (cf. *luiula*)

P.   At beginning of inscription: *pilulae; pinguedo; pommade; pulpa; pulvis.* At end of inscription: *praecipitatus; praeparatus*

Paeonia   Common Peony (*Paeonia officinalis*). Petals, root and seeds used

Palma   1. The Date Palm. Fruit used (cf. *dactylus*). 2. The Coconut Palm. Fruit used. 3. The Palm-oil Tree. Oil expressed from kernels of fruit (*oleum palmae*) used

Palma Christi   Castor Oil Plant (*Ricinus communis*). Seeds used

Panacea   A metallic substance prepared by a chemical process, e.g. *panacea mercurii rubra* (red oxide of mercury)

Panchymagogum, extractum   Purgative preparation made from colocynth pulp, agaric, scammony, aloes, black hellebore and other ingredients

Panis, emplastrum de crusta   See *crusta panis, emplastrum de*

Papaver album   Opium Poppy (*Papaver somniferum var. album*). Leaves, seeds, flowers, capsules and dried latex of capsules (opium) used

Papaver erraticum   Wild Poppy, Red Poppy (cf. *papaver rhoeas*)

Papaver nigrum   Probably denotes the Black-specked Opium Poppy (*Papaver somniferum var. nigrum*)

Papaver rhoeas; papaver rubrum   Red Poppy, Field Poppy, Corn Poppy (*Papaver rhoeas*). Petals used

Paralysis Cowslip, Paigle, Palsywort (*Primula officinalis*). Flowers and root used

Paralysis, syrupus Syrup made from cowslips and other ingredients. Used in treatment of nervous disorders

Paralyticos, unguentum ad Ointment for the treatment of palsy

Paregoricum, elixir Alcoholic tincture of opium, flavoured with aniseed oil and other ingredients. Used for relief of coughs

Pareira Pareira. Root of the plant *Chondodendron tomentosum*

Parietaria Pellitory of the Wall (*Parietaria officinalis*). Herb used

Pas d'âne (French) Coltsfoot (cf. *tussilago*)

Passula Raisin

Pavot (French) Opium Poppy (cf. *papaver album*)

Pece (Italian) Pine tar, pitch, rosin

Pêche (French) Peach

Pêcher (French) Peach tree

Pectorale, electuarium; pectorale, emplastrum; pectorale, unguentum Electuary, or poultice, or ointment used for treatment of disorders of the chest

Pediculos, unguentum contra Ointment made from sulphur, stavesacre seeds and other ingredients. Used for eradication of hair parasites

Pedis cati Cat's-foot, Mountain Cudweed (*Antennaria dioica*). Flower-heads used

Peganum See *harmala*

Penidiae; penidium Confection made by melting sugar over a low heat, cooling and drawing out the product into strands

Penninckwater (Dutch) Pennyroyal-water. Liquor distilled from the leaves of pennyroyal (cf. *pulegium*)

Pentaphyllum Cinquefoil, Five Fingers (*Potentilla reptans*). Herb and root used

Peonia (Italian) Peony (cf. *paeonia*)

Pepe (Italian) Pepper (cf. *piper*)

Pepo Pumpkin (*Cucurbita pepo*). Seeds used

Pera (Italian) Pear

Perfoliata Hare's-ear, Thoroughwax (*Bupleurum rotundifolium*). Herb used

Persica malus See *persicus*

Persicaria Water-pepper, Smartweed (*Polygonum hydropiper*). Herb used

Persicorum, syrupus de floribus Syrup of peach blossom

Persicum, Philonium See *Philonium Persicum*

Persicus Peach-tree (*Amygdalus persica*). Fruit and blossom used

Peruvianum, balsamum Balsam of Peru. Balsam exuded from the trunk of the tree *Myroxylon pereirae*

Peruvianus, cortex Cinchona bark, Peruvian bark, Jesuit's bark. Dried bark of trees of the genus *Cinchona*[12]

[12] *Cortex Peruvianus, balsamum Canadense, balsamum copaivae, balsamum Peruvianum, balsamum*

Pervinca   Periwinkle. Plant of the genus *Vinca*. Herb used

Pesca (Italian)   Peach

Pestacchio (Italian)   Pistachio

Pestem, pilulae contra; pestilentiales, pilulae   Anti-pestilential pills, made from aloes, myrrh, saffron and other ingredients (cf. *pilulae Rufi; trochisci hedychroi*)

Pesto (Italian)   Crushed, ground

Petasites   Butterbur (member of genus *Petasites*). Root used

Petroselinum   Parsley (*Petroselinum sativum*). Herb, root and fruit used

Petum   Tobacco

Peucedanum   Hog's Fennel, Sulphurwort (*Peucedanum officinale*). Rhizome used

Phellandrium   Water Hemlock, Cowbane (*Cicuta virosa*). Herb used

Philonium Londinense; Philonium Persicum; Philonium Romanum   Polypharmaceutical preparations, made from opium and other ingredients. Used in relief of pain and to induce sleep. Named after Philon of Tarsus (first century B.C.), a physician

Philosophorum, oleum   Name an allusion to brick furnaces used in philosophical (alchemical) operations. Philosophers' Oil, Oil of Bricks. Oleaginous liquid obtained by distillation of a mixture of powdered brick or tiles and olive oil

Phu   Probably the plant *Valeriana phu*. Root used

Phylonium   See *Philonium*

Piantaggine (Italian)   Plantain (cf. *plantago*)

Pice, unguentum e; piceum, unguentum   Ointment of tar. Used in treatment of skin disorders

Pied-de-chat (French)   Cat's-foot (cf. *pedis cati*)

Pillola (Italian)   See *pilula*

Pilosella   Hawkweed, Mouse-ear (*Hieracium pilosella*). Herb used

Pilula   1. Pill. 2. Pill mass. Mixture of drugs and excipients which was held in stock by pharmacist for rolling into pills as the need arose (cf. *massa pilularum*)

Pilulae sine quibus esse nolo   See *sine quibus esse nolo, pilulae*

Pilule (French)   See *pilula*

Pimento   Pimento, Jamaica Pepper, Allspice. Fruit of the tree *Pimenta officinalis*

Pimpinella   Probably the Burnet Saxifrage (*Pimpinella saxifraga*). Root used

Pinea   See *pinus*

Pinguedo   Fat, grease

Tolu, hamamelis, ipecacuanha, matico, pareira, pimento, quassia, ratanhia, serpentaria Virginiana, simarouba, urucu, and a few others, denote drugs which are obtained from plants or trees indigenous to the American Continent or the West Indies. Pharmacy vessels inscribed with such names (e.g. Plate 36c) cannot be of date earlier than the seventeenth century, when these medicaments began to enter European medical practice.

Pini, nucleus Pine-kernel, pine-seed

Pini, turio Pine-cone

Pino, lohoch de Anti-tussive and anti-asthmatic remedy, made from pine-kernels and other ingredients

Pinus Member of genus *Pinus*, Pine

Piombo (Italian) Lead

Piombo, unguento di (Italian) See *plumbo, unguentum de*

Piper Pepper, especially Black Pepper (*Piper nigrum*)

Pirethrum See *pyrethrum*

Pirum See *pyrum*

Pisilio See *psillio*

Pistachia, nux; pistacia Pistachio

Pitimo See *epitimo*

Pivoine (French) Peony (cf. *paeonia*)

Pix Tar, pine tar, pitch, rosin

Pix Burgundica Burgundy Pitch. Resinous substance exuded by the spruce-fir

Plantago Greater Plantain (*Plantago major*) and certain other species of *Plantago*. Herb used

Pleres arconticum, electuarium; pliris arconticum, electuarium Electuary made from pearls, red coral, musk, aloë-wood, cinnamon, cloves, nutmeg, roses, violets and other ingredients. Used as a tonic and in treatment of melancholy

Pll. (Italian) Abbreviation for the word *pillole* (pills)

Plumbo, unguentum de Ointment made from calcined lead, litharge, ceruse, antimony, rose oil, turpentine and yellow wax. Used in treatment of ulcers

Plumbum Lead

Polmone di volpe, loch di (Italian) *Lohoch* of fox's lung (cf. *pulmone vulpis, lohoch de*)

Polvere (Italian) Powder

Polychreste; polychrestum, sal (from Greek πολύ, much + χρηστός, useful, i.e. a drug effective against a number of ailments) 1. (Also known as *sal polychrestum Glaseri*, after Christopher Glaser, a seventeenth-century apothecary to the King of France, who introduced the preparation into medical practice.) Potassium sulphate (see also *arcanum duplicatum*). 2. (Also known as *sal polychrestum de Seignette*, after Elie Seignette, born in 1632 at La Rochelle, France.) Seignette Salt, Rochelle Salt, potassium sodium tartrate

Polygala Common Milkwort (*Polygala vulgaris*). Herb used

Polygonum Knot-grass, Knot-weed (*Polygonum aviculare*). Herb used

Polypodium Common Polypody (*Polypodium vulgare*). Rhizome used

Polytrichum Probably denotes the fern Maidenhair Spleenwort (*Asplenium trichomanes*). Leaves used

Pomfolice (Italian); **pomfolige** (Italian)   Crude zinc oxide (cf. *pompholyx*)

Pomis compositus Regis Saporis, syrupus de; pomis R.S., syrupus de   Syrup having purgative action, prepared from senna leaves, borage, apple juice and other ingredients. Supposedly named after Sabur Ben Sahl, Persian physician of the ninth century A.D.

Pommade (French)   Pomade (scented ointment)

Pomme (French)   Apple

Pommes composées R.S., sirop de (French)   See *pomis compositus Regis Saporis, syrupus de*

Pomo (Italian)   Apple

Pomo arancio (Italian)   Orange (fruit)

Pomo granato (Italian); **pomo punico** (Italian)   Pomegranate

Pompholyx   Crude zinc oxide, tutty

Pomum   Apple

Populeon, unguento (Italian); **populeum, unguentum**   Ointment made from poplar buds, black nightshade, henbane leaves and other ingredients. Used as an emollient, and in treatment of burns

Populus   Poplar-tree (*Populus nigra*, Black Poplar, and perhaps other species of *Populus*). Buds, *gemmae populi*, used

Porcus   Hog, pig

Porrum   Leek (*Allium porrum*)

Portulaca   Purslane (*Portulaca oleracea*). Herb and seeds used

Potentilla   See *argentina*

Poterii, antihecticum   See *antihecticum Poterii*

Poudre (French)   Powder

Pourpier (French)   Purslane (cf. *portulaca*)

Praecipitatus   Precipitate, precipitated

Praeparatio   Substance prepared for medicinal use

Praeparatus   Prepared

Prassium   See *marrubium*

Primula veris   Primrose (*Primula vulgaris*). Herb and root used

Prunella   Self-heal (*Prunella vulgaris*). Herb used

Prunellae, sal   See *sal prunellae*

Prunus   Plum, prune

Prunus sylvestris   Blackthorn (*Prunus spinosa*). Fruit (sloe) used

Psillio (Italian); **psyllium**   Fleawort (*Plantago psyllium*). Seeds used

Ptisana   Ptisan. Herbal decoction or infusion

Pulegium   Pennyroyal (*Mentha pulegium*). Leaves used

Pulicaria   Probably the composite plant Small Fleabane (*Inula pulicaria*). Seeds used

Pulmonaria   Lungwort (*Pulmonaria officinalis*). Leaves used

Pulmone vulpis, lohoch de   *Lohoch* whose chief ingredient was the fox's lung

Pulpa   Pulp (of fruit)

Pulsatilla Pasque-flower, Pasque-anemone (*Anemone pulsatilla*). Herb used
Pulvis Powder
Pumex Pumice
Punica; punica malus Pomegranate-tree (cf. *granata malus*)
Pyrethrum Pellitory of Spain (*Anacyclus pyrethrum*). Root used
Pyrola Plant of the genus *Pyrola* (Wintergreen). Herb used
Pyrum Pear

Quassia Quassia, Bitter Wood. Stem-wood of the trees *Picrasma excelsa*, native in the West Indies, and *Quassia amara*, indigenous to South America
Quercetanus (Latinised form of) Joseph du Chesne (*chêne* (French), and *quercus* (Latin) = oak tree); French chemist (1544–1609). Introduced calomel into medical practice
Quercinum, viscum See *viscum quercinum*
Quercus Oak-tree. Bark, buds, leaves and acorns used
Quinquefolium See *pentaphyllum*
Quinque radicibus, syrupus de Syrup made from the roots of five plants, viz. Butcher's broom (cf. *ruscus*), smallage (cf. *apium*), fennel, parsley and asparagus
Quinquina See *Peruvianus, cortex*
Quodit See *conditum*

R. At beginning of inscription: *racine; radice; radix; raíz; resina*. At end of inscription: *Rhazes; rheum* (as in *syrupus rosarum cum r.*); *Romanum* (as in *Philonium R.*); *rosatum* (as in *mel r.*); *ruber*
R.S. *Rex Sapor* (see *pomis compositus Regis Saporis, syrupus de*)
Rabarbaro (Italian) Rhubarb (cf. *rheum*)
Racine (French); **radice** (Italian) Root
Radicibus, syrupus de duabus See *duabus radicibus, syrupus de*
Radicibus, syrupus de quinque See *quinque radicibus, syrupus de*
Radix Root
Rafanus See *raphanus*
Ragia (Italian) Venice turpentine (cf. *terebinthina Veneta*)
Raiz (Portuguese); **raíz** (Spanish) Root
Raleighana, confectio Raleigh's Confection, Raleigh's Cordial. Polypharmaceutical preparation said to have been devised by Sir Walter Raleigh during his imprisonment in the Tower of London from 1603 to 1616.[13]
Ramich, trochisci Lozenges having tonic properties; composed of rose petals, cloves, nutmeg, yellow sandalwood, gum Arabic and other ingredients
Ramno (Italian) Buckthorn (cf. *rhamnus*)

[13] A. C. Wootton, *Chronicles of Pharmacy*, London, 1910, vol. 1, pp. 310–15; C. H. LaWall, *Four Thousand Years of Pharmacy*, Philadelphia and London, 1927, p. 217; L. G. Matthews, *The Royal Apothecaries*, London, 1967, p. 113.

Ramolaccio (Italian)   Horse-radish

Ranich, trochisci   See *ramich, trochisci*

Raphanus hortensis   Garden-radish

Raphanus rusticanus   Horse-radish

Rapontico (Italian)   Rhapontic Rhubarb (cf. *rhaponticum*)

Rases   See *Rhazes*

Rasura   Shavings

Rasura eboris   Rasped ivory, ivory shavings

Ratanhia   Rhatany (the South American shrub *Krameria triandra*). Root
used

Razes   See *Rhazes*

Rea   See *rhea*

Realgar   Realgar, red sulphide of arsenic, arsenic disulphide

Refrigerans Galeni, ceratum   Cerate compounded from oil of roses (or oil
of sweet almonds), white wax and chilled water. Used as an emollient and for
treatment of inflammations

Regius, syrupus   'The Royal Syrup'. Syrup made from rose-water

Réglisse (French); **regolitia** (Italian)   Liquorice (cf. *glycyrrhiza*)

Requies magna Nicolai; requies Nicolai   'Nicholas's Repose'. Opiate
whose formula was devised by Nicolaus Myrepsus (q.v.)

Resina   Resin

Resina pini   See *pix Burgundica*

Resumptivum, unguentum (from Latin *resumptivus*, restorative)
Ointment made from seeds of fenugreek, oil of violets, oil of sweet almonds,
chamomile oil, yellow wax and other ingredients. Used in treatment
of asthma and pleurisy

Reubarbaro (Italian); **rhabarbarum**   Rhubarb (cf. *rheum*)

Rhamnus   Buckthorn (*Rhamnus cathartica*). Fruit used

Rhaponticum   Rhapontic Rhubarb (*Rheum rhaponticum*). Rhizome used

Rhases; Rhazes   Celebrated Persian physician and medical author
(A.D. 865–925). Planned the rebuilding of the great hospital at Baghdad (see
page 24). A treatise by Rhazes, entitled *Kitab-al-hâwi*, and translated into
Latin under the name *Liber Continens*, had a considerable influence on
European medical thought

Rhea   Poppy

Rheum   Chinese Rhubarb (*Rheum palmatum* and certain other species of
Rheum). Rhizome used

Rhodia radix   Rose-root, Rose-wort (plant of genus *Sedum*). Root used

Rhodii, lignum; rhodium   Rosewood

Rhoeados, syrupus   Syrup of red poppies

Rhus   See *sumach*

Ribe (Italian); **ribes; ribesia**   Red currant (*Ribes rubrum*). Sometimes
denotes the Black Currant (*Ribes nigrum*)

Ricini, oleum   Castor oil (cf. *Palma Christi*)

96 Nueva Botica (New Pharmacy) of Carlos IV in Royal Palace, Madrid. The drug
jars, of porcelain, were made in 1794 at the Royal Factory of Buen Retiro; they are
emblazoned with the arms of Castile and Aragon.* *See page 29*

Riso (Italian)   Rice
Rob   Juice of a fruit, usually sweetened with sugar or honey, concentrated by
evaporation to a syrupy consistency
Romanum, Philonium   See *Philonium Romanum*
Romarin (French)   Rosemary (cf. *rosmarinus*)
Rorismarini, flores   Flowers of rosemary
Rosa alba   White Rose (petals used)
Rosa canina   Dog-rose (cf. *cynorrhodon*)
Rosaceum, unguentum   See *rosatum, unguentum*
Rosaceus solutivus, syrupus   See *rosatus solutivus, syrupus*
Rosa Damascena   Damask Rose
Rosa Hiericontea   Rose of Jericho (*Anastatica Hierochuntica*)
Rosa pallida   Pale Rose
Rosa Provincialis   Rose grown at Provins, to the east of Paris. Petals used
Rosa rubra   Red Rose
Rosarum solutivum, syrupus   See *rosatus solutivus, syrupus*

* Rafael Palma Pradillo, 'Museo y Real oficina de farmacia en el Palacio de Oriente', *Boletin de la
Sociedad Española de Historia de la Farmacia*, vol. 15, 1964, pp. 127–30.

Rosatum, unguentum   Ointment made from rose petals, or rose-water, and other ingredients. Used as a skin emollient

Rosatus solutivus, syrupus.   Syrup having aperient action; prepared by infusing rose petals with water, followed by straining, adding sugar and evaporating the product

Rosmarinus   Rosemary (*Rosmarinus officinalis*). Leaves and flowering tops used

Ros solis (from Latin *ros*, dew, and *solis*, genitive of *sol*, sun)   Common Sundew, Round-leaved Sundew (*Drosera rotundifolia*). Herb used

Rotula   Lozenge of irregular shape

Ruber, rubra, etc.   Red

Rubia tinctorum   Madder (*Rubia tinctorum*). Root used

Rubrum desiccativum, unguentum; rubrum, unguentum   Ointment made from lead oxide, lead carbonate, calamine, Armenian bole and other ingredients. Used to promote healing of wounds, especially of chapped chilblains

Rubus idaeus   Raspberry Bush (*Rubus idaeus*). Fruit and leaves used

Rudii, pilulae   (Pills of Rudius). Purgative pills made from Socotra aloes, colocynth, scammony, black hellebore root and other ingredients. Used in treatment of quartan fever, melancholy and lethargy

Rufi, pilulae   Anti-pestilential pills, containing Socotra aloes, myrrh and saffron. Named after Rufus of Ephesus (first century A.D.), an anatomist and physician

Ruperti, herba   See *Gratia Dei*

Ruscus   Butcher's Broom (*Ruscus aculeatus*). Root used

Ruta   Rue, Herb of Grace (*Ruta graveolens*). Herb used

Ruta capraria   Goat's Rue (*Galega officinalis*). Flowering herb used

Ruta muraria   Wall Rue, White Maidenhair (*Asplenium ruta-muraria*)

S.   At beginning, or in middle of inscription: *sal; sciroppo; sel; seme; semen; sine; sirop; siropo; siroppo; species; spiritus; succus; syropo; syrupus.* In middle, or at end of inscription: *Salomonis; semplice; siccus; simplex; solutivus; Sylvius*

S.A.   At end of inscription: *sine agarico* (as in *confectio Hamech s.a.*)

S.C.   *Syrupus corticis*

S.O.   At end of inscription: *sine opio*

S.S.   *Syrupus simplex*

Sabina   Savin (*Juniperus sabina*). Young shoots used

Saccaro (Italian); **saccharum**   Sugar

Saccharum hordeatum   Barley sugar

Saccharum penidiatum   See *penidiae*

Saffran de Mars apéritif (French)   Red iron oxide obtained by prolonged exposure of iron to action of moisture (cf. *crocus Martis; Martis limatura praeparata*)

Sagapenum   Gum resin furnished by *Ferula Persica* and certain other species of *Ferula*

Sal   A solid substance, usually inorganic in nature

Sal absinthii   Residue obtained in calcination of wormwood (*absinthium*), ashes of wormwood

Sal ammoniacum; sal Armeniacum   Sal-ammoniac, ammonium chloride

Sal catharticus Glauberi   Sodium sulphate, Glauber's salt (named after Johann R. Glauber (1604–70), German chemist who introduced the compound into medical practice)

Sal commune   Table-salt

Sal de duobus; sal duobus; sal duplicatum   See *arcanum duplicatum*

Sal gemmeum   Rock-salt

Salix   Tree of the genus *Salix* (Willow). Bark used

Sal mirabile   See *sal catharticus Glauberi*

Salomonis, opiata   See *opiata Salomonis*

Sal petrae   Saltpetre (cf. *nitrum*)

Sal polychrestum   See *polychrestum, sal*

Sal prunellae   Preparation of fused nitre

Salsepareille (French)   Sarsaparilla

Sal tartari   Salt of Tartar, impure potassium carbonate. Residue obtained from calcination of Cream of Tartar

Salvia   Garden Sage (*Salvia officinalis*). Leaves used

Sal vitrioli   See *vitriolum album*

Sambucinum, oleum   Liniment made by boiling elder flowers in olive oil and discarding the insoluble matter

Sambucus   Common Elder (*Sambucus nigra*). Flowers, fruit, leaves and bark used

Sanctum, lignum   See *guaiaci, lignum*

Sandalum   See *santalum*

Sandaraca   1. (Also known as *sandaracha Graecorum*.) Realgar, arsenic disulphide. (Not used in this sense after the seventeenth century.). 2. Also known as *sandaracha Arabum*.) Sandarac. Gum resin obtained from certain trees of the genus *Tetraclinis*

Sanguis   Blood

Sanguis draconis   Dragon's blood. Resinous exudation formed on the fruit of climbing palms of the genus *Daemonorops*

Sanicula   Sanicle (*Sanicula Europaea*). Leaves used

Sano et esperto, loch (Italian)   See *sanum et expertum, lohoch*

Santalum   Tree or shrub of the genus *Santalum* (Sandalwood), especially *Santalum album* (White Sandalwood). Heartwood (*lignum santali*) used

Santonicum   Wormseed. Dried flowerheads of the composite plant *Artemisia cina*

Sanum et expertum, lohoch   Anti-tussive and anti-asthmatic medicament, made from hyssop, fenugreek, maidenhair, fennel, iris, cinnamon, liquorice, raisins, dried figs, sweet almonds and other ingredients

Sapo   Soap

Saponaria   Soapwort, Fuller's Herb (*Saponaria officinalis*). Herb and root used

Sapo tartareus   'Soap of Tartar'. Unctuous mass prepared by heating a mixture of saltpetre and tartar with oil of turpentine

Sarcocolla   Sarcocolla. Gum resin of Eastern origin; probably an inferior grade of gum tragacanth

Sarsaparilla   Sarsaparilla. Root of certain plants of the genus *Smilax*

Sassafras   Sassafras. Inner bark of the root of the tree *Sassafras officinale*

Satureia   Summer Savory (*Satureia hortensis*). Herb used

Saturni, salis   Salt of Saturn, sugar of lead, lead acetate

Saturninum, unguentum   Ointment of lead acetate

Satyrion; satyrium   Term denoting certain plants of the genus *Orchis*, especially *Orchis morio* (Green-winged Orchid). Tuberous root used

Savina (Italian)   Savin (cf. *sabina*)

Saxifraga   Meadow Saxifrage (*Saxifraga granulata*). Plant used

Scabiem, unguentum contra   Anti-scabies ointment, made from sulphur, white lead, calcined lead, litharge, frankincense and other ingredients

Scabiosa   Field Scabious (*Scabiosa arvensis*). Leaves used

Scabiosum, unguentum   See *scabiem, unguentum contra*

Scammonia; scammonium   Scammony. Gum resin obtained from the root of the plant *Convulvulus scammonia*. Sometimes termed *Scammonium de Aleppo*, since much of the drug was imported from the Levant

Scarabeus   Dor-beetle

Scariola   See *endivia*

Scecachul; scecacul   See *secacul*

Schaenanthum; schénanthe (French)   See *schoenanthum*

Schilla   See *scilla*

Schoenanthi, herba; schoenanthum   Grass of the genus *Andropogon*, e.g. *Andropogon schoenanthus*, native in North Africa and certain Eastern countries. Sometimes known as Camel's Hay

Scilla   Squill, Sea-onion (*Urginea maritima*). Bulb used

Sciroppo (Italian)   Syrup

Scolopendrium   Hart's-tongue (*Scolopendrium vulgare*). Fronds used

Scordium   Water Germander (*Teucrium scordium*). Herb used

Scorpio   Scorpion

Scorza (Italian)   Bark, rind, peel, crust (of bread)

Scorzonera   Viper's Grass, Black Salsify (*Scorzonera hispanica*). Root used

Scylla   See *scilla*

Sebesten   Sebesten. Plum-like fruit of the tree *Cordia myxa*

Secacul; secacul Arabum   Name applied to an Eastern plant of uncertain identity

Secale Rye

Sedum Term denoting the House-leek (*Sempervivum tectorum*), and the Wall-pepper (*Sedum acre*). Herb used

Seignette, sal polychrestum de See *polychrestum (de Seignette), sal*

Sel (French) Salt

Seme (Italian); **semen** Seed

Sempervivum See *sedum*

Semplice (Italian) Simple, not mixed

Sena; senna Senna. Shrub of the genus *Cassia*, especially *Cassia senna*. Leaves used

Sepia Cuttle-fish, cuttle-bone

Sericum Cocoon of the silkworm

Serpentaria Virginia; serpentaria Virginiana Serpentary, Virginian Snake-root. Rhizome and root of the plant *Aristolochia serpentaria*

Serpyllum Wild Thyme, Mother of Thyme (*Thymus serpyllum*). Herb used

Sesamino (Italian); **sesamum** Sesame (*Sesamum Indicum* and *Sesamum Orientale*). Seeds used

Seseli Plant of the genus *Seseli*, Hartwort. Leaves and seeds used

Siccativus Siccative, drying

Siccum; siccus, etc. Dry, dried

Sigillum Salomonis; sigillum Solomonis Solomon's Seal (*Polygonatum officinale*). Root used

Siler montanum Term denoting the umbelliferous plants Mountain Laserwort (*Laserpitium siler*) and Lovage (*Levisticum officinale*), and possibly other plants

Silvius See *Sylvius*

Simarouba Tree of the genus *Simaruba* (indigenous to South America), especially *Simaruba officinalis*. Bark of root and of trunk used

Simphitum See *symphytum*

Simplex Simple, not mixed (as opposed to *compositum*)

Sinapi Mustard

Sine Without (preposition)

Sine quibus esse nolo, pilulae 'The pills I would not wish to be without.' Purgative pills made from Socotra aloes, scammony, larch agaric, senna leaves, myrobalans, dodder, petals of red roses, mastic and other ingredients

Sirop (French); **siropo** (Italian); **siroppo** (Italian); **sirupus** Syrup

Sisarum Skirret (*Sium sisarum*). Root used

Smaragdus Emerald (gem)

Socotrina, aloe See *aloe Socotrina*

Solanum Black Nightshade (*Solanum nigrum*). Leaves used

Solanum dulcamara; solanum lignosum See *dulcamara*

Solatrum See *solanum*

Solfo (Italian) Sulphur

Solimato (Italian) Sublimate of mercury, chloride of mercury

Solomonis, opiata   See *opiata Salomonis*
Solomonis, sigillum   See *sigillum Solomonis*
Solutif (French); **solutivum; solutivus**   Aperient
Sonchus; sonco (Italian)   Common Sow-thistle (*Sonchus oleraceus*), and certain other plants of the genus *Sonchus*. Herb used
Sorbus   Tree of the genus *Pyrus* (formerly genus *Sorbus*), especially the Service-tree (*Pyrus domestica*). Fruit used
Soufre (French)   Sulphur
Soufre, fleurs de (French)   Flowers of sulphur, sublimed sulphur
Spagyrica, conserva   Polypharmaceutical preparation, used for treatment of quartan fever and jaundice
Sparagio (Italian)   Asparagus
Species   Mixture of powdered plants, spices, etc., for use in preparation of herbal teas
Specificum antihecticum Poterii   See *antihecticum Poterii*
Spica   Spike Lavender (*Lavandula latifolia*). Flowers or flowering tops used
Spicae, oleum   Spike Lavender oil
Spica Indica   See *nardus Indica*
Spica nardi; spiga nardo (Italian)   See *nardus*
Spina alba   Hawthorn, Whitethorn (cf. *oxyacantha*)
Spina cervina   Buckthorn (cf. *rhamnus*)
Spiritus   Liquor obtained by distillation of an aromatic drug, or mixture of such drugs, with alcohol or wine
Spodio (Italian); **spodium**   (From Greek σποδός, ashes) Spodium. Powder obtained by calcination of ivory and certain other substances
Spodium Graecorum   Crude zinc oxide
Squilla   See *scilla*
Squinante (Italian); **squinantho** (Italian)   See *schoenanthum*
Staechados; staechas   See *stoechas*
Stannum   Tin (metal)
Staphisagria   Stavesacre, Lousewort (*Delphinium staphisagria*). Seeds used
Starkei, pilulae   Pills devised by George Starkey, an English seventeenth-century physician. Made from opium extract, black and white hellebore, liquorice and other ingredients. Used in treatment of mental illness, and as a sedative
Stecade (Italian); **stecados** (Italian); **stechas**   French Lavender (cf. *stoechas*)
Sternutatorius, pulvis   Sternutatory powder, errhine
Sticade; stichas   See *stoechas*
Stillatica; stillaticus, etc.   Distilled
Stipes   Stalk, stem
Stipticae, pilulae   See *stypticae, pilulae*
Stirax   See *storax*
Stoechade; stoechas   French Lavender, Cassidony (*Lavandula stoechas*). Flowers or flowering tops used

Stomachale, ceratum; stomachicum, ceratum   Cerate (ointment) for treatment of gastric disorders

Stomatico, cerotto (Italian)   Poultice for treatment of gastric disorders

Storace (Italian); **storax**   Storax. Gum resin obtained in classical times from the trunk of the tree *Styrax officinalis*, and in later times from *Liquidambar orientalis*

Stramonio (Italian); **stramonium**   Thorn-apple (*Datura stramonium*). Leaves and seeds used

Stypticae, pilulae   Pills serving to arrest haemorrhages

Styrax   See *storax*

Styrax calamita   Storax packed in reeds for shipment

Sublimato (Italian)   Sublimate of mercury (cf. *solimato*)

Succaro   See *zuccaro*

Succedaneum   A drug substituted for another

Succinum   Amber (fossil resin)

Succo (Italian); **succus; sugo** (Italian)   Juice; evaporated juice

Sulfur; sulphur   Sulphur

Sulphuris, balsamum   See *balsamum sulphuris*

Sulphuris, flores   Flowers of sulphur (sublimed sulphur)

Sulphuris, lac   Precipitated sulphur

Sumach   Sumach (*Rhus coriaria* and certain other species of the genus *Rhus*). Berries used

Summitates   Young shoots of a plant or shrub, e.g. *summitates sabinae* (young shoots of Savin, Savin tops)

Sureau (French)   Elder (cf. *sambucus*)

Sylvestris, malum   See *malum sylvestris*

Sylvestris, prunus   See *prunus sylvestris*

Sylvius   Franciscus de le Boë (or du Bois; latinised to *Sylvius*). Iatrochemist and Professor of Medicine at the University of Leyden (1614–72)

Symphytum   Common Comfrey (*Symphytum officinale*). Root and rhizome used

Synapi   See *sinapi*

Syropo (Italian); **syrupus**   Syrup

Syrupus corticis . . .   Syrup of bark (or peel) of . . .

T.   *Tabellae; theriaca; tinctura; triaca; trochisci*

Tabella   Tablet lozenge

Tacamahaca, gummi   Tacamahac. Resin furnished by *Bursera tomentosa* and certain other resiniferous trees

Tamarindus   Tamarind. Fruit of the tree *Tamarindus Indica*

Tanacetum   Tansy (*Tanacetum vulgare*). Leaves, flowers and seeds used

Tapsus   See *verbascum*

Tarassico (Italian); **taraxacum**   Dandelion (*Taraxacum officinale*). Root and leaves used

Tartarum emeticum   Tartar emetic, potassium antimonyl tartrate

Tartarum vitriolatum   Vitriolated tartar, crude potassium sulphate. Product obtained by chemical treatment of tartar with sulphuric acid

Tartarus   Tartar, argol, crude potassium hydrogen tartrate

Tartarus vitriolatus   See *tartarum vitriolatum*

Taurus   Bull, ox

Taxus   1. Yew-tree. 2. Badger

Terebinthina   Turpentine. Oleo-resin obtained from the pine-tree

Terebinthina Veneta   Venice Turpentine, Larch Turpentine. Oleo-resin furnished by the larch-tree

Teriaca; teriacum; tériaque (French)   See *theriaca*

Terra Japonica   See *catechu*

Terra Lemnia; terra sigillata   See *bolus*

Tetrapharmacum, unguentum   'Ointment of the four ingredients'. Salve made from pine resin, tar, wax and olive oil. Used as a vulnerary

Thalictrum   Common Meadow-rue (*Thalictrum flavum*). Herb and root used

Thapsia   Root of the umbelliferous plant *Thapsia Garganica*

Therebinthina Veneta   See *terebinthina Veneta*

Theriaca   1. Theriac. Polypharmaceutical preparation (electuary), reputedly introduced into medical practice by Nicander of Colophon (second century B.C.), Greek poet and priest of Apollo, as an antidote against poisons, especially the bite of serpents. The preparation was reformulated in subsequent centuries and became gradually to be regarded as a universal remedy. Theriac of Andromachus (q.v.) contained seventy-three ingredients, the most important of which was the flesh of vipers. *Theriaca* was one of the five sovereign remedies, the others being *confectio alkermes, confectio de hyacintho, Mithridatium* and *Orvietanum* (cf. page 84).

The principal varieties of theriac were *theriaca Andromachi, theriaca caelestis* or *coelestis* (celestial theriac), *theriaca Damocratis, theriaca Edinensis* (theriac formulated according to the Edinburgh Pharmacopoeia), *theriaca Germanorum, theriaca Londinensis* (theriac formulated according to the London Pharmacopoeia), *theriaca Veneta* (theriac of Venice) and *theriaca diatessaron*. The last-named variety of theriac (from the Greek διὰ τεσσάρων, composed of four ingredients) was intended for the use of the poor, and contained only myrrh, bay-laurel berries, root of gentian and root of round birthwort.

2. (In nineteenth-century use, principally in England.) Treacle

Thériaque (French)   Theriac

Thlaspi   Name applied to the cruciferous plants Mithridate Mustard (*Thlaspi arvense*) and Treacle Mustard (*Erysimum cheiranthoides*). Seeds used

Thus   See *olibani, gummi*

Thymelaea   Spurge-flax (*Daphne gnidium*)

Thymus   Garden Thyme (*Thymus vulgaris*). Herb used

Thyriaca   See *theriaca*

Tiglio (Italian); **tilia**; **tilleul** (French)   Tree of the genus *Tilia*, especially *Tilia Europaea* (Lime-tree, Linden-tree). Flowers used

Tinctura   Tincture. Alcoholic or aqueous extract of one or more drugs, usually of vegetable origin

Tiriaca   See *theriaca*

Tolu, balsamum   Balsam of Tolu. Balsam obtained from the trunk of the tree *Myroxylon toluiferum*

Tormentilla   Tormentil, Septfoil (*Potentilla tormentilla*). Rhizome used

Tragacantha   Tragacanth. Dried gummy exudate obtained from certain species of *Astragalus*

Trementina (Italian)   Turpentine (cf. *terebinthina*)

Triaca (Italian)   Theriac

Triapharmacum, unguentum   Ointment made from three ingredients, viz. litharge, olive oil and vinegar. Used in treatment of skin disorders

Tribus, pilulae de   Pills composed of three purgative drugs, viz. Socotra aloes, agaric and rhubarb

Tribus, syrupus de   Syrup made from three purgative drugs, viz. senna leaves, agaric and rhubarb

Trichomanes   See *polytrichum*

Trifera magna (Italian)   See *tryphera magna*

Trifera Persica (Italian)   See *tryphera Persica*

Trifolium fibrinum; trifolium paludosum; trifolium palustre   Buckbean, Bogbean, Marsh Trefoil, Water Trefoil (*Menyanthes trifoliata*). Leaves used

Trifolium pratense   Clover

Tripharmacum, unguentum   See *triapharmacum, unguentum*

Triphera   See *tryphera*

Triticum   Wheat

Trochisci albi Rhasis   See *albi Rhasis, trochisci*

Trochiscus   Lozenge, trochisk

Tryphera magna   Electuary compounded from opium, cinnamon, galangal rhizome, zedoary rhizome, henbane seeds and other ingredients. Used to relieve gastric pains, and to induce sleep

Tryphera Persica   Electuary made from senna leaves, larch agaric, rhubarb, thyme dodder, hops and other ingredients. Used as a mild purgative, as an antidepressant, and in treatment of jaundice

Tucia (Italian)   Tutty, crude zinc oxide

Tunicae, flores   Clove-scented Pink, Clove-gillyflower (*Dianthus caryophyllus*). Flowers used

Turbith   See *turpethum*

Turio pini   Pine-cone

Turpethum   Turpeth. Root of the plant *Ipomoea turpethum*

Tussilago   Coltsfoot (*Tussilago farfara*). Leaves and flowers used

Tussim, pilulae ad   Anti-tussive pills, composed of liquorice, opium, frankincense, myrrh and saffron

Tutia   Tutty, crude zinc oxide

Tutia pro oculis, unguentum de   Eye-ointment, made from zinc oxide and other ingredients

Tuzia (Italian)   Tutty, crude zinc oxide

U.   At beginning of inscription: *unguento; unguentum*. At end of inscription: *usta; ustum*

Ulmaria   Meadow-sweet, Queen of the Meadows (*Filipendula ulmaria*). Leaves used

Ulmus   Tree of the genus *Ulmus* (Elm). Bark and leaves used

Umbilicus Veneris   Pennywort, Navelwort (*Cotyledon umbilicus*). Herb used

Unguento (Italian); **unguentum**   Ointment

Ungula   Hoof

Ungula caballina   Coltsfoot (cf. *tussilago*)

Universale, balsamum   Ointment compounded from lead acetate, white wax and olive oil

Ursus   Bear

Urtica   Plant of the genus *Urtica* (Nettle). Leaves and seeds used

Urucu   Anatta, arnatto. Dye obtained from the seeds of the Roucou tree, *Bixa orellana*

Usta; ustum, etc.   Calcined, ashed

Uva   Grape, raisin

V.   At beginning of inscription: *vinum; vngvento (unguento); vngventvm (unguentum)*. In middle, or at end of inscription: *Veneris* (as in *capillus V.*); *Veneta* (as in *theriaca V.*); *verde; verum; vino; violatum; viride; vstvm (ustum)*

Vaccinium   See *myrtillus*

Valeriana   Common Valerian (*Valeriana officinalis*). Root and rhizome used

Verbascum   Plant of the genus *Verbascum* (Mullein). Petals and leaves used

Verbena   Vervain (*Verbena officinalis*). Herb used

Verde (Italian)   Green

Verderame (Italian)   Verdigris

Vermes, unguentum contra; vermifugum, unguentum   Ointment having anthelmintic action, made from wormseed, rue, oil of wormwood, wax and other ingredients

Vermifugus   Vermifuge, anthelmintic

Vermis   Worm (generally in the sense of an intestinal worm)

Veronica   Common Speedwell (*Veronica officinalis*). Herb used

Verum, verus, etc.   Genuine

Vesicatorium, emplastrum See *epispasticum, emplastrum*

Vigo, emplastrum de Poultice for treatment of wounds, devised by Giovanni da Vigo (1460–1525), surgeon to Pope Julius II

Vincetoxicum Swallowwort (*Vincetoxicum officinale*). Rhizome used

Vinum Wine

Vinum destillatum Brandy

Viola Plant of the genus *Viola* (Violet). Petals, leaves and seeds used

Violato (Italian); **violatum** Made from violets

Vipera Viper

Viperina Viper's Bugloss (*Echium vulgare*). Root used

Virga aurea Golden-rod (*Solidago virgaurea*). Herb used

Viride Green

Viride, balsamum Lotion made from verdigris, oil of linseed and oil of turpentine. Used for treatment of ulcers

Viride, oleum Liniment made by heating leaves of bay-laurel, rue, chamomile, marjoram and wormwood with olive oil, followed by straining to remove insoluble matter

Viride aeris See *aerugo*

Viscum Mistletoe (*Viscum album*, White mistletoe, and *Loranthus Europaeus*, Yellow-berried mistletoe). Twigs and leaves used

Viscum quercinum Oak Mistletoe

Vitae, aqua Alcohol, brandy

Vitae, lignum See *guaiaci, lignum*

Vitellum ovi Egg-yolk

Vitis Vine (*Vitis vinifera*). Leaves used

Vitrioli, oleum Oil of vitriol, sulphuric acid

Vitriolum, oleum See *vitrioli, oleum*

Vitriolum album White vitriol, zinc sulphate

Vitriolum caeruleum Blue vitriol, copper sulphate

Vitriolum viride Green vitriol, ferrous sulphate

Vitulus Calf

Volpe (Italian); **vulpes** Fox

Vultur Vulture

Xylobalsamum Fragrant wood of the tree *Commiphora opobalsamum* and of certain other balsamiferous trees

Yera picra See *hiera picra*

Yrino, olio See *irino, olio*

Yssopus See *hyssopus*

Yva arthritica See *chamaepitys*

Zafferano (Italian) Saffron (cf. *crocus*)

Zedoaria Zedoary. Rhizome of the zingiberaceous plant *Curcuma zedoaria*

Zenzero (Italian)   Ginger (cf. *zingiber*)

Zibethum   Civet. Unctuous substance, having a musky smell, obtained from the civet cat

Zingiber; zinziber   Ginger. Rhizome of the plant *Zingiber officinale*

Zizyphus   See *jujuba*

Zolfo (Italian)   Sulphur

Zuccaro (Italian); **zucchero** (Italian)   Sugar

Zucchero buglossato (Italian)   Candied confection made from bugloss

Zucchero rosato (Italian)   Sweetmeat made from sugar and petals of red roses or oil of red roses

Zucchero violato (Italian)   Candied confection made from violets

Zwelfer   Johann Zwelfer (1618–68). Apothecary and physician who practised in Germany, Italy and Austria; author of works on pharmacy including a revision of the Augsburg *Pharmacopoeia* (1652)

BIBLIOGRAPHY

Only the more important books and articles are cited; additional sources will be found in the notes to the individual chapters. References are arranged by country in chronological order.

General

B. Reber, *Considérations sur ma Collection d'Antiquités au Point de Vue de l'Histoire de la Médecine, la Pharmacie et les Sciences Naturelles*, Geneva, 1905

P. Dorveaux, *Les Pots de Pharmacie. Leur Historique, Suivi d'un Dictionnaire de leurs Inscriptions*, 1st ed. Paris, 1908; 2nd ed. Toulouse, 1923

W. Maskew, 'Pharmacy pots of the XVth to the XIXth centuries. A selection from the finest European collections', *Chemist and Druggist*, vol. 102, 1925, pp. 959–78

C. Benito del Caño and R. Roldán, y Guerrero, *Cerámica Farmaceutica. Apuntes para su Estudio*, Madrid, 1928

B. Rackham, *Catalogue of the Glaisher Collection of Pottery and Porcelain in the Fitzwilliam Museum, Cambridge*, 2 vols., Cambridge, 1935

G. Urdang and F. W. Nitardy, *The Squibb Ancient Pharmacy*, New York, 1940

J. Chompret, *Les Faïences Françaises Primitives d'après les Apothicaireries Hospitalières*, Paris, 1946

W. B. Honey, *European Ceramic Art from the End of the Middle Ages to About 1815*, 2 vols., London, 1949–52

Agnes Lothian, 'Drug jars and their inscriptions', *Chemist and Druggist*, vol. 153, 1950, pp. 805–7

Agnes Lothian, 'Saints on drug jars', *Chemist and Druggist*, vol. 159, 1953, pp. 598–603

Agnes Lothian, 'Pharmacy jars', in *The Concise Encyclopaedia of Antiques*, ed. L. G. G. Ramsey, London, 1955, vol. 2, pp. 263–9

J. Nicolier, 'Les pots de pharmacie', *Connaissance des Arts*, 15 October 1955, pp. 50–5

B. Rackham, *Islamic Pottery and Italian Maiolica: Illustrated Catalogue of a Private Collection*, London, 1959

Jeanne Giacomotti, *La Majolique de la Renaissance*, Paris, 1961

Agnes Lothian, 'Two centuries of dated drug jars', *Chemist and Druggist*, vol. 177, 1962, pp. 722–5

H. E. Thomann, 'Die "Roche"-Apotheken-Fayencen-Sammlung', *Keramik-Freunde der Schweiz*, Nos. 58–9, 1962, pp. 11–32

Brigitte Klesse, *Majolika*, Cologne (Kunstgewerbe-Museum), 1966

(Sir) Victor Negus, *Artistic Possessions at the Royal College of Surgèons of England*, Edinburgh and London, 1967, pp. 79–118

H. Stafski, *Aus Alten Apotheken*, 4th ed., Munich, 1967

R. J. Charleston (ed.), *World Ceramics: An Illustrated History*, London, New York, Sydney, Toronto, 1968

H. Curtil, *Les Pots de Pharmacie*, Paris, 1971

G. Conti, *Museo Nazionale di Firenze, Palazzo del Bargello: Catalogo delle Maioliche*, Florence, 1971

H.-P. Fourest and Antoinette Faÿ, 'Majoliques Européennes de la Renaissance', *Cahiers de la Céramique*, No. 51, 1972, pp. 10–37

T. Hausmann, *Majolika. Spanische und Italienische Keramik vom 14. bis zum 18. Jahrhundert*, Berlin, 1972

A. Caiger-Smith, *Tin-Glaze Pottery in Europe and the Islamic World. The Tradition of 1000 Years in Maiolica, Faience and Delftware*, London, 1973

G. Kallinich, *Schöne Alte Apotheken*, Munich, 1975

A. V. B. Norman, *Wallace Collection. Catalogue of Ceramics. Part 1. Pottery, Maiolica, Faience, Stoneware*, London, 1976

C. Frégnac, *La Faïence Européenne: Le Guide du Connaisseur*, Fribourg, 1976

Italy

H. Wallis, *Italian Ceramic Art. The Albarello. A Study in Early Renaissance Maiolica*, London, 1904

W. Bode, *Die Anfänge der Majolikakunst in Toskana*, Berlin, 1911

A. Castiglioni, 'La farmacia Italiana del Quattrocento nella storia dell'arte ceramica', (a) *Faenza*, vol. 10, 1922, pp. 76–88, (b) *Bollettino Chimico Farmaceutico*, vol. 64, 1925, pp. 65–92

B. Rackham, *Guide to Italian Maiolica*, London (Victoria and Albert Museum), 1933

C. Pedrazzini, *La Farmacia Storica ed Artistica Italiana*, Milan, 1934

Genoa, Palazzo Reale, *Mostra de l'Antica Maiolica Ligure dal Secolo XIV al Secolo XVIII*, Genoa, 1939

B. Rackham, *Catalogue of Italian Maiolica*, 2 vols., London (Victoria and Albert Museum), 1940

J. Chompret, *Répertoire de la Majolique Italienne*, 2 vols., Paris, 1949

G. Morazzoni, *La Maiolica Antica Ligure*, Milan, 1951

G. Polidori, *La Maiolica Antica Abruzzese*, 2nd ed., Milan, 1952

B. Rackham, *Italian Maiolica*, London, 1st ed. 1952; 2nd ed. 1963

G. Liverani, 'Di alcuni vasi da farmicia nel Museo Internazionale delle Ceramiche di Faenza', *Keramik-Freunde der Schweiz*, No. 26, 1953, pp. 21–3

Agnes Lothian, 'Drug jars of Northern Italy', *The Alchemist*, vol. 17, 1953, pp. 323–8

G. Russo Perez, *Catalogo Ragionato della Raccolta Russo-Perez di Maioliche Siciliane*, Palermo, 1954

G. Morazzoni, *La Maiolica Antica Veneta*, Milan, 1955

N. Ragona, *La Ceramica Siciliana dalle Origini ai Giorni Nostri*, Palermo, 1955

G. Liverani, *Five Centuries of Italian Majolica*, New York, Toronto, London, 1960

G. Pesce, *Maioliche Liguri da Farmacia*, Milan, 1960

M. Bellini and G. Conti, *Maioliche Italiane del Rinascimento*, Milan, 1964

C. Barile, *Antiche Ceramiche Liguri: Maioliche di Albisola*, Milan, 1965

O. Ferrari and G. Scavizzi, *Maioliche Italiane del Seicento e Settecento*, Milan, 1965

Ilona Pataky-Brestyánszky, *Italienische Majolikakunst: Italienische Majolika in Ungarischen Sammlungen*, Budapest, 1967

G. Donatone, *Maioliche Napoletane della Spezieria Aragonese di Castelnuovo*, Naples, 1970

Laura Campanile, *I Vasi di Farmacia*, Milan, 1973

G. Conti, *L'Arte della Maiolica in Italia*, Milan, 1973

G. Cora, *Storia della Maiolica di Firenze e del Contado. Secoli XIV e XV*, 2 vols., Florence, 1973

Jeanne Giacomotti, *Catalogue des Majoliques des Musées Nationaux (Musées du Louvre et de Cluny; Musée National de Céramique à Sèvres; Musée Adrien-Dubouché à Limoges)*, Paris, 1974

A. Ragona, *La Maiolica Siciliana dalle Origini all'Ottocento*, Palermo, 1975

France

E. Garnier, 'Les anciens vases de pharmacie des hôpitaux et hospices de Paris', *Gazette des Beaux-Arts*, vol. 38, 1888, pp. 127–36

J. Chompret, J. Bloch, J. Guérin and P. Alfassa, *Répertoire de la Faïence Française*, 6 vols., Paris, 1933–5

J. Thuile, *La Céramique à Montpellier du XVIᵉ au XVIIIᵉ Siècle; ses Rapports avec la Faïence Nîmoise*, Paris, 1943

A. Lane, *French Faience*, London, 1st ed. 1948; 2nd ed. 1970

J. Hossard, 'Abaquesne, premier faïencier français au service de la pharmacie', *Revue d'Histoire de la Pharmacie*, vol. 11, 1953–4, pp. 147–51

E. Tilmans, *Faïences de France*, Paris, 1954

Montpellier, Musée Fabre, *La Faïence de Montpellier*, 1962

L. Cotinat, 'Les faïences pharmaceutiques des ateliers de Rouen 1540–1800', *La Pharmacie Française*, vol. 67, 1963, No. 2, pp. 11–17

Jeanne Giacomotti, *French Faience*, London, 1963

H.-P. Fourest and Jeanne Giacomotti, *L'Oeuvre des Faïenciers Français du 16e à la Fin du 18e Siècle*, Paris and Lausanne, 1966

The Low Countries

B. Rackham, *Early Netherlands Maiolica*, London, 1926

Agnes Lothian, 'Dutch drug jars and their marks', *The Alchemist*, vol. 16, 1952, pp. 216–21

D. A. Wittop Koning, *Delftse Apothekerspotten*, Deventer, 1954. Published also, with a synopsis in English, under the title *Delft Drug Jars*

H. E. Thomann, 'Die "Delftse Pottenkamer" der J. R. Geigy A.G., Basel', *Keramik-Freunde der Schweiz*, No. 65, 1964

H. E. Thomann, 'Gibt es spezifische Kennzeichen für Haarlemer Apotheken-gefässe?', *Vrienden van de Nederlandse Ceramiek*, No. 47, 1967, pp. 1–3

D. A. Wittop Koning, 'Van Antwerpse majolica tot Delfts aardewerk', *Antiek*, vol. 1, No. 8, 1967, pp. 26–35; vol. 1, No. 9, 1967, pp. 22–31; vol. 2, No. 1, 1967, pp. 3–10; vol. 2, No. 6, 1968, pp. 265–70

Dingeman Korf, *Nederlandse Majolica*, Bussum n.d. (1969?)

J. K. Crellin, *Medical Ceramics: A Catalogue of the English and Dutch Collections in the Museum of the Wellcome Institute of the History of Medicine*, London, 1969

C. H. de Jonge, *Delft Ceramics*, London, 1970

Leeuwarden, Fries Museum, 'Antwerps plateel', *Vrienden van de Nederlandse Ceramiek*, Nos. 62–3, 1971; Nos. 66–7, 1972

England

G. E. Howard, *Early English Drug Jars*, London, 1931

Agnes Lothian, ' "Observables" at the Royal College of Surgeons. English delft drug jars bequeathed to the College by Sir St. Clair Thomson in 1943', *Annals of the Royal College of Surgeons of England*, vol. 7, 1950, pp. 497–502

Agnes Lothian, 'The armorial London delft of the Worshipful Society of Apothecaries', *The Connoisseur*, vol. 127, March 1951, pp. 21–6

Agnes Lothian, 'Vessels for apothecaries: English delft drug jars', *Connoisseur Year Book*, 1953, pp. 113–21

Agnes Lothian, 'Bird designs on English drug jars', *Chemist and Druggist*, vol. 161, 1954, pp. 672–7

Agnes Lothian, 'The pipe-smoking man on seventeenth century English delft drug jars', *Chemist and Druggist*, vol. 163, 1955, pp. 566–8

Agnes Lothian, 'Angels in the design of seventeenth century English delft drug jars', *Chemist and Druggist*, vol. 163, 1955, pp. 732–6

Agnes Lothian, 'Cherub designs on English delft apothecary ware', *Chemist and Druggist*, vol. 165, 1956, pp. 608–13

Agnes Lothian, 'English delftware in the Pharmaceutical Society's Collection', *Transactions of the English Ceramic Circle*, vol. 5, part 1, 1960, pp. 1–4

H. Tait, 'Southwark (alias Lambeth) delftware and the potter, Christian Wilhelm', *The Connoisseur*, part I, vol. 146, August 1960, pp. 36–42; part II, vol. 147, February 1961, pp. 22–9

A. Nisoli, 'Apotheker-Fayencen in England', *Schweizerische Apotheker-Zeitung*, vol. 102, 1964, pp. 310–15

J. K. Crellin, *Medical Ceramics: A Catalogue of the English and Dutch Collections in the Museum of the Wellcome Institute of the History of Medicine*, London, 1969

J. K. Crellin, 'Medical ceramics: their scope and significance', *Transactions of the English Ceramic Circle*, vol. 7, part 3, 1970, pp. 191–9

L. G. Matthews, 'Apothecaries' pill tiles', *Transactions of the English Ceramic Circle*, vol. 7, part 3, 1970, pp. 200–9

J. F. Wilkinson, 'Old English apothecaries' drug jars', *Proceedings of the Royal Society of Medicine*, vol. 63, 1970, pp. 137–44

Agnes Lothian Short, 'Apothecary jar inscriptions—their interpretation', *Proceedings of the Royal Society of Medicine*, vol. 63, 1970, pp. 145–7

F. H. Garner and M. Archer, *English Delftware*, London, 1972

Spain

Alice W. Frothingham, *Talavera Pottery with a Catalogue of the Collection of the Hispanic Society of America*, New York, 1944

M. González Martí, *Cerámica del Levante Español: Siglos Medievales*, Barcelona, etc., 1944

A. Batllori i Munné and L. M. Llubiá i Munné, *Ceràmica Catalana Decorada*, Barcelona, 1949

Alice W. Frothingham, *Lustreware of Spain*, New York, 1951

J. Ainaud de Lasarte, *Ars Hispaniae*, vol. 10 (*Cerámica y Vidrio*), Madrid, 1952

Laboratorios del Norte de España, *Museo Retrospectivo de Farmacia y Medicina*, Masnou, 1952

M. Almagro Basch and L. M. Llubiá Munné, *La Cerámica de Teruel*, Teruel, 1962

G. Folch Jou, 'La collección de botes de farmacia en el Museo de la Farmacia Hispana', *Boletin de la Sociedad Española de Historia de la Farmacia*, No. 66, 1966, pp. 51–77. Published also by the Museo de la Farmacia Hispana as a monograph under the title *Catálogo de los Botes de Farmacia*

R. Jordi González, *Cerámica Farmacéutica en el Museo de Arte de Cataluña*, La Bisbal, 1971

R. Jordi González, *Historia de una Botica: La 'Farmacia-Museo' del Pueblo Español*, La Bisbal, 1972

Portugal

José Queirós, *Cerâmica Portuguesa*, 2nd ed., 2 vols., Lisbon, 1948
R. Dos Santos, *Faiança Portuguesa. Séc. XVI e XVII*, Oporto, 1960
Lisbon, Biblioteca Nacional, *Exposição de Faianças Portuguesas de Farmácia*, Lisbon, 1972

Germany

H. Kohlhaussen, G. Schiedlausky and H. Stafski, *Alte Apothekengefässe*, Biberach an der Riss, 1960
A. Nilsoli, 'Apothekenfayencen in Deutschland', *Schweizerische Apotheker-Zeitung*, vol. 101, 1963, pp. 400–4
W. H. Hein and D. A. Wittop Koning, *Deutsche Apotheken-Fayencen*, Frankfurt, 1977

Switzerland

A. Nisoli, 'Winterthurer Apotheker-Fayencen', *Schweizerische Apotheker-Zeitung*, vol. 108, 1970, pp. 611–20
Robert L. Wyss, *Winterthurer Keramik: Hafnerware aus dem 17. Jahrhundert*, Berne, 1973

Denmark

A. Øigaard, *Fajancefabriken i Store Kongensgade*, Copenhagen, 1936
Dannesboe Andersen, *Gammelt Dansk Apoteksinventar*, Copenhagen, 1944
K. Baerentsen, 'Apoteksfajance fra fabriken i Store Kongensgade', *Farmaceutisk Tidende*, vol. 75, 1965, pp. 1253–61

China

M. Beurdeley, *Porcelain of the East India Companies*, London, 1962

INDEX